OUT OF THE
MOUTH OF BABES

OUT OF THE MOUTH OF BABES

REVIVED
A Family's Ultimate Challenge

Annie Boddie

Library of Congress Control Number:		2022920418
ISBN:	Hardcover	978-1-6698-5010-6
	Softcover	978-1-6698-5009-0
	eBook	978-1-6698-5008-3

Print information available on the last page.

Rev. date: 11/21/2022

To order additional copies of this book, contact:
Xlibris
844-714-8691
www.Xlibris.com
Orders@Xlibris.com
847294

In Remembrance
of
My Mother
Clara Bullock
April 27, 1931–October 2, 2004
My Father
Rev. David A. Tyson, SR.
October 12, 1928-August 7, 2018
My Mother's Brother (My Uncle)
James Turner Cooper

April 20, 1933–February 13, 2014
and

My Father's Brother (My Uncle)
Rev. Jesse Walter Tyson

June 29, 1944–March 28, 2014

To my Lord and Savior Jesus Christ, who is the head of my life. My husband James Boddie, my sons: Donald Cooper, Minister Demond (Tiffany) Cooper, their sons: Devin Cooper, Elijah (Cheyenne) Cooper, their son Emmanuel Cooper, My sister Shaunay Tyson her children Malikai McDowell and Ta'Nya Cole, Sgt James and Prof Sheril Rogers, My niece Jessica Heath.

CONTENTS

ACKNOWLEDGMENTS

I want to thank two of Edgecombe County's finest Dr. R. Brooks Peters and Denise Poland-Torres, PA-C for their expertise in the medical field as well as their friendship. Mrs. Lydia Wilkins, my former neighbor and a friend of the family. I recognize my pastor, Bishop Annie (Jasper) Pettaway of the St. Mark Deliverance Church. Pinetops, N.C. Pastor Alice D. (William) Hinton of Princeville, N.C., Apostle Dr. Marvin (Sylvia) Smith of Spring Lake, N.C., Pastor Lathan Woods of Tom River, N. J., Pastor Larry and Evangelist Jessie Kendrick of Omaha, Nebraska, Elder Paul and Mother Betty Everette of Wilson, N.C. I thank you all for your love, wisdom, guidance, patience, and friendship you all bestowed upon me over the years.

I also want to thank Rev. Thomas and Ernestine Jones for being with me when my mother passed. On that day, Rev. Jones told me that I was one of his adopted daughters and since that day, I call him "Papa Jones!" To my dear friends of twenty-plus years Princess and Fredrick Woodard, Cassandra and Johnny Frank Lyons, Bettye Davis, and her son Brandon Davis, you all have made me laugh when I felt like crying. You all listened to my childhood stories and have been with me in good times as well as bad times. All of my friends knew I could make up a story in a minute and when they heard it they would laugh and say, "Girl you have a very good imagination. In fact, as we listen, we can't help but laugh at you." Finally, I want you to know you are my friends until the end. You have truly been a blessing to me, and I pray that the blessings of the Lord will continue to follow you all ways.

INTRODUCTION

O*ut of the Mouth of Babes: A Family's Ultimate Challenge REVIVED* is a fictional story about a couple that met in high school and became sweethearts. They were a very strong-willed, compassionate couple that came from families with extremely strong, moral backgrounds. Their families weren't by any means rich in substance; however, they were rich with love, joy, peace, and all the things that mattered in life.

After dating for a few years, they made a mutual decision to get married and through their union, they were blessed with four awesome children. They weren't any different than the average children their age. All of them had their own unique personalities. One of the children was totally an exception to the rule, she was truly a babe. A babe is described as a very young child or even a native couple. But this couple was certain this child had a sense of "being here before." She truly was wise beyond her years and was truly in a class all by herself. She was more advanced than her peers.

How many times as adults have, we ignored a child because we classified them as a talker or presumed whatever they had on their minds was unimportant or silly? Or perhaps we were too busy doing our own thing to take a few minutes to listen. Regardless of our age, race, creed, or color, we were all created equal. Children shouldn't be considered insufficient, little mouth pieces because they have lots of things on their minds. When these children spoke, their parents paid close attention to every word that proceeded out of their mouths. However, they were flabbergasted to hear such wisdom and knowledge flowing out of the mouth of this little babe. She was extremely outspoken, bold, and quite a visionary as you will soon see.

Whatever these children set their minds to do, they worked until their visions were accomplished. Failure wasn't a part of their vocabulary. What the couple didn't learn from their other children they definitely learned from this one. Due to circumstances beyond their control, the parents experienced several challenges. Although the challenges were both positive and negative, there were times when their mother contemplated pulling her hair out. But her faith always kicked in just in the nick of time. She learned quite a few lessons from her offspring's experiences, some of that changed her family tremendously.

As you read this book, you will find that the course of events that take place are designed to cause you as the reader to feel what each character felt. Despite the emotional aspects you may feel, this story was created to make you think about the life you are living currently. Some may change their views while others may choose to remain the same. Unfortunately, there are some that will definitely adopt the "I don't care" syndrome." Whatever the case may be, your life could very well depend on it.

Annie C. Boddie

INTRODUCING THE BARNESWORTHS

Albert and Ta'Nelle met in high school. Although Albert was a year older, the two soon became high school sweethearts. While living at home with their families and attending high school, they both worked part-time jobs and saved as much of their money as they could. After they finished high school, they went to college. Once again, they started working part-time jobs off campus. At the end of Albert's junior year of college, he started submitting resumes online to various companies in hopes of seeking full-time employment.

During Albert's senior year of college, he was blessed with a full-time job in his field of study. When Ta'Nelle became a junior, she also submitted resumes. After she became a senior, she landed a full-time job and started working a week after graduating. Albert and Ta'Nelle made plans to wed eighteen months after she graduated from college. They decided to have a small, yet special wedding accompanied by two bridesmaids, two groomsmen, a maid of honor, the best man, a flower girl, and a ring bearer. In their minds, the size of the wedding wasn't important. The most important thing was being together and making a vow before God and their loved ones.

After making wedding plans, the couple began shopping

for their dream home. They wanted to gain an idea of how much of an investment they would need to make in order to purchase this home. They wanted to have at least four children so they knew they would need enough space to accommodate their family. Once they were given the estimates, they decided to work as much overtime as they possibly could to accomplish their dream. Albert also began working a part-time job on the weekends. They were very resourceful when it came to saving their money. They were determined to remain focused on their dreams. Regardless of their demanding work schedules, they always made time to spend with each other whenever possible to maintain a strong relationship.

A few months before the wedding, Albert and Ta'Nelle decided to begin shopping for their new home. They searched and searched but couldn't seem to find what they were looking for. They learned of a contractor building houses nearby where they both worked and decided to stop by on their way home from work. They informed the contractor they were looking to purchase a home that would be ready to move in immediately after returning from their honeymoon. The home they wanted had to be large enough to accommodate a family of six with a formal dining room, a den (sitting area), and an additional room for out-of-town guests. The contractor showed the couple several homes that his crew was working on in the area that would be ready for closing before their wedding day. After examining the houses in the area, they didn't find exactly what they considered to be the home of their dreams. The contractor also had other homes being built across town that he felt would be sufficient according to their plans. The couple made an appointment to meet the contractor the next week at the same time at the new location.

The next week, Albert and Ta'Nelle had high hopes of

finding their home. Although all the houses were attractive, none of them stood out, but they refused to give up. There were three houses remaining. Finally, the couple saw the front of a house from a distance and looked at each other, something on the inside clicked. They had to see the inside of that house because from the looks of things, it appeared to be exactly what they wanted. They were so excited and started praising God that very moment. They put their faith in action ("Faith without works is dead," James 2:17). The house had five bedrooms and four bathrooms, and was a split-level home with both formal and informal dining areas as well as a large living room, den, and study (or could be used as an extra bedroom). The master bedroom was equipped with two large walk-in closets, a master bathroom with a Jacuzzi, his and her sinks, and a stand-up shower with a bench. To top it off, there was a three-car garage attached, which the couple identified as abonus. Ta'Nelle looked at Albert and said, "Honey, that bench in the master bathroom was put there for you. Since you are the oldest, you will have something to sit on when you get too old to stand." He said, "If I were you, I wouldn't laugh too hard, after all, you are right behind me, who knows you might sit on it before I do." As the two shared a big laugh, the contractor could see that the couple loved each other dearly and had a great sense of humor.

After viewing the home Albert and Ta'Nelle were hooked. The next day, the contractor had papers delivered to a real estate lawyer at the couple's request. The closing of the house was tentatively scheduled for one week after their marriage. After meeting with their lawyer, they put all the finances in one account at the bank that was needed for the closing. Once they received an okay from the realtor that there wouldn't be any problems purchasing the house, they proceeded with their plans. They wanted to take two weeks off from work. One week would be used for the honeymoon, and the second week would be set aside for closing and moving into their dream home. A few weeks before the wedding, Albert and Ta'Nelle went to pick out new furniture to complement each room. They purchased enough furniture to fill two bedrooms, the living room, the den, and the informal dining room, which would be enough to start.

A few days before the wedding, Ta'Nelle received a very important phone call. It was a call from their lawyer letting her know that they could close on the house immediately. The next day, Albert and Ta'Nelle completed all the necessary paperwork, and she was given the keys. Due to the wedding approaching so rapidly, Albert felt it would be best to have the furniture delivered after they returned from their honeymoon as originally planned. However, as a surprise for Albert, Ta'Nelle, along with her parents, (Carson and Brittany Whitehead), they returned to the furniture store that afternoon.

After arriving at the store, Ta'Nelle set up an appointment with the store manager (with her parents' approval) to have the furniture delivered to their new home while they were away on their honeymoon. She walked through the store and showed her parents the furniture they purchased. She was careful to make a list of the furniture and the exact room, she wanted everything placed in as well as how she wanted it done.

Due to the couple's large purchase and their delightful personalities, the store manager (with permission from the owner) gave the couple a set of bunk beds with box springs and mattresses along with two dressers. He told Ta'Nelle to consider it an early wedding present. After dropping her father (Carson) off at their house, the women ventured to the mall to purchase the drapes and bedding needed to complete the rooms. Ta'Nelle was very satisfied with the things she had purchased. Ta'Nelle and her mother (Brittany) returned to her parent's home to gather some of her things before going to her new home. They would only be there a short period of time, just long enough to hang the drapes and to place some of her clothes in the closet.

Finally, they were finished, and Ta'Nelle turned to her mother (Brittany) and said, "Mom, I love it! I can't wait to see Albert's face when we return from our honeymoon. I am so glad he doesn't have a key to this house yet!" Her mother (Brittany) replied, "I am too honey. I want him to be totally surprised, I don't want anything to get in the way of your happiness." The wedding was going to take place in less than three days. Ta'Nelle was so excited she had finished everything she needed to do. The ladies stopped by one of their favorite restaurants and picked up the food they ordered for supper. Ta'Nelle could now go home and relax until it was time to go to their final wedding rehearsal, which was scheduled for the next evening at the church. After eating supper and cleaning up the kitchen, she excused herself and took a long hot relaxing bathe. Ta'Nelle told her mother she was going to lie down for a few minutes and get a nap. When she awakened, it was the next day, the crack of dawn to be exact. As she looked around, she thought she was dreaming, only to learn that a few minutes of sleep had turned into hours. Ta'Nelle could not believe she was so tired, but she was awakened refreshed. She then prepared for her morning run. She ran her normal six miles before preparing for her final day at work as a single woman.

When Ta'Nelle went to work, she knew she wouldn't be able to concentrate, but she was determined to give it her best shot. All her co-workers could sense the love and excitement that she expressed about her new future. She planned to get off work at 3:00 p.m., but her co-workers decided to surprise her with a bridal shower during their lunch hour at 11:30 a.m. She was so shocked that she cried. They loved Ta'Nelle and made sure she knew it. There were not any words she could say that would express the appreciation she felt in her heart at that very moment. The gifts included: his and her identical bath robes with their names engraved on them, bath cloths, engraved silverware, dishes, glasses, cooking utensils, toasters, canisters, night gowns, a coffee maker, bedding sets, a microwave oven, gift cards, dish towels, gels, candles, scented oils, and various items that the women believed the couple would need.

After the shower, the co-workers assisted Ta'Nelle with taking her gifts to her car. Her boss knew that she was excited and overcome with emotions, therefore, he let her go home immediately. When she returned to her parents' home, all the gifts were repacked and stacked in her room until after the wedding. Everything was going as planned, and Ta'Nelle could hardly wait to marry the man of her dreams. There were just two things left to do before the wedding: the wedding rehearsal and the dinner. The wedding rehearsal was planned for 6:30 p.m., and it went off without a hitch. The directress of the wedding (Ta'Nelle's Aunt Brenda Connors) was quite pleased with the way things were going. Aunt Brenda said, "Ta'Nelle and Albert, I am well pleased. If everything goes as we practiced, this will be a sensational wedding." Ta'Nelle and Albert thanked everyone. Ta'Nelle said, "This has been a shocking, yet formidable day! Now let us see what the rehearsal dinner has in store for everyone! I honestly believe this night will be one that Albert and I will never forget! To God be the glory!" The dinner was scheduled at one of the local restaurants at 8:00 p.m.

At the dinner, everyone decided to order from the menu. Once the meal was completed, the wedding couple gave their guests gifts. The brides maids' (Destiny Harris and Makaila Richardson) and the maid of honor, Ta'Nelle's sister (Rosalyn

Whitehead-Williams) were all given matching jewelry. The flower carrier, "Miss Giggles" (Cassandra Barker) were given a beautiful gold and white princess crown, and white gloves. She was so happy, Ta'Nelle placed the crown on her head until they were ready to leave the restaurant. Albert gave the ring bearer, "Mr. Smooth" (Joseph Roundtree), his very first top hat and a cane. Naturally, he had to wear his hat as he practiced his moves. Pictures of Mr. Smooth and Miss Giggles were taken together and separately. The groomsmen (Gregory Rogers and Terry Edwards) along with the best man (Ja'Von Walker) were all given gold cufflinks. All the items would be worn during the wedding ceremony.

After the rehearsal dinner was over, it was time for everyone to depart to their separate homes. When Albert stopped to drop Ta'Nelle off, she tried her absolute best to get Albert to reveal where they were going on their honeymoon. Albert's lips were closed. The more determined Ta'Nelle became, the more Albert ignored her. Naturally, like most women, she had to try at least two or three more times. After about ten minutes, she gave up and Albert walked her to the door of her parent's home as they said their good nights. She did not have a clue where they were going on their honeymoon, but she believed wherever they were going had to be someplace incredibly special. She went inside and prepared herself for bed however, she was so excited that she could not sleep. She decided to recheck her luggage to make sure she packed everything she thought she would need for her honeymoon. She started playing a variety of her favorite gospel singers music as she lay across the bed. Before long, she was fast asleep. When she awakened it was the day of her wedding, time to get up.

TA'NELLE'S WEDDING DAY

There was not any time to waste. Everyone's hair appointment was scheduled with their own hairdressers. There was so much to do and little time to do it before the wedding, which would begin at 3:00 p.m. Ta'Nelle and her wedding party were going to be dressed at the church. Ta'Nelle wanted to make sure that no one would be seen before the wedding, (especially Ta'Nelle) all the girls were to be ready and picked up by 1:00 p.m. so they could arrive at the church no later than 1:30 p.m. The bride wanted everyone to be ready no later than 2:30 p.m. Once the wedding party had finished dressing, they would remain in a private room until the wedding began. The bride would dress in a separate room with the assistance of her maid of honor, her sister, Rosalyn Whitehead-Williams, as well as her mother Mrs. Brittany Whitehead.

Once the limousine driver arrived, Ta'Nelle and Rosalyn's wedding attire were carefully placed in the trunk. The limousine was a white stretched with twelve passengers that was fully equipped with a color HDTV, CD player, a full bar, snacks, and all the latest games. The driver was elegantly dressed in a black tuxedo with a white shirt, black tie, and black shoes. He was a very well-mannered young man. Once he escorted the women to the limo, he made sure they were comfortable before proceeding to his next destination. Next, he picked up Destiny

Harris, and Makaila Richardson followed by Cassandra Barker. Everything was going just as planned.

Finally, it was time for the wedding. The ushers were dressed in cream tuxedos, along with black shirts, cream bow ties, and black patent leather shoes. The ushers were on point, they seated all the guests and then quickly returned to their posts at the entrance of the sanctuary. All the quests knew that Albert and Ta'Nelle believed in being on time. When Ta'Nelle sent word that she was ready the outside doors were shut, and were to remain shut until the conclusion of the ceremony. Any latecomers would be seated in the church's fellowship hall to watch the wedding ceremony on the monitors. The couple meant what they said and said exactly what they meant. They were not going to allow anything or anyone to ruin or interrupt their momentous day.

Ta'Nelle's Aunt Brenda Connors (directress) entered the doorway. She was dressed in a cream-colored square neckline, embroidered, A-line gown with cut-out red apple roses, with green stems on her skirt. She topped it off with a gold necklace, bracelet, earrings set, and gold two-and-a-half-inch pumps. She shook her head up and down to let the musicians know they were ready to start the ceremony. The ushers entered the sanctuary to light the candles. While the ushers were exiting the sanctuary, the soloist Camella Walters took her place. Once the ushers returned to their posts, the directress signaled to the musicians to start playing the music for the soloist. As Camella started to sing her version of, "I'm still holding on," Mr. and Mrs. Alston and Belinda Barnesworth and Mr. and Mrs. Oliver and Cynthia Thomas (the parents and grandparents of Albert) was seated. Mr. and Mrs. Carson and Brittany Whitehead and Mr. and Mrs. Tyrone and Julia Bryant (Ta'Nelle's parents and grandparents) were seated next. Upon the completion of the solo the minister, groom, and best man entered the sanctuary and took their places at the altar. Mrs. Brenda Connors then closed the doors of the sanctuary to prepare for the wedding precession.

The presiding minister was Apostle Renee Woods. She wore a white ministerial robe with gold trim, and two-and-three-fourth-inch gold closed-toe pumps, with gold and white, diamond earrings. Albert wore a black tuxedo with a penguin tail, a black bow tie, a white shirt, black patient leather shoes, with a black top hat (worn until the bride entered the sanctuary) and he held a black cane with a gold tip in his right hand. Albert believed he was the cleanest man in the sanctuary (as he should have) and he was oh, so ready to see his bride. He was as people would say, "as sharp as a tack!" Ja'Von Walker, the best man wore a black tuxedo with a white shirt, a gold cummerbund, a black bow tie, and black patent leather shoes, with gold cufflinks.

It was time for the wedding processional to begin. The soloist (Camella) stood at the microphone while Mrs. Connors opened the doors to the sanctuary. Once the musicians started to play their mixed version of "Flesh of My Flesh," the bridesmaids and the groomsmen entered the doorway. The two bridesmaids (Destiny Harris and Makaila Richardson) were dressed in red apple satin, strapless, floor-length gowns draped with detachable gold and white sashes tied in a bow around their waists on the left-hand side. Their shoes were gold, satin, peep-toe pumps, with two-and-a-half-inch heels. They wore gold necklaces, with earrings and bracelets to match the maid of honor (which was given as gifts from the bride). Their bracelets were worn on their left wrists. The bride maids were escorted down the aisle by the two groomsmen Gregory Rogers and Terry Edwards. The groomsmen wore black tuxedos with white shirts, red cummerbunds, and black patent leather shoes. They marched at least four rows apart.

The maid of honor Mrs. Rosalyn Whitehead-Williams wore a floor-length gold, strapless dress draped with red apple, gold, and white sash. She wore red apple satin peep-toe pumps with a two-and-a-half-inch heel. All the bouquets were red apple, gold, and white silk roses with red apple and gold ribbons. After the maid of honor reached her position at the altar, the ring bearer entered. Joseph Roundtree was an extremely outgoing young man that loved to dress up. People that knew him considered him to be a natural clown (or comedian). As Mrs. Brenda Connors directed him to enter the sanctuary, it was as if he was modeling on a runway. He was the tender age of five, but he had the personality of a grown man. When Joseph was old enough to stand on the bed, he discovered the mirror. Once he realized he was seeing himself, he quickly learned how to pose from the day he discovered the mirror. Soon thereafter he gained the nickname, "Mr. Smooth." He truly lived up to his name on that day. He was dressed exactly like the groom. He wore a black tuxedo with a penguin tail, black bow tie, white shirt, and black patent leather shoes. He also sported a black top hat that was neatly tilted to the right side of his head and carried a black cane with a gold tip in his left hand. You can rest assured that he had the right walk to fit the occasion.

Mr. Smooth entertained everyone in attendance. In fact, he had everyone eating out of his hands. Once Mr. Smooth started walking and realized everyone was watching him, he made sure he stopped along the way to pose for the photographer. After he completed his walk, the sheet rollers rolled the sheet to the altar. As the sheet cleared the doorway, the doors were closed in preparation for the flower carrier and the bride. Everyone was so excited to see what the little flower carrier had up her sleeves.

As the doors were re-opened to the sanctuary, the musicians started to play soft music. The flower carrier, Cassandra Barker, aka "Miss Giggles" entered the doorway. She wore a white three-fourth inch princess dress with gold, and red apple miniature flowers and a gold and red apple sash with a white crinoline (can can) slip underneath. She wore her gold and white crown on her head and short white gloves on her hands with flat black pumps. Her basket was filled with fresh red apples, gold, and white rose petals.

Miss Giggles (Cassandra) was a sweet little girl that would make the average person smile, and that day was not any different. She was only three years old but was wiser than you could ever imagine. Being bashful was not a word in her vocabulary. She knew how to work for a crowd, and that day, she was determined to do just that. Under the direction of Mrs. Connors, she yelled as loud as she could, "The bride is coming! The bride is coming! The bride is coming!" She stood at the doorway yelling over and over, "The bride is coming! The bride is coming! The bride is coming!" She placed her hand on her hip and said, "The bride is coming! The bride is coming! Do you hear me? I said the bride is coming!" Everyone laughed as hard as they could, they could not wait to see what she would do next.

As she started to walk down the aisle, she realized that she had forgotten to drop the rose petals. She suddenly decided to put the basket down on the sheet and grabbed her little mouth with both hands. She said with a loud voice, "Uh-oooooh, uh-oooooh, I forgot!" She placed her hands in the basket and grabbed a handful of rose petals as her little hands could hold. She quickly walked back to the door and threw all the rose petals up in the air and watched as the petals fell on her little face. At that point, she noticed that everyone was watching her, and she laughed and laughed.

She returned to the basket of flowers and yelled loudly once more, "The bride is coming!" Miss Giggles, truly lived up to her to her name on that day. She returned to her job of grabbing the rose petals and continued to throw them up in the air until she had finally reached her destination. Once she reached the altar she yelled, "The bride is coming! The bride is coming!" By that time, everyone had laughed so hard that they were in tears including the Apostle. Everyone in attendance knew that Albert and Ta'Nelle had made the right choice when they selected the flower carrier and the ring bearer.

It was time for the bride to make her entrance. Although she was not in the sanctuary yet, she was also in tears from hearing the events that had taken place with the ring bearer (Mr. Smooth) and the flower carrier (girl) (Miss Giggles). She could not wait to see the video, she knew she would laugh even harder. The bride marched in on a revised version of "Here Comes the Bride." The bride was escorted by her father Carson Whitehead. He wore a black tuxedo with a black cummerbund, a black bow tie, a white shirt, and black patent leader shoes. Miss Giggles (Cassandra) was very attentive, once she saw the bride, she pointed toward the door and yelled, "See I told you the bride is coming, there she is, there she is! Mommy, the bride is coming, I told you! There she is! There she is!" Her mother replied, "We see her sweetie." The bride wore a white lace taffeta, dropped waist A-line gown with a Scoop neckline, elongated bodice, a bubble skirt, and sweep detachable train, with a matching veil. She wore white stockings with a two-and-three-fourth-inch white pumps with a rhinestone ornament across the front of her shoes.

The bride (Ta'Nelle) carried two bouquets, one with

artificial flowers (to keep), and the other one was real flowers (to be thrown at the reception). The bouquets were red apple, gold, and white roses draped with gold, red apple, and white ribbons. The bride decided to go with the traditional wedding with something old, new, borrowed, and blue. For something old, she wore her diamond princess ring. For something new, she wore white gloves. For something borrowed, the bride wore a three-piece diamond and gold necklace, earrings, and bracelet set that belonged to her mother. For something blue, she carried a blue flowered handkerchief that belonged to her grandmother. She was finally ready to make her grand entrance, and she did.

As the groom (Albert) watched his bride enter the doorway, he could not believe how absolutely stunning she looked. He had never seen her more gorgeous than that very minute. As their eyes met, Ta'Nelle saluted Albert and he responded with a big thumbs up as he motioned to her, "I love you!" She then proceeded down the aisle as the two continued to flirt with each other. When she was about halfway to the altar, she stopped briefly and threw him a big kiss. Of course, he put his hand out and caught it and immediately responded with a kiss of his own. Once she reached the altar, she bowed down to her groom.

As Albert and Ta'Nelle displayed their love for each other, Albert could no longer contain himself. Once Ta'Nelle approached the altar, Albert started singing his version of, "You are so beautiful to me. I wish you could see-eee. You mean the world to mee-eee. You are so beautiful to mee." He could care less that they were in the middle of the ceremony. Naturally, every woman in the sanctuary began wiping their eyes, and gasping, "ah, ah, that's so sweet!" The wedding guests were utterly amazed at the love and devotion that the couple was showing one another. Although the song was not a part of the original program, the couple placed a footnote at the bottom of the program stating, "Program subject to change under the direction of the Holy Spirit!"

After the groom finished singing, Apostle Renee Woods began the wedding ceremony with the following:

"Dearly beloved, we are gathered here in the sight of God, and in the presence of this company, to join together, this man and this woman in holy matrimony, which is commanded by God to be honorable among all men. Therefore, it is not to be entered into, unadvisedly or lightly; but reverently, discreetly, advisedly, and in the fear of God. Into this holy estate, these two persons present come now to be joined. If anyone can show any reason why, these two should not be lawfully joined together, let him (or her) speak now, or forever hold his (or her) peace."

At that moment, Albert turned to his guests and gave them such a horrible stare as if he were saying, "Do not you say nothing, I mean nothing! Do not even think about it! I double dare you to open your mouth!" When Albert was satisfied that he had gotten his point across he turned around to the apostle. Apostle Woods looked at Albert and smiled. Without a doubt, he was caught. Apostle Woods proceeded with the ceremony. Ta'Nelle, the bride, was given in marriage by her parents Mr. and Mrs. Carson Whitehead.

The Apostle informed everyone in attendance that the couple had written their own vows. They were asked to join hands as Albert began saying his vows.

"Baby, from the first day I saw you, I knew you were someone incredibly special. I wanted so many times to talk to you, but I wanted to do things decently and in order. While we were in high school, I watched you for a year. I prayed that one day, you would be an especially important part of my life. I asked the Lord for his direction and guidance so that I would not make the wrong move. You see, I watched my close friends as they disrespected, abused, and hurt seven or eight of my classmates and I did not want that to be a part of my life. I love you too much to hurt you. I read in the Word of God in Proverbs 31:10–12, that a virtuous woman is worth far more than rubies. She does her husband good and not evil all the days of her life. I stand here today before my God, our families, and friends to declare that I have found virtue in you. I promise you that I will love, honor, protect, and cherish you for the rest of my life. The Bible says, "That when a man finds a wife, he finds a good thing." Thank you for being my good thing. In sickness and health, whether we are rich or poor, you will always be my good thing. I love you, baby, today and always!"

Ta'Nelle stood there attentively listening as the tears rolled down her face. When Albert finished, she had to take a few moments to recompose herself. She was finally ready to say her vows. To everyone's surprise, she opened her mouth, but nothing came out. She tried three times to speak, but only her lips moved. Suddenly she was able to speak lightly, so the apostle, handed her the microphone. Once she calmed herself down, she began speaking so clearly that the microphone was no longer needed. Ta'Nelle looked into Albert's eyes smiled and said:

"Honey, when we first met, I knew you were a very mature, well-respected, young man that seemed to have his head on straight. Although you are a year older, I admire the love and determination you possess. Whenever we are together, I know that you love me. And today, I stand to announce to the entire congregation that you are the man of my dreams. I love you more than you can ever imagine. I love you as a man of God, a friend, a companion, and a protector. You have helped me to stay focused and you never asked me to compromise, and for that, I thank you. You have been there to encourage me, and to uplift me thru all my challenging times. It gives me great honor to become your wife. And I promise you that I will love you and respect you even when you are old and gray (which will occur, ten or twenty, years before I become gray). If you become bald, blind, crippled, or crazier than you are right now, you will always be my man, until death do us part, and do not forget it!"

After the vows, Apostle Woods asked for the rings and prayed over them before placing them in the couple's hands. The rings were exchanged individually, beginning with the groom and then the bride. They were both asked to repeat the following while exchanging the rings:

"As a pledge and in token of the vows between us made, with this ring, I thee wed: In the name of the Father, and of the Son, and of the Holy Ghost. Amen."

They were then directed to kneel down at the altar as the apostle, prayed for their union. After the prayer was complete, "James Boddie and the Faithful Few sang The Lord's Prayer." The couple then lit the unity candle and returned to the altar. Apostle Woods told the groom that he could kiss his bride, and boy, oh boy, did he lay one on her. The groom kissed his bride so long and passionately that the musicians started playing their final song. "To God Be the Glory!" The soloist sang two verses of the song, and the groom was still embracing his new bride. The best man (Jay'Von Walker) could not take it any longer, he sprang into action. He touched the groom and said, "Man, do not kill the woman! You just got married, you have hundreds of time to kiss her later. Let the woman breathe p-l-e-a-s-e!" At that point, the sanctuary was filled with laughter, lots, and lots of laughter. One of the guests in the audience yelled, "We got the message, we know you love her, now please, please, please lose her and let her go in the name of Jesus!"

The groom finally let his wife breathe. She was totally breathless after that long, passionate, and powerful affection of love. Once the bride recuperated, she and her husband turned to their guests. Apostle Woods introduced the couple as Mr. and Mrs. Albert and Ta'Nelle Barnesworth while the soloist continued singing, "To God Be the glory!" Ta'Nelle grabbed the train on her dress and Albert quickly grabbed her left arm.

Ta'Nelle knew Albert had two or three more gimmicks up his sleeve, but she had no idea what he would do next. Just when everyone had calmed down from their laughter, Albert's new gimmick were put in play. Anyone that did not know him personally and was not familiar with his comical side was in for a treat. He reached down, picked Ta'Nelle up off the floor, and twirled her around three times yelling, "In the name of the Father, the Son, and the Holy Ghost, I thank God I finally have the woman of my dreams!" Truly, Albert started a fire in that place that only God could put out. He put Ta'Nelle down and the two of them immediately started dancing for the Lord. The musicians started playing and singing, "I, I got a praise, I got praise, and I got to get it out, I got a praise!"

At that point, the Holy Ghost (Spirit) was moving throughout the sanctuary. Apostle Woods, the wedding party, the parents of the couple, along with seventeen of the guests could not contain them-selves any longer. God was truly being glorified. They danced and danced for ten minutes while it was all captured on tape. As the Spirit of God lifted off the couple, it fell on someone else. Forget the reception for the time being the party had already started in the church. Talking about a time, good God Almighty, they had a time!

The rolled sheet that was so skillfully placed down the aisle was not anymore, it was simply a piece of paper to be disposed of. Albert and Ta'Nelle could not have planned their wedding any better. Without a doubt, the Lord had set his approval on their marriage. And what God had joined together, let no man put asunder. Amen! Amen! And Amen! While the guests were praising God, the Barnesworths along with the wedding party proceeded out of the sanctuary. They were led into the restroom to redo their hair and makeup in preparation for the photographer.

After five minutes, everyone danced until their heart was content. Meanwhile, the mothers of the couple were busy explaining to the caterers they would be arriving thirty or forty minutes later than planned. Before long, the wedding party had re-entered the sanctuary and was ready to be photographed. There were twenty-five guests waiting in the sanctuary to see what other surprises the couple had planned. They were enjoying themselves tremendously and did not want to miss a single thing. The photographer took dozens of pictures. Half of the pictures were serious while others were completely comical. The couple was determined to make sure the wedding party was enjoying themselves to the fullest. They pulled out every stunt that came to their mind, nothing within reason was off limits. There were thirty pictures taken unaware ft the wedding party as well as the guests.

Finally, everyone was on their way to the reception and was looking forward to a continuance of entertainment from the newlyweds. If Albert had his way, they would thoroughly be surprised, or extremely shocked by his personality. Due to the large response from the invitations, the reception was moved to a private hall to accommodate the huge crowd of guests that were expected to be in attendance. The wedding procession was so long that the traffic was lined up for twelve blocks.

Once the wedding couple reached the reception hall, they remained in the limo. The newlyweds wanted everyone to have an opportunity to get comfortable, served appetizers, and have a half-hour to mingle among themselves before they entered the establishment. As the guests arrived at the reception hall the wedding party, ushers, and twenty of the immediate family members escorted them to their assigned seats. The caterers assisted the guests with their drinks and appetizers. All the tables were covered with white tablecloths and decorated with red apple, gold, and cream-colored artificial rose pedals. There were six eight-inch apple red, gold, and cream-colored vases with fresh roses and candles, placed on each table, along with small bags of pillow mints for all the guests to enjoy. "James Boddie and the Faithful Few" provided the music until the wedding couple arrived.

The reception was catered by D&D Catering Service of Brooksville, North Carolina, which is owned by Donald and Demond Cooper. The couple wanted to have a variety of food to satisfy the taste buds of everyone in attendance. Under the advice of the Coopers, they provided their guests with the following menu:

The appetizers

    Tossed salad
    Swiss meatballs
    Fruit salad (A combination of various fruits)
    Cheeses: white and cheddar with crackers
Finger sandwiches

The main course

Fried chicken	Shrimp
Macaroni and cheese	Mashed potatoes
Chopped barbecue	Cole slaw
Chicken drum lets	String beans
Pulled beef with gravy	Lima beans
A variety of bread	

Drinks

| Fruit punch | Tea |

Unsweetened tea

Sparkling white grape Water/fruit drinks
juice

Various types of sodas   No Alcoholic
Beverages

Desserts

Red velvet cake   Chocolate cake
Apple and peach cobblers Banana pudding
Pineapple upside-down
cakes
The traditional wedding
cake

While the guests patiently waited for the arrival of the couple, they could only imagine in their minds what events would shortly come into play. Before they knew it, the wedding party was entering the building. As the Barnesworths started to approach the doorway of the reception hall, the directress (Brenda Connors) proudly introduced them. Their guests saluted them with a standing ovation, cheers, and very loud applause. They were immediately escorted to their seats, the wedding party, the parents of the wedding couple along with Apostle Renee (Richard) Woods were seated, at a table on a stage that overlooked all the guests. Albert and Ta'Nelle wanted to make sure they could see and be seen by their guests. They were determined to be the perfect host and hostess.

To maintain the same atmosphere as the wedding, James

Boddie and the Faithful Few started singing a rearranged version of, "We have come this far by faith." Upon completion of the song, Apostle Woods asked everyone to bow their heads as she blessed the food and the caterers started serving everyone. While everyone was enjoying their meal and each other, music was softly playing on a flash drive that was handpicked, by the couple. Everything was going as planned, and the reception started without a hitch. Finally, it was time to move on to the next phase of the reception. The caterers were very attentive. Whenever someone was finished with their meal; their dishes were cleared and their glasses were refilled.

Ta'Nelle's Aunt, Brenda Connors directed the couple to position themselves for their toast to each other. They were directed to the center of the stage so everyone would have a clear view. As they crossed their arms in preparation for their toast, Albert leaned over and whispered a private message in Ta'Nelle's ear. Before he knew it, she was laughing uncontrollably. Albert looked at her in amazement as he wondered what was so funny. He believed that something or someone had captured her attention. What could it be? Or Ta'Nelle was trying to play a trick on him. Whatever the case may be, Albert knew there wasn't any way to prepare himself, all he could do was stand there and watch as things unfolded. As the two of them posed for the photographer, Ta'Nelle continued to laugh. By the reaction on Albert's face, everyone knew to brace themselves.

As the couple raised their glasses, Ta'Nelle continued to laugh uncontrollably while rubbing her abdomen. At that point, Albert said, "Honey, what is wrong with you? Why are you laughing?" She tried her best to compose herself and after thirty or forty seconds, she was finally able to speak. Ta'Nelle said, "I know that all of you thought I was going to play a trick on Albert, but that was far from the truth. What you thought was a prank was a vision from the Lord that happened immediately. God is! Not was, but is a right-now God, and I can prove it! You see the Lord showed me that Albert was going to spill the grape juice on my dress. When we raised our glasses for the toast, the more tickled I became until my laughter became uncontrollable. I want you to know that the Holy Ghost is in this place. I did not leave the Holy Ghost at home on the shelf, or outside, I brought him with me because he lives in my heart. While Albert was standing there shivering trying to figure out what I was going to do, I was busy preparing myself."

She continued by saying, "Maybe you noticed when I placed my hand on my abdomen. Shortly thereafter, as we attempted to toast each other, Albert turned the glass up to my chin and proceeded to pour the freezing cold juice on my dress. As the juice ran down my dress, a cold chill ran up and down my spine. At that time, all I could do was rub my abdomen until the warmth returned to my body. To those of you that do not believe as I do, here is my proof." She turned around until everyone in the reception hall witnessed the stain on her dress. The Barnesworths and their guests had to take a much-needed station break, it was time to praise and glorify the Lord. Ta'Nelle praised the Lord so much that she danced out of her shoe. Albert usually gets embarrassed easily, but he had another agenda at that time, he had to praise and magnify his God. It was a joyful and miraculous day. Thank you, Jesus!

Next, it was time to cut the cake. But before the cake was cut, I wanted to place a picture of it below, so everyone could see just how elegant it was.

The bride and groom statue are included as an added bonus so you can really see the detail and thought the artist put into her work. I could not have selected a more talented artist. The picture was drawn by Mrs. Pat Montgomery, Wilson, NC.

And where do you think you are going?

Albert and Ta'Nelle approached the wedding cake, he became a little uncomfortable. Although he poured the grape juice on Ta'Nelle's dress accidentally, he believed she would retaliate somehow with the cake. Everyone acquainted with the couple was familiar with their actions, and they were confident it was show time. While Albert and Ta'Nelle stood in front of the cake, their guests sat at the edge of their seats anticipating their next move. Everyone in the room became completely silent as the coupled looked at each other. They tried their absolute best to exhibit a serious face in hopes of surprising their guests as well as each other. Suddenly, they grabbed the knife with their right hands and positioned themselves for the picture. After ten or twelve pictures were taken, the caterers removed the top layer of the cake, the couple would keep it until their first anniversary.

Albert and Ta'Nelle read each other's minds for truly it was show time! The couple proceeded to cut a slice of cake and placed it on a plate. Shortly thereafter, the two of them picked up a large piece of the cake. As their eyes met, they both pondered in their mind what they thought the other would do. Before they completed their thoughts, they were in the middle of a small cake fight. Frosting was everywhere. Their parents could not believe their adult children were acting so childish; however, everyone could see the love they shared for each other. The groom's black mustache, beard, mouth, nostril, and a small portion of his left eye were suddenly covered with red, white, green, and cream-colored frosting. The bride was adorned with a beautiful new shade of makeup around her mouth, eyelid, and cheek. To the groom's surprise, his wife had won the battle and now they were even. Albert quickly learned that when Ta'Nelle makes up her mind to win, she wins! Albert and Ta'Nelle had everyone in stitches from laughing so hard. While everyone continued to laugh, they slipped out privately to clean up from the mess they made. Shortly thereafter, they returned to the room where everyone was finishing their desserts and enjoying everything that had taken place thus far.

The cake was magnificent! It was tasty too if I say so myself, in fact, it was so delicious that fifteen or twenty of the guests quickly started licking their fingers and saying, "Humm, Humm mm good!" Truly it is impossible for any of you to taste the cake, but I wanted you to see the picture before it was cut. I did not want to tease you by showing you the crumbs that remained. One of the caterers reached for the cake tray to throw it out when a woman grabbed her hand. As their eyes met the woman said, "Honey, what are you going to do with that?" She replied, "Throw it out!" The lady said, "No, no, no, no, no! Daughter, I will not let you throw those good old crumbs away! Rake them on my plate. You young folks do not know you cannot be throwing away food. Daughter, when I was a child, Momma and Daddy better not see us throwing away tasty food when there is nothing wrong with it. Do you know there are hundreds hungry people in this world that would love to have this food even if it is crumbs, those are big pieces too! We here in America take too many things for granted. Now put it right here on my plate. You're not going to throw those good crumbs away; you surely are not!" When she got the crumbs, she grabbed her fork and started eating until there was nothing left.

LORD, LET THE GOOD TIMES ROLL/PAYBACK

It was now time for the toasts, the wedding couple toasted their guests. First they wanted to thank their Lord Jesus Christ for blessing their beautiful union and all their guests. Next, it was time to hear from the best man Ja'Von Walker. As he stood up, he said, "Can I have your attention, please? Will everyone please stand, and lift your glasses as we toast the wedding couple? To Albert and Ta'Nelle, may you find the joy, peace, and happiness that you both deserve! I pray that the joy you experienced today will continue to follow you throughout your marriage. May the Lord favor you the remainder of your lives as you continue to walk with him!"

Next, it was time for the maid of honor Rosalyn Whitehead Williams to toast the couple. Oh, this should be very, very, good. Remember Albert is now her brother-in-love! I cannot even imagine what is going thru Albert's mind right now, not to mention how nervous he must be. Rosalyn cleared her throat, just to make Albert uncomfortable, and yes it worked! She said, "I want to thank you my dear little sister for choosing me as your maid of honor. I thank God I was able to share on such a sensational occasion. Albert and Ta'Nelle, may you continue to be as happy as you are now!" Albert began to let out a huge breath, he believed everything was going to go smoothly, but would it? Only time would tell. Rosalyn continued by saying, "To Albert, in a wedding, there is a best man and a best woman! The best woman is the maid of honor, which is little old me! The most important duty for the maid of honor is to take care of the bride until the wedding is completed. However, I want you to know I will work o-ver-time, did you hear me, Albert?" All he could do was nod his head. "I will work o-ver-time, if one tear, just one tear fall, from my sister's eyes, just one, that is not a tear of joy. Then it is on! Remember I know where you live! To the newlyweds' happiness, bottoms up!

After the laughter that filled the entire room in response to Rosalyn's remarks Mr. Barnesworth went on to say: "On behalf of the entire Barnesworth family, I stand to welcome this beautiful young, anointed woman of God into our family. Ta'Nelle, we are honored to call you, our daughter. Albert, you could not have chosen a more delightful woman. The joy of the Lord is your strength. Everything you set your hands to do will prosper. If there is anything you need, Belinda and I, are a phone call away. To Albert and Ta'Nelle, we speak blessings over you now and forever in the name of the Father, the Son, and the Holy Ghost!"

Everyone clapped as things continued to go quite smoothly, maybe too smoothly. It was time to hear from Ta'Nelle's parents. The first time Albert met the Whiteheads, Carson made sure he knew the dos and don'ts where Ta'Nelle was concerned. They pride themselves on being a religious, close-knit, protective family. Mr. Whitehead started by saying, "Albert, we love you, and we welcome you into our family. We watched you as well as Ta'Nelle as you dated, and we found you to be a true man of God. Now, Albert, Ta'Nelle is a valuable commodity to her mother and me, and you should never take her for granted. I want the two of you to call and visit as often as you like, but any calls or visits from my daughter that are not pleasant due to your actions are not acceptable." As the room remained silent, Mr. Whitehead cleared his throat and said in a deep thunderous voice, "Do you understand, son?" Albert replied in a weak voice, "Yes, sir!" Mr. Whitehead raised his glass and said, "To Albert and Ta'Nelle, may God continue to bless this union." Albert grabbed his handkerchief and wiped the sweat off his face while feeling relieved. One of the guests said, "Albert, better behave because Daddy do not play!" One of the ladies replied, "Big sister Rosalyn don't play either!"

Shortly after everyone had finished toasting the couple, the church secretary, Mrs. Butterfield, moved to the microphone. She began by saying, "Good afternoon. Currently, I stand to give a special tribute to the wedding couple. First, I want to congratulate you on your new marriage. The following events that are about to take place were designed with you in mind. Albert and Ta'Nelle, your parents handpicked a group of young ladies to entertain you by way of dance. I ask you to pay remarkably close attention. The young ladies range from the tender age of thirteen to twenty years old. Although you have only been married two hours, it is important that you know you will experience life's trials and tribulations.

"During those times, you will need to encourage each other so you will be victorious over all obstacles the enemy place in your path. So, to help you on your journey of wedded bliss, we put together a special program that we believe you and your guests will enjoy. The young ladies will perform three dance routines. The first one is, "Be Encouraged." There may be times when you rethink your marriage. You may say to yourselves, what was I thinking? We want you to remember that things are not always the way they appear. Look to the Lord, think of the good things you love about each other, and focus on your dreams.

"After you have encouraged each other, remember that you both said yes! That yes was to each other, but most importantly, you said yes to the Lord. You said yes to the Lord's will and his way. The second song is "Say Yes." Finally, after saying yes, you must recognize that you are no longer two individuals, but one flesh. And in so doing, Albert, you are not Albert without Ta'Nelle. Ta'Nelle, you are not Ta'Nelle without Albert. You are family, and you need each other to survive. And to help you keep your love fresh, the young ladies will perform their final dance, "I need you to survive." Now without any further ado, we ask Apostle Woods to come and introduce our special musical guests."

Apostle Woods said, "We came out to celebrate a marriage between Albert and Ta'Nelle. This marriage is not an ordinary marriage, you see, there are thousands of people getting married every day. But there are few marriages ordained by God, and this one is! When God ordains a marriage, the couple is ready to be committed to one another. The couple is not easily swayed, or tempted by others. You know God is well pleased with this union because his presence has been with this couple throughout their courtship. God's glory has been revealed in the church and here in this reception hall. And God's glory is all over this couple. So, whenever you need a pick-me-up, he is there! Just in case you did not know, God is good all the time! Come on everyone put your hands together for the Anointed Praise Dancers under the direction of Elderess Gabrielle Shoemaker."

The girls danced with their whole hearts. They were given a standing ovation and thunderous applause. To show their appreciation, the girls humbled themselves and bowed in reference to the Lord. Ta'Nelle was all to pieces. When she

saw the young ladies' faithfulness, she let out a huge hallelujah.
Before she knew it, she was doing a praise dance of her own.
All Apostle Woods could say was, "The fire of the Holy Ghost
is in this place." The Holy Ghost filled that reception hall
and even the servers, were praising God in the in the spirit.
Once everyone recuperated and returned to their prospective
places, the program continued. Mrs. Butterfield, the church
secretary, said, "Albert and Ta'Nelle there will be times, when
you will become upset with each other. During those times,
your mind may take you places you have no right to go. While
going through this, you will need to seek guidance from the
Lord. Here are four verses of scripture that we feel will help
you get a grip on every situation. Psalm 51:10, "Create in me
a clean heart, O God; and renew a right spirit within me,"
And if you believe what you have asked of the Lord, you will
stand on his word. Mark 11:22–24, 'And Jesus answering saith
unto them, Have faith in God. For verily I say unto you, that
whosoever shall say unto this mountain, be thou removed, and
be thou cast into the sea; and shall not doubt in his heart but
shall believe that those things which he saith shall happen; he
shall have whatsoever he saith. Therefore, I say unto you, what
things soever ye desire, when ye pray, believe that ye receive
them, and ye shall have them.' After obtaining the victory, you
can say without a doubt, he keeps on blessing me repeatedly.
After everything has been spoken and done, you can testify,
"Lord, I know you've been so good to me!"

"At this time, I would like to introduce a group of young
men, that can and, will sing. They will bless the Barnesworths
with four selections: 'Give me a clean heart. Have a little
faith. You keep on blessing me. And Lord, I know you have
been so good' Put your hands together for Mr. James Boddie
and the Faithful Few!" As the guests applauded, the group

gathered around the microphones. Mr. Boddie congratulated the Barnesworths on their marriage and thanked them for the opportunity to perform on such a joyous occasion. Once they started singing, the guests were overjoyed and wanted more. However, Mr. Boddie thanked everyone and let them know that the group genuinely believed, in being obedient and turned the microphones back over to Mrs. Butterfield.

The Barnesworths were very satisfied with everything that had taken place, but there were three or a four more things left to do before they could leave on their honeymoon. First, they thanked everyone for coming out and sharing in the celebration of their new life together. Secondly, they wanted the guests to know the importance of marrying a saved, sanctified, and Holy Ghost-filled mate. They stated if they would have had a theme for their wedding, it would have been, "To God Be the Glory!" For truly, all honor and praise solely belong to our Lord and Savior Jesus Christ!

At last, it was time to throw the bouquet and the garter belt. Ta'Nelle asked all the single ladies to gather in front of her and away from the other guests as she prepared to throw the bouquet. She had no idea there were so many single women in attendance. She turned her back to the ladies and counted to three, threw the bouquet up, and caught it immediately after it left her fingertips. The ladies believed she was playing with them, but she was double-checking to make sure she was throwing the bouquet with the fresh flowers. If nothing else, the ladies had a quick practice run. When Ta'Nelle finally threw the bouquet, she heard a loud commotion. At that moment, she believed it was a suitable time to move as far away from the ladies as possible. As she turned to see what was happening, to her surprise, seven of the ladies were on the floor struggling over the bouquet.

Destiny Harris and Makaila Richardson (the bridesmaids), had to put their two senses into the festivities. Although they had no desire to marry any time soon, they made sure they edged the women on to get the most out of the situation. It did not take much; the women were on a mission. One thing is for sure, the women were focused and dedicated, to their cause. The ladies forgot they were wearing formal attire, all they thought about was getting the bouquet. The way they were acting, you would think they were wearing pants. Destiny and Makaila continued to cheer the women on after all the girls just wanted to have a little fun.

The ladies struggled, and struggled, they were determined to get the bouquet at all costs. They forgot where they were and disregarded the video camera. But rest assured, the camera man did not miss a thing! Everyone in attendance laughed as hard as they could. Even the caterers stopped working to enjoy the view. It was truly a sight for sore eyes, or should I say, a picture that no one would soon forget. It was down to the last three women, and all of them thought they had the bouquet. Two of the women gathered themselves off the floor and declared themselves winners only to learn that they were holding a five or six pieces of flesh flowers in their hands. The bride's lovely bouquet suddenly became bits and pieces of shredded flowers. The winner emerged holding the plastic holder with four flowers remaining in tack. Ta'Nelle and the other guests laughed so hard they were in tears once again. The ladies could not wait to see how the guys would act. Of course, they knew whenever Albert threw the garter, there would surely be a show. Albert was determined to steal the spotlight from the women, but truly, he had huge shoes to fill.

Albert took a short break to recover from the ladies' show, at least that is what he wanted everyone to believe. While everyone was gathering themselves, Albert was busy taking the time allotted to think of something to top the ladies. One thing you could count on Albert was going to show his true self. Albert took his time getting the garter off Ta'Nelle's leg. He pulled and pulled, in between pulls, he stopped to see who was watching. He was an entertainer: it took him almost three and a half minutes to finally complete such an easy task. One of the guys said, "Albert, the longer it takes you to remove the garter belt, the longer it will take you to start your honeymoon." Now those words caught Albert's attention. It was as if the guys had lit a bomb under him.

Before they knew it, Albert had removed the garter and was standing up with his back to the guys ready to throw it. Without any notice, he threw the garter into the air. In fact, it was so fast that at least eleven of the guys were totally caught off guard. While they were waiting, they soon learned someone had already caught it. Albert grabbed Ta'Nelle's hand as he looked back at the men and started singing, "It is over now. I feel like I can make it, the reception is over now!" The crowd busted out into laughter at Albert's comical song as he and Ta'Nelle walked out hand in hand to change out of their wedding attire in preparation for their honeymoon. Well as you can see, Albert was unable to outdo the women. Nothing could take away the experience of witnessing women on the floor in formal attire fighting over a bouquet of flowers. You would have thought a fine, rich, athletically fit man of God was going to appear for whoever caught the bouquet. No but at least that is how they acted. I am telling you that sure was hilarious and embarrassing to the women that were fighting.

Meanwhile, as Albert and Ta'Nelle were changing out of their wedding attire, their family members were packing their gifts in their parents' vehicles. The guests on the other hand were busy plotting what would be the best way to pay Albert and Ta'Nelle back, they wanted to send them off with a bang. All the guests were equipped with bags of birdseed and positioned themselves in what they thought was just the right spot to attack the couple. Once the Barnesworths entered the doorway, it was on. It was time for all the guests to repay the couple for the old and the new and they did. As the limo driver opened the door to the limo, Albert and Ta'Nelle produced what they thought was a good plan. They were both in incredibly decent shape, physically so they decided to run as fast as they could to escape their guests' fury.

Unfortunately, for Albert and Ta'Nelle, their guests had plans as well. The guests were lined up on both sides of the establishment ready to attack immediately. They had an abundance of bird seeds under their arms, behind their backs, and in their pockets. At that moment, I am sure they regretted inviting so many guests to their big day, even the children joined in the activities. What was a couple to do? Their physical shape was no longer an advantage, the limo was too far away, and they could not protect each other! Wow! The photographers and the video recorders were ready to film every ounce of footage and they did. The older guests were ready with their cameras, they wanted to have something to remember as well.

Albert tried to bribe his groom men and co-workers to help shield them, but they were on their own. They were technically in more trouble than they ever imagined. Albert and Ta'Nelle ran as fast as they could, but not fast enough to get away bird seed attacks. It appeared that their guests had gotten the last laugh, but did they? Ta'Nelle made a B-line for the limo only to be captured by Destiny and Makaila. The young ladies were at it again, they were determined to give Ta'Nelle as much grief as possible. They wanted her to believe they were trying to rescue her, but not so! You see, they had four co-conspirers waiting in the limo to perform their final attack on Ta'Nelle and they laughed uncontrollably. Shortly, the wedding party was content with their attack on Ta'Nelle and let her relax in the limo.

But what about Albert? I can only imagine the songs that came to his mind at that time, rest assured the most fitting song was, "Trouble in my way! I have to cry sometime, so much trouble in my way, I have to cry sometime! But that's all right! I know Jesus will fix it after while!"

While Albert was trying to escape the fury of his guests, Ta'Nelle was busy enjoying the view. Although they were concerned for each other, they knew they truly were not in any danger. The guests just wanted to have a wonderful time. Albert was on his own, he was looking for a way out of his dilemma. Finally, the poor man surrendered, he said, "Ok you got me I give up!" At that moment, the guests unleashed all their tricks on Albert. Truly they were sending the couple off to start their honeymoon with a bang. Now that is what I call a big send-off! Nobody was mad but the devil!

Although Albert was exhausted and wanted to take a long shower, he still had a little more fight left, and you know he had to strike one more time. Albert shook all his bird seeds off onto Ta'Nelle's lap, and quickly gathered as much as he could. He asked the limo driver to let the window down so he could rid himself of the seeds. He wanted everyone to think he was going to throw the seeds on the ground. (Yeah right.) He stuck his head out the window and started throwing the seeds again. He had forgotten that his friends knew him very well and he would not go down without a fight. Remember he prides himself on winning any task that is before him. As he turned to get some more seeds, his friends came closer to the window. When Albert turned back to the window, he got the surprise of his life. He did not realize that his mouth was wide open, and before he could close it, they loaded it with all the seeds they had left. He laughed and laughed the first time, oh, but the surprise was on him. He motioned for the driver to go so he could rid his mouth of the seeds. Once the limo was around the corner away from the guests, the driver stopped so Albert and Ta'Nelle could rid themselves of the seeds. There were hundreds of happy birds that day. Whoa! Just think this was only the beginning of an adventurous life for Mr. and Mrs. Albert and Ta'Nelle Barnesworth!

Quick Update

Mr. Smooth, the ring bearer, became a professional child model at the tender age of seven. Once he married and became a father, he modeled three or four times a week. He was a role model for his children, a great resolute family-oriented person, and most importantly, a true man of God. His children grew up to be successful adults, and they continued their parent's legacy.

Miss Giggles, the flower carrier, was the center of attention for plenty weddings as a flower carrier. When she became older, she went on to college where she became a successful surgeon. She married and gave birth to three sons and a set of identical twin girls. The boys were very protective over their sisters as well as their mother.

THE BARNESWORTHS
START THEIR NEW LIFE

Albert and Ta'Nelle were off to start their new life. They spent the night in one of the local hotels. Early the next day, they drove to the Raleigh Durham International Airport (RDU) and boarded a plane. They were on their way to New Orleans, Louisiana. Albert planned everything perfectly. They arrived in New Orleans, just in time for Mardi Gras. They could feel the excitement as they checked into their hotel. Albert wanted Ta'Nelle to enjoy their honeymoon in the elegant city of New Orleans, Louisiana. He made sure Ta'Nelle knew that he loved and cherished her from the beginning of their marriage. He was determined to make sure his new bride was happier than she had ever been in her adult life.

While honeymooning, the Barnesworths enjoyed everything New Orleans had to offer. They went on tours of the city. They visited the French Quarters, the home of Tulane and Loyola Universities, the Pontchartrain Hotel, Victorian houses, museum shows of old Mardi Gras costumes, and wax models of pirates. They enjoyed the city parks and sampled different foods from the cooking styles of Creole and Cajun. Distinct items of the foods, although tasty, were a bit too spicy for Ta'Nelle. She was a very health conscience young woman that prided herself in maintaining her girlish figure.

The Barnesworths passionately admired the Mardi Gras. As the jazz bands played, they found themselves moving to the beat of the music. To their surprise, all the newlyweds in attendance were honored as incredibly special guests of the city of New Orleans. The Barnesworths knew their honeymoon would be a celebration they would always remember. They were determined to take full advantage of every opportunity presented to them while on their honeymoon. So, they decided to take a large quantity of pictures and videos as possible to share their special trip with their families and friends. Albert and Ta'Nelle went shopping to get souvenirs, pictures, clothing, whatnots, and memorabilia to be delivered shipped, to their new home. They also purchased items for family and friends that would show their unique personalities. After shopping, the packages were prepared and mailed at the local post office a couple of days before the Barnesworths' return flight home. To Albert's surprise, Ta'Nelle announced she wanted a bite to eat, he could not get into the restaurant fast enough. In his mind, the shopping trip was finished, unfortunately, the shopping resumed immediately after the meal. That day, Albert certainly learned the true meaning of shop until you drop.

Albert was a good man and truly proved it that day, he let Ta'Nelle shop until she was satisfied. Naturally, her satisfaction took five hours longer than Albert ever imagined. Finally, the shopping trip was complete. Albert was exhausted; he could not get to the hotel fast enough. When they entered the room, poor Albert fell on the bed and slept for two and a half hours. Ta'Nelle on the other hand was good to go. While Albert slept, Ta'Nelle took time to pack up the things they purchased. When she finished packing, she decided to watch a little TV until Albert recuperated.

Once Ta'Nelle found something on the tube to watch, it was

as if Albert sensed he was no longer the center of attention. He snored and snored, the more he snored the louder he became. Ta'Nelle knew she had to produce a new plan, watching TV was only a figment of her imagination. Being a character, she decided to pull out the camcorder to tape her husband. She pondered in her mind what she wanted to name her new movie. She said to herself, "Oh my goodness I have the perfect name, "The Orchestra Alberto!" As Albert continued to snore Ta'Nelle decided it would be great if she named the tune that she felt would best describe the sounds she was hearing. Shortly thereafter, Albert was awakened by Ta'Nelle's constant moving. She quickly cut the camcorder off and pretended to be watching TV. "Oh man! He messed up my video, but that is all right, I got him!"

As the saying goes, all good things must end. In less than twenty-four hours, the honeymoon would officially be over. Albert and Ta'Nelle would be boarding a plane back to North Carolina. On their final night, they decided to bid farewell to all the locals and the other couples they met. Afterward, they had dinner followed by a romantic stroll on the beach before calling it a night. The next day, they were up early to start their trip home. The plane was right on schedule, and before long, they were on their way to their new home. Ta'Nelle was so excited she could not wait to see Albert's face when he saw all the trouble, she went through to make their new home special.

As Albert opened the door, he quickly picked Ta'Nelle up and carried her across the thresh hole. He planted a big enthusiastic kiss on her lips. Before he could finish his kiss, he heard, "Surprise! Surprise!" As he opened his eyes, he looked directly into a video camera. He put Ta'Nelle down and then looked around the room only to see it was filled with their relatives and close friends. As Albert and Ta'Nelle made their way around the room to greet their guests, Albert noticed the living room was filled with the furniture the two of them had purchased.

Albert quickly realized Ta'Nelle had tricked him. Although he did not want to be rude to his guests, he wanted to see what else Ta'Nelle had up her sleeve. She grabbed Albert's hand and guided him thru the remainder of the house. She showed him all the furniture the two of them had purchased all neatly in place. He was not satisfied until they walked thru the entire house. She tried her absolute best to convince Albert that all the other rooms were empty but due to her sense of humor, he thought she was joking. As Albert and Ta'Nelle continued to walk thru the house, they saw that the formal dining room and one of the other bedrooms were completely furnished (as a surprise by their parents). They could not thank the Lord or their parents enough. The joy they displayed on their faces was all their parents needed.

Albert and Ta'Nelle's parents had prepared enough food to feed everyone in attendance and had food left over. After they ate, Albert and Ta'Nelle excused themselves for a brief time. They believed it was the perfect time to surprise their guests with their individual gifts. Ta'Nelle had her fragile gifts in their suitcases and her parents placed the other gifts in their bedroom. They also wanted to share the flash drive of their incredibly special honeymoon. That afternoon was filled with surprises. The guests' reactions to their gifts were just what the couple expected. But the best was yet to come! Ta'Nelle could not imagine how surprised Albert would be when he realized that all his snoring was caught on tape. Once again, Albert was tricked, and everyone enjoyed it. He was teased for months about, "The Orchestra Alberto!"

Right when Albert was rejoicing from his newfound freedom,

he saw an old college friend he had not seen since their college years. As they greeted each other, the man said, "Hey, man, I am so sorry we lost touch for a while. I graduated a year before you. I heard that you got married to the whitehead girl, I forgot her first name. Congratulations, man! You have a good woman and I was told you had a nice size wedding too. I would love to stay connected with you. I got married too, but it did not work out. I know you and Mrs. cut up at the wedding." Albert said, "Thanks, man. Yes, we cut up a little bit. You know me, man, I had to be myself. We had lots of fun, everyone got a good laugh. Man, me and Ta'Nelle had the place rocking. We praised God in the church and at the reception. You know, if you start out right, then everything will fall into place! We love and respect each other. I could not have asked the Lord to give me a better wife than Ta'Nelle!"

The friend said, "That's good, man. I was not as smart as you. I married a girl for the wrong reason. Neither one of us had the Lord in our lives. She was beautiful, with a nice figure, and I just had to have her, so I thought. Whenever I thought about her, I could not sleep, I could not eat without seeing her on my plate. Wow man, she just rocked my world. I had to talk to her every few hours, and I could not go anywhere without having her on my arm. So, I married her, and boy, oh boy, she rocked my world all right! That beautiful face and that fine figure did not mean a thing! She had the nastiest attitude, in fact, everything I thought I loved was all lust. She pretended to be something that she was not, and silly me fell for it. Man, I could not get rid of her fast enough. Today, I can honestly say I learned my lesson. I did a complete turnaround. I have accepted the Lord Jesus Christ as my Savior. I have a call on my life, and I am waiting for the manifestation of his Spirit. I told the Lord as I was going thru with my divorce, if he gets me out of the mess I had gotten myself into, I would wait on him. Hey man, we must stay in touch this time. I need you in my life. You were a profound influence on me while we were in college. Oh Man, I was informed you have a new nickname, 'Orchestra Alberto.' I heard about that when I asked someone how could I reach you. Your wife got you good! *Ha, ha, ha, ha.* Man, I am sorry but whenever I think about you, it just makes me laugh. Here is my card, call me sometimes. Chat later, Alberto!"

The Barnesworths' New Arrival

After Albert and Ta'Nelle were married for almost three years, they were confident that they had saved up enough money to start their family. They wanted their first child to be a son, but regardless, of the child's gender if the child was healthy, that is all that mattered. Once the decision was made, an appointment was made to see the doctor. After the examination, the doctor informed them that they could proceed with their plans. They were positive that within a two or three months, they would be expecting their first child. After three or four few weeks, Ta'Nelle noticed some changes in her body, she was experiencing several things that she had never felt before. Unknowing to her husband, she ventured to the drug store and purchased a pregnancy test. She read the instructions on the box, unfortunately, she had to maintain her cool until the following morning before administering the test. She could hardly wait until morning, but she tried her best not to disturb her husband. Before long, Ta'Nelle was awakened by the alarm clock, it was time to get up. She set the alarm thirty minutes earlier so she could take the test before going to work. While Albert was fast asleep, the test results revealed a positive sign, she was indeed pregnant.

She was so excited she started rejoicing immediately. She

yelled so loud that Albert awakened out of his peaceful sleep. He yelled, "Honey, what is wrong? What is wrong?" All she could say was, "Oh my god! Oh my god!" As she pointed to the test in her hand she said, "Look! Look! Look!" Albert jumped up out of his comfortable bed, ran into the bathroom, and said, "What? What?" She said, "Ooh, ooh, ooh," while pointing to the test. The poor man thought his wife was losing her mind, he had absolutely no clue to what she was pointing. She finally was able to speak the English language and said, "Honey, we are pregnant! We are having a baby!"

Ta'Nelle could barely wait for the doctor's office to open. Meanwhile, they went to work and after about an hour, Ta'Nelle received a call from the receptionist stating they could come in the following week. However, she asked the receptionist to call her if there were any cancellations. She also left a message on the nurse's voicemail to ask the doctor to order the necessary lab work, so she could get the results on her visit. Albert and Ta'Nelle were finally on their way to the doctor's office. Immediately after their arrival at the office, Ta'Nelle checked in at the desk. In five minutes, they were on their way to the examination rooms. Shortly after, the nurse recorded all Ta'Nelle's vital signs and returned to the nurse's station, the doctor entered the room. He was determined not to keep Ta'Nelle and Albert in suspense any longer than necessary. As he sat on the stool, he opened his laptop to review the lab tests. The doctor said, "Your vital signs are exceptional, just where they need to be for an expectant mother!" Although that was the news the Barnesworths was expecting, it went right over their head. In other words, they did not hear a thing! Albert and Ta'Nelle looked at each other, and looked back at the doctor. It was as if they did not hear or understand a word he said. At that point, the doctor said in a noticeably clear, slow voice, "Congratulations! You are having a baby!"

Albert and Ta'Nelle were overjoyed. They were told to expect the baby on or around July 12. They were given a copy of a diet of things that would be good for the health of the baby and, a prescription for prenatal vitamins. Ta'Nelle would return to the doctor's office in one month. She was almost five weeks, but in her mind, July was quite a distance away. She informed the doctor that she had been experiencing morning sickness for two weeks, and it was unbearable. The doctor told her to snack on crackers to help with the morning sickness until she enters her second trimester.

When Albert and Ta'Nelle left the doctor's office, they went directly to the drugstore to get the prenatal vitamins. Afterward, they went to a restaurant to grab an early lunch before going to work. Ta'Nelle wanted to start her vitamins immediately, but when she saw the size of the pills: she had second thoughts. After a few days on the pills, she could not decide which was worst, the morning sickness or the vitamins. In her words, the pills, "smelled terrible and tasted like raw eggs," but she would take the pills for the baby's sake! Thankfully after three months, the morning sickness was a thing of the past.

By the time Ta'Nelle was four months, she had a pretty baby bump. Soon thereafter, she was given an ultrasound to make sure the baby was growing properly. Everything was going great, the baby's growth was right on schedule. Unfortunately, the baby was not positioned correctly to determine the sex. Finally, after two months, a second ultrasound was performed, and the couple was assured that the baby was a girl. Before long, the couple was going to the doctor every two weeks. When Ta'Nelle's pregnancy entered the end of the eighth month, the doctor's appointments increased to once a week until the baby was born.

On June 29, the doctor revealed to the Barnesworths that it would not be long before their bundle of joy arrives. On July 1, the labor pains started, and when the pains were ten minutes apart, the couple checked into the hospital. Ta'Nelle had what was considered to be truly short labor. The baby was born at 12:05 a.m. on July 2, and she weighed 5 lbs. and 3 ounces. She was completely healthy and given the name Ta'Nya Monae. Ta'Nya's complexion was pecan tan, her eyes were deep brown, and she had black, thick, curly hair just like her parents. They were very, very happy with their newborn baby.

Ta'Nya was growing so fast, she was a good baby. She was starting to resemble her mother increasingly more every day. When she became sleepy, she would play in her hair until she knocked herself out. Her mother tried to discourage her from playing in her hair by removing her hand and rubbing her fingers until she was asleep. As she grew older, she would be put in the crib with a bottle. At times, she would grab her hair and twist it until she was fast asleep. When she was three months old, her mother placed her in daycare so she could return to work. She hated to leave her baby, but she knew it was time.

The more Ta'Nya grew, the more independent she became. She loved to find her own way. Whenever she tried something and it did not work, she would work at it until she ran out of ideas, then and only then would she ask for assistance. Her parents jokingly called her Miss Independent. The Barnesworths had no idea that their little girl would truly live up to that name. As Ta'Nya continued to grow older, she developed a deeper love for her hair. It seemed that in every free moment she had, she played and pulled her hair. Ta'Nelle tried to stop her, but there was no way possible to watch her every move and shortly there were four spots on her head that was completely bald, thanks to her fingers. Ta'Nelle could only comb Ta'Nya's hair after she had fallen asleep.

When Ta'Nya was almost two years old, she became a big sister to her parents' second baby. Once again, the baby was a girl and she was named Alanta Ja'Nae. Ta'Nya was a little jealous of her baby sister but after a couple weeks, her parents believed she had recovered from it. To their surprise, Ta'Nya's whole attitude changed for the worst. She truly was living up to her nickname, she was very stubborn and disobedient, however, she was smart enough to try to fool her parents. While returning to the daycare, Ta'Nya began showing jealousy toward the other children. She became very selfish and wanted all the attention. When the teacher worked with the other children, Ta'Nya would do whatever she could to disrupt the class. She started pulling the other girl's hair, fighting, throwing things across the room, and tearing up the other children's work. The teacher tried to calm Ta'Nya down but once she left her presence, she started acting out again. The teacher went home before Ta'Nelle came to pick her up but she wrote a note and placed it in her backpack. When Ta'Nelle questioned her, she said the teacher was lying to her and she did not like her. After listening to her, Albert and Ta'Nelle made it clear that she goes to the daycare to learn not to start trouble, and they would not stand by and let her have her way! The next day, Ta'Nelle received another note about Ta'Nya. Ta'Nelle decided it would be best to go to the school and watch Ta'Nya. She could not believe the things she was seeing. Ta'Nya was hitting the students as well as the teacher. At that moment, and to Ta'Nya's surprise, Ta'Nelle entered the classroom and confronted her. On occasions, the Barnesworths would spank Ta'Nya's hands, take away her dolls, take her snacks, or put her in time-out, but nothing worked. They prayed

and asked the Lord to show them what was making their little
girl's attitude change so drastically in such a brief time. As they
pondered in their minds the things Ta'Nya was doing and when
she started to change, the Lord revealed to them what was going
on with her. Ta'Nya was still jealous of her baby sister and was
taking it out on everyone she met.

Albert and Ta'Nelle knew it was time for a reality check.
Ta'Nya had to come under submission immediately. She had
to learn finally that she was a child and would remain in a
child's place one way or another. Although they were upset with
her, they understood and started including her when feeding,
holding, and changing her baby sister Alanta. However, they
made sure they always kept a close eye on her. Ta'Nya began to
calm down once more and her teacher sent notes of improvement
home every week. Ta'Nya's family was so proud of her and
showered her with all the love they could muster up.

After a two and a half years, the Barnesworths welcomed
their third child. She was named Jamberlyn Latrice. Ta'Nya
was fine with the new baby. She was growing up and was no
longer jealous of her siblings, in fact, she welcomed them. When
she became eight, she entered a new chapter of her little young
life. She was a pretty, little girl, but in her mind, she did not fit
in with the crowd at school. She wanted to do something about
it, so she started doing her hair. She would leave home with her
hair freshly done by her mother, only to return with a style of
her very own. Her mother tried to stop her from combing her
hair, she talked to her, but it seems to have fallen on deaf ears.

One day, Ta'Nya decided she wanted to go a little further
so she cut her hair. When she returned home from school,
her mother could not believe what her daughter had done, all
she could do was take her to the hairdresser to get her hair
trimmed. Ta'Nelle understood why Ta'Nya was changing her

hair, she did the same thing when she was her age. Ta'Nya wanted to look more mature. Alanta said, "Mommy, Ta'Nya will be an um, um what you call the lady that comb ladies' hair in her house?" Ta'Nelle said, "A beautician, or a hairdresser." Alanta said, "Yes, a what you just said. Mommy she will comb hair in her own house. She will have so many girls' hair to comb that they will have to wait a long time to get their hair done. People will come from state to state to let Ta'Nya do their hair, even the people with lots of (rich) money. People from TV will come too, they will get on airplanes to come to her house. Mommy some of the people will live around here. People will hear about the respectable job Ta'Nya does and will fly her to their house so she can comb their hair. She will be one of the best hair ladies in the whole wide world. She will name her house, "Nya's House of Styles!" Ta'Nelle was surprised yet empowered, all at once as she listened to her baby. She said, "Well whatever she wants to do as long as she is happy is fine with your dad and I!"

While Ta'Nya was going thru her hair issues and growing pains, Ta'Nelle was facing something she thought she would never have to deal with. She was experiencing discomfort in her abdomen and scheduled an appointment to see her doctor. During her appointment, she informed the doctor that her menstrual cycle was normal, and she had no complaints about morning sickness, or anything related to pregnancy. Therefore, the doctor did not see any reason to order a pregnancy test. She was examined, and additional tests would be ordered over the next few weeks, she would receive a call from the doctor if there were any positive results. He believed it was something as simple as a hormonal imbalance. Whatever the case, the doctor assured Ta'Nelle that she had nothing to worry about. She went about her normal routine: she took aspirin or another mild pain reliever when necessary. She was not a worrying person she truly lived and walked by her faith.

While Ta'Nelle was waiting on her test results, Ta'Nya was busy searching for ways to look more mature. She noticed that ten of the girls in her class had long, pretty hair, and she wanted to wear the hairstyles they were wearing. She wanted her hair to grow and while waiting, she practiced styling the hair on her dolls. Once the doll's hair became bald, Ta'Nya no longer had any use for it. She then asked her parents to buy her dolls with thick long hair. At that point, Ta'Nelle was grateful that her daughter had learned that a girl's hair is a very important part of her appearance. She was quite comfortable letting her mother or the hairdresser maintain her hair.

At last, Ta'Nelle received the call she was patiently waiting for from her doctor. All the tests came back negative. She was still having a little discomfort, so the doctor told her to come to the lab the next day to submit a urine and blood specimens. He would call her as soon as he receives the results. The next day, Ta'Nelle showed up at the lab at 8:00 a.m. After ten minutes, she was on her way to work, Ta'Nelle was terribly busy and before she knew it was lunch time. The doctor was busy in the delivery room delivering a set of twins, and he took an early lunch before going to his office. By the time the doctor made it to the office it was 12:30 p.m. He quickly ran into his office to put on his lab coat and check on Ta'Nelle's test results. While putting his arm in the sleeve of his coat, he glanced at the results and was totally caught off guard. He was so shocked that he fell in his seat, and said, "Well, you do not say! I would have never thought about that!" The doctor was a man of his word, he immediately picked up the phone and called Ta'Nelle. She was both shocked and relieved when she received the test results.

Albert had no idea that his wife was having abdominal

discomfort. She did not want to trouble him over something that may very well turn out to be nothing. Although Ta'Nelle's tests were done secretly, she knew Albert had to be informed, immediately. After getting off work, she picked up the girls and went home to start their dinner. About thirty minutes before she finished cooking, Albert walked into the house. She wanted to tell him her news but she felt it would be best after the girls were asleep, and the two of them were preparing for bed. As Ta'Nelle sat on the edge of the bed, she grabbed Albert's arm and pulled him next to her. He wondered what was on her mind. As he sat there attentively, Ta'Nelle began to explain to him all she had endured the last few weeks. She was not the kind of woman who prolonged things; she was straightforward. She was careful to make sure Albert understood everything she word that was spoken.

After having Jamberlyn, the Barnesworths thought they were finished having children. Jamberlyn was merely eighteen months old when Ta'Nelle learned she was expecting again. They used precautions so there would not be any more children soon. But to their surprise, she was carrying what she hoped would be her final baby. Naturally, after the initial shock wore off, the Barnesworths had high hopes, that they would finally give birth to the son they wanted so desperately. After a month the girls were told the news. Ta'Nya and Jamberlyn wanted a little brother. Alanta on the other hand said, "Mommy and Daddy, I know you want the baby to be a boy badly, but unfortunately, the new baby is another girl. You will name her Anointia Denise!" Although they listened and were amazed at Alanta's prediction, they truly hoped she was wrong. After a few months, the Barnesworths was disappointed when the ultrasound clearly showed that the baby was indeed another girl. Regardless of their disappointment, they declared the baby as another blessing from God. They were incredibly happy with their family. At birth, all the girls were almost identical, except for their complexion and their own unique personality.

After the baby was born, Ta'Nya's priorities changed. She made sure she stayed focused at school and maintained straight A's until she completed high school. She was determined to be the best big sister she could be by setting a good example for her sisters both in school and at home. Although she loved to style hair, she outgrew the dolls and replaced them with mannequins. When Ta'Nya entered high school, the young boys tried to whisper in her ear, but she remained focused on her dreams. She was adamant that she would not let anything or anyone stand in the way of her dreams.

Ta'Nya was sixteen years old when she graduated from early college. In addition to her high school diploma, she also received a certificate in cosmetology. After a couple of weeks, Ta'Nya received the papers needed to take her state boards. She was so excited that she called and scheduled an appointment as soon as possible. She talked to five of the local beauticians to let them know she was going to take her tests on the next available date. Two of the shop owners informed Ta'Nya that she could work in their shop as a shampooer until she received her license. They also had a booth open if she was interested in collaborating with them.

Ta'Nya could not wait to take her state board exam, she was so excited and ready to start her new career. Finally, it was the day of the test, and before she knew it, she was at the office. Ta'Nya took the test and breezed thru it. She believed that she had aced the test. That afternoon, she reported to one of the hairdressers to work as a shampooer until she became a full beautician. On the thirtieth day after taking the test, Ta'Nya received notification in the mail, she was a licensed beautician. Ta'Nya was a very humble young lady that were instructed by her parents, to be the best she could be, in order to be successful. She planned to work in that shop until she built up her reputation with her clients. Meanwhile, at night, she returned to college for business administration and received her associates degree. She planned to open her business one day and wanted to make sure she knew all the aspects of business.

In two months after Ta'Nya started working she made a name for herself. People were coming from the surrounding areas for Ta'Nya to style their hair. She had a reputation as one of the best beauticians in the state, just as Alanta predicted less than six years ago. She had more customers than she could manage, but would do whatever she could to work others in. Shortly she had to get her own telephone line because the other stylist's customers could never contact them. She was booked up for weeks at a time and had customers on standby in hopes of a cancellation. Ta'Nya's dream of having her own beauty salon was in her grasp. She was confident her business would be successful because she was taught by the best parents, the best instructors, and the best beauticians. She wanted her business to be her very own and decided it would be best to build her salon rather than rent one. She hired a contractor to draw up plans for her new salon and to let her know how many acres of land she would need. She was given an estimate of the finances needed to accomplish her goals. Ta'Nya's parents saved money in an account for all their girls to be used for their college education. If you remember, Ta'Nya attended college on scholarships. However, since Ta'Nya did not use any of the money set aside for her, she had a jump start on her finances. She added to her finances by saving as much money, as she could. After about a year, she was able to purchase the land she needed for her business. Six months later, she had saved enough money to start the building by using her land as collateral. The contractor informed Ta'Nya that her salon would be ready to occupy in six months or less. The building would be twelve feet by twenty-five square feet with an eight feet ceiling and totally equipped with all the necessities. If everything went as planned, the building would be ready to occupy in five or six months. She wanted three stalls in each bathroom and each to be wheelchair accessible. She was overjoyed and planned to name her new business, "Nya's House of Styles." Ta'Nya wanted her new salon to be big enough to accommodate other stylists. She hoped to hire two beauticians and three barbers.

Once the word spread that Ta'Nya was opening a new salon, she hired one experienced hairstylist and one experienced barber. Ta'Nya wanted to give back to the community and help new stylists and barbers get established. She returned to the beauty school to talk to her former instructors. She informed them that she was looking for only the best workers she could find to fill the positions in her salon her reputation truly depended on it. Because she expected the absolute best, she required that all her new employees graduate at the top of their class. She wanted the students to know that she would be interviewing barbers as well as stylists within the next few weeks. She would only need one stylist and two barbers. She already had a well-established hair stylist and a barber to start immediately upon the opening of her salon. She would consider hiring two stylists that could manage both men and women. She would not tolerate rude, or ill-mannered individuals.

When Ta'Nya opened her business, she was twenty years old. Her parents were extremely proud of her and made sure she knew it. The salon was decorated with twelve spiritual pictures, ornaments, and a variety of green prayer plants, peace lilies and blooming cactus plants. Ta'Nya wanted the customers to feel welcomed the moment they entered the establishment. The day before the shop opened, Ta'Nya, and all her employees, had a grand opening. She invited her pastor, the town council members, including the mayor, and the families and friends of the staff along with her former teachers at the early college. Once the shop opened; it was fully staffed. As the customers entered the shop, they were asked to sign in and put the time of their appointment. To keep down confusion, all the stylists or barbers had their own sign-in book. Ta'Nya wanted to make sure the customers were in the stylist's chair within five or ten minutes of their appointment. Nya's House of Styles would be open six days a week. On Mondays, Tuesdays, Thursdays, and Fridays, the shop would open from 8:00 a.m. to 6:00 p.m. However, on Wednesdays, and Saturdays, she would open from 6:00 a.m. to 2:00 p.m. She wanted to do anything that she could do to make her customers happy.

No matter how tired Ta'Nya became, she was available to be faithful and active in her church. She was a member of the church all her young life. She developed quite a singing voice and was a soprano as well as one of the lead singers. Her pastor often told her that she was the life of the choir because of her unique singing style. When the congregation was not lively enough for the pastor, he always asked Ta'Nya to sing. In his eyes, she knew how to bring the congregation to their feet. I guess you could say, she rocked the house. As the pastor preached her morning message, Ta'Nya was always in the amen corner. She had a way of provoking her pastor into letting the Lord use her and she truly did. When the invitation was given to the congregation to accept Jesus Christ as their Lord and savior, or join the church, the choir always managed to put the icing on the cake by singing a soul-searching song.

Ta'Nya was successful in every aspect of her life. She was

growing spiritually, physically, financially, and mentally. Once or twice, she had to discipline one of her employees. They did not want to obey her because of her age, in their eyes, she was a child. She kindly let them know they would obey her rules and regulations, or they could work someplace else. Ta'Nya had a lot on her plate, but yet she knew how to manage her business. Ta'Nya made sure she stayed busy but still found time to have a social life. She was dating; however, she was waiting for that special man of God to come and sweep her off her feet. She was determined to stay in the will of God. She had hopes of marrying one day but was not in any rush. The man that she would marry had to confess Jesus as his Lord and Savior and be, Holy Ghost-filled, and exhibit the same love, affection, and understanding as her father. She wanted the same love to exist in her life that she had witnessed from her family and would not settle for anything less. Ta'Nya's parents set ambitious standards for her and her sisters to live by. Due to her home training, Ta'Nya also set high ambitions for herself in whatever she became involved with.

Nya's House of Styles continued to prosper. Ta'Nya and her co-workers extended their hours to two or three days a week especially due to special occasions or funerals. Because of the love that Ta'Nya displayed among her employees and customers, she led eighty-five percent of her clients to Christ. The clients considered Nya's House of Styles a filling station for the Lord when they needed an encouraging word, tell a testimony or just be a witness for the Lord. Who would have thought you can serve the Lord, get delivered, and get a right now word while getting your hair styled/cut? God moves wherever He is welcomed! Amen somebody!

Ta'Nya and her staff were so well-known that the rich and famous would fly in to get their hair done. Sometimes, Ta'Nya would make trips to California, Chicago, and Washington, D.C., to further prosper her business. Ta'Nya remained humble in everything the Lord blessed her with, and she hung signs above her doors that read, "Without God, I Can Do Nothing and to God Be the Glory!"

ALBERT AND TA'NELLE EXPECT THEIR SECOND CHILD

On December twenty-fourth the Barnesworths welcomed their second child, just in time for Christmas. She was referred to as their Christmas miracle. She was 8 lbs. and 5 oz. and was named, Alanta Ja'Nae. Ta'Nya was fine with having a little sister until she was released, from the hospital. Whenever Alanta cried, so did Ta'Nya. Their parents truly had double for their troubles and had to find a way to close one of those mouths, Ta'Nya's. Ta'Nelle said, "Albert, Momma often said out of the mouth of babes, and she would explain it as knowledge or wisdom, but all I hear out of this child's mouth is a bunch of noise!" Albert started laughing and said, "Honey, you are a mess, you will make me crack my side laughing so hard!" Ta'Nelle was doing her absolute best to help Ta'Nya adjust to having a new baby in the house. When Alanta was sleeping, Ta'Nelle made sure she spent as much quality time as she could with Ta'Nya.

Alanta was a complete handful, Ta'Nelle believed she would learn quite a bit from her, but she did not know the extent of it. She was a very observant, or some people may say, nosy baby. It seemed as if she saw everything and everyone that came into her view. She was an exceptionally light sleeper and a simple tip-toe would awaken her. Once she awakened, she would rotate her eyes around the room to see what was going on. There were times when Ta'Nelle would enter the room thinking her baby was asleep only to see her pretty eyes scoping the room. She decided to call her by her middle name Ja'Nae. Although she was a quiet baby, she was the opposite of Ta'Nya. Three hours after her birth, she was turning over and making baby noises. When she reached the tender age of one week, she had a way of letting her mother know when she was not comfortable. She would squirm, wiggle, and make such an ugly face until her blanket were on her correctly. Once Alanta was comfortable she would reward her mother with a big smile. She was in a class all by herself.

When Albert entered the room, he was told of all the things Ta'Nelle discovered about their baby in just one week. Albert could not picture his baby doing all the things Ta'Nelle mentioned, he had to see it for himself. As Albert stood there watching the baby, he was shocked. As he shook his head, he said, "Wow! This is unbelievable, I know we have the right baby because she looks just like Ta'Nya. However, she appears to be, much older than one week. She is doing things that babies do at six or even nine months old!" Albert and Ta'Nelle soon realized that Ja'Nae had a way of getting what she wanted, whenever she wanted it. They were curious to find out what else their baby would teach them in the not-so-distant future. Ta'Nelle looked at Albert and said, "Honey we better hold on because I believe we are in for a bumpy ride!" And ride they did as you will soon see.

At the tender age of one month, Ja'Nae was sitting up and holding her bottle. Ta'Nelle became deeply concerned due to the baby's recent activities. Although she was loved by everyone, she was good baby until she started teething. The poor baby tried everything she could to get some relief, from the agony she was experiencing. Ta'Nelle brought a teething ring and teething gel to put on her gums along with medication for her fever. She gummed everything that was within her reach. Once she cut her first teeth, she seemed to calm down. She did not know what happened, all she knew was that the agony was gone.

When Ja'Nae started cutting her third and fourth teeth, she became unbearable. After the fourth teeth came in, she was a complete biting machine, no one was safe around her. She would bite anything and anyone that came close enough to her. Once she realized she was causing pain to others, she would bite until she became amused, and she laughed and laughed. Ta'Nya was constantly on the defense against her. When her cousins came to visit, she would attack them as well. They became so angry with her that they started to retaliate by hitting her, remember Ja'Nae had a way of getting what she wanted, but would she, this time? She would cry so sadly that her family members could not bear to hear her and would quickly comfort her. Unfortunately, for the relatives, Ja'Nae would take advantage of every opportunity. Before they knew it, she was biting them yet again. Ta'Nelle had enough; she made up her mind that she was going to do whatever was necessary to put a stop to her bad habit. She picked Ja'Nae up and tried to calm her down. Ta'Nelle was ready for any trick Ja'Nae would attempt to do. Once Ja'Nae calmed down, she started playing with her mother's fingers. While Ta'Nelle was talking to their relatives, Ja'Nae believed it was a suitable time to strike. While holding her mother's fingers, Ja'Nae reached down and tried to bite her. Ta'Nelle warned her to stop but she had to continue until she won the battle. Doesn't that sound familiar, Ta'Nelle at her wedding reception?

Ja'Nae was stubborn and determined to win every battle regardless of who she struggled against. She was smart but not as smart as she thought. As she placed her mother's fingers in her mouth, she pretended to suck on them in hope of catching Ta'Nelle off guard. To Ja'Nae's surprise when she put her mother's finger in her mouth, she had two of her own as well. After ten or twelve seconds, she bit down on the fingers with all her might. She had highly hoped that she was biting her mother's fingers but shortly thereafter felt the pain on her own. Poor Ja'Nae had lost the battle yet again and was ready to retire, the pain proved to be more than she could tolerate. To the delight of the Barnesworths and the other relatives, that, was the end of Ja'Nae's biting frenzy.

Immediately after Ja'Nae surrendered, Ta'Nelle went into the kitchen to prepare dinner. She knew it was time for her baby to find another way to exercise her gums. That afternoon, Ta'Nelle prepared baked chicken, broccoli and cheese, and mashed potatoes. Ja'Nae's chicken and broccoli were chopped into small pieces. For dessert, she would eat baby peaches while the other family members would eat a fruit salad. After Ja'Nae finished her meal, she was given a chicken bone to nibble on. That day, Ta'Nelle managed to satisfy Ja'Nae's stomach and her gums at the same time. Oh, happy day!

One afternoon Ta'Nelle got off work and went to the daycare to get the girls and three of their cousins; the children were to help keep Ja'Nae occupied so Ta'Nelle could cook their dinner. The TV was turned on to Ja'Nae's favorite cartoons so she could watch the TV while the children were doing their homework. When Ta'Nelle started cooking she opened up the windows, cut the vent on and closed the door tightly in order to prevent the smell of food from traveling into the living room. Within an hour the kitchen was filled with the odor from the food.

Ja'Nae smelled something but she did not know what it was, so she returned to her cartoons. The children knew that Ta'Nelle's time was almost up, so they started playing with Ja'Nae. Before long the smells were strong. Ta'Nelle heard

he children playing so she rushed and grabbed two small bowls to put food in to cool, she knew Ja'Nae was getting impatient. By the time Ta'Nelle finished placing the food in the second bowl, Ja'Nae was pushing on the door as hard as she could. The door opened after the third try s, and Ja'Nae climbed up on the chair and looked at her mother running around the room. She had enough, she yelled, "Mama eat! Mama eat! Mama, Mama eat!" Ta'Nelle grabbed the first bowl and placed it on the table so her baby could eat. Ja'Nae was eating so fast that she was grabbing the second bowl when Albert entered the kitchen. She was truly a daddy's girl, when she laid her eyes on Albert, nothing else seemed to matter, not even her stomach. Ja'Nae reached for her daddy and that was all she wrote. She jumped and jumped until Albert picked her up. Forget about the food, Albert was all she needed or wanted at that moment. You can best believe Ta'Nelle was glad to see her husband come into the kitchen.

Every day, Albert tried his best to get home from work as soon as possible to help with Ja'Nae. He would enter the back door to have a few minutes to shower before Ja'Nae realized he was home. Regardless of how exhausted Albert was, he always was available for his family, especially Ja'Nae. Once he entered the family room, he could see that Ta'Nelle needed rest. Ja'Nae had worn her out. Ta'Nelle on the other hand never admitted she was tired, however, when she sat down, she was out like a light. Albert was determined to muster up all the energy he could to be the best father he could be and to help raise his children. He was truly a good man that stepped in whenever and wherever needed.

Ja'Nae was a very smart and energetic little girl. Whenever she set in her highchair and ate with the family, she always made sure her mother knew how thankful she was for her meals by saying, "Mommy, yummy, yummy, yum, yum!" Then she would let out a huge chuckle. She was determined to enjoy herself every day. When family and friends came to visit, they were in for a treat. Ja'Nae had a sense of humor that surpassed any child they had ever seen. The visitors often videotaped Ja'Nae so they would have something to laugh at when they were not quite themselves. Ja'Nae would laugh until she fell asleep, usually, the visitors were ready for a nap themselves.

Every Saturday, the Barnesworths would visit the area's nursing homes and convalescent centers to pray and minister to the residents. They were concerned that Ja'Nae would be afraid of the residents, but to their surprise, she was the complete opposite. Once they arrived at the center, the residents would reach for Ja'Nae, and she would embrace them with a beautiful smile. She loved all the attention she received from the residents as well as the staff. She quickly became the life of the establishment. As the residents reached for her, she went from arm to arm and lap to lap. When it was time to leave, she would look around the establishment to make sure everyone had a smile on their face. However, if she noticed a resident looking sad, she would cry and plead for her parents to give her a little more time. Ja'Nae would say, "Mommy, something is wrong with that lady. She doesn't look so good. Can I please talk to her? I want to make her smile!" Ta'Nelle would put Ja'Nae down and let her do whatever was in her heart.

Ja'Nae went to work immediately. She approached the lady and with her little baby voice, she said, "What is wrong? You do not feel good? Do you have a tummy ache?" The lady replied, "No, baby, I am fine. I am so happy to see you and your family come, and I hate to see you leave. But I am all right. I will see you the next time, okay?" Ja'Nae gave the lady a big hug and, the lady was smiling from ear to ear. Ja'Nae refused to leave until she had done everything in her power to put a smile on every resident's face. Once Ja'Nae had accomplished her goal, she was ready to leave. That day, Ja'Nae's love and compassion for others were overwhelming. Albert and Ta'Nelle were immensely proud of their baby.

Before long, Ta'Nelle was expecting her third child and as usual, she and Albert wanted a son. Once the girls were told they were getting a new baby, Ja'Nae said, "Mommy and Daddy, I had a dream last night that we would be getting another baby sister in a little while. I also dreamed about the baby's name. Do you want to know what you are going to name her?" Ta'Nelle said, "Baby, what name did you hear in your dream?" "Mommy, the new baby's name is Jamberlyn Latrice. Mommy, when you go to the doctor in a little while, you will see for yourself it is a girl!" Ja'Nae replied. "Surely little Ja'Nae was correct the baby was a girl and named Jamberlyn Latrice. Wow! Out of the mouth of babes, who would have believed Ja'Nae's dreams were accurate, after all, she was merely a toddler." She loved her sister, and she looked forward to helping Ta'Nya watch Jamberlyn while their mother was busy doing chores. They would help feed the baby but when it came time to change the diaper, they left that up to their parents. When Jamberlyn was almost three, the Barnesworths welcomed their fourth child, and yes, Ja'Nae was correct yet again, the baby was another girl. This child according to Ja'Nae would be the Barnesworths' final child, and she would be named Anointia Denise. And so it happened just as Ja'Nae had spoken.

JA'NAE'S DREAMS
ARE REVEALED

Ja'Nae was growing so fast that the Barnesworths could not wait to see what she would say or do next. Before long, she was evaluated for kindergarten and passed all her tests with excellence. She would be joining Ta'Nya at the elementary school in the fall. Shortly, a few weeks before school started, Ta'Nelle went shopping for the girls' school clothes. She tried her absolute best to pick out the prettiest things she could find for Ta'Nya and Ja'Nae. She made sure she matched the items with socks, shoes, hair bows, headbands, and all the latest accessories. She was quite satisfied with all her purchases. That evening when she returned home, she let the girls try on the clothes to make sure they fit properly. All Ta'Nya's clothes fit perfectly, so she would be able to wear them for several months. She was so excited and was ready to start her new school with Ja'Nae. Oh, what fun they would have together learning new things about the school and each other. Some of Ja'Nae's clothes needed altering, however, she loved what was chosen for her.

The next day, Ja'Nae seemed troubled. Unbeknownst to Albert and Ta'Nelle, she had another dream. As they began to ask her what was going on, she told them she could not quite explain it to them at that moment but would explain when she received clarity. They knew she was not sick so they prayed to the Lord that he would give them insight into what Ja'Nae was trying to reveal. Ja'Nae dreamed the same dream seven times and was finally ready to talk to her parents. She was confident that the dream would soon happen. You see Ja'Nae did not know at the time, but she was walking by faith, the same faith that her parents taught her. That night after dinner, Ja'Nae informed her parents that she was ready to talk to them. She wanted to talk in regard to going to the new school. They gave her their undivided attention. She said, "Mommy and Daddy, I know I have been a little quiet lately, but I have been dreaming the same dream for days. I want you both to know that I love you very much. I am so sorry if I worried you. I had a dream about the outfits, and in the dreams, I saw that something was missing. I truly could not explain it until now. Mommy, I want to look different than the other girls at school." Ta'Nelle said, "Baby, what do you mean you want to look different? You are merely a little girl! Your dad and I have rules that all our children will live by. Now we must see what you are talking about before we can say it is all right!"

Ja'Nae said, "Mommy, I know we have rules. But I want my clothes to be accessorized, I want an object put on all my clothes. I want the object to be placed right below my knee on the left-hand side. As I grow taller, I want the objects to move up until it reaches my heart. It would be like my own little angel or an angel wing. You see, I want something that will let me know that I am never alone. Daddy, do you remember reading us a Bible story about Jesus being in our hearts and that he is with us all the time?" Albert said, "Yes, baby, I remember!" "Well, I want an angel or an angel wing on all my clothes so I can look at it when I am away from home. It will reassure me that everything is going to be all right. Daddy, I believe it will help me to concentrate on my schoolwork, and I will make good grades like Ta'Nya. When I take my tests and start to get nervous, it will help me to calm down. As I look at it, I will remember how Jesus said in his word, 'That I can do all things through Christ which strengthens me! (Phil. 4:13)' You know what? I believe just what Jesus said. Mommy and Daddy, if you cannot find an angel or an angel wing, then whatever you find for me it will be called my own personal angel. Okay? That is all I wanted so if it's all right with you I will go play with my sisters." She hugged them and told them she loved them. As Ja'Nae hugged, Ta'Nelle, tears rolled down her face. Albert said, "We love you too, baby, and thank you so much for talking to us! Whenever you need to talk to us, we are here."

As Albert and Ta'Nelle talked among themselves, they could not help but notice how confident, sweet, and humble Ja'Nae was. They looked at each other and said, "Out of the mouth of babes flows such wisdom and knowledge!" Ta'Nelle said, "Honey, do you remember when we brought her home from the hospital, how advanced she was for her age? I told you what we did not learn from Ta'Nya, we would surely learn from Ja'Nae! Well, we just learned another valuable lesson. Wow! The joy of the Lord is all over me. Hallelujah!" "Surely you are right!" said Albert.

Ja'Nae was the second bundle of joy that was born the day before the birth of their Lord and Savior Jesus Christ. The Barnesworths knew they were blessed with all their girls, but they could not comprehend how vast the Lord's blessings were until that very moment. You see the Barnesworths was a praying family. They remember hearing that a family that prays together stays together. They never took the Lord for granted regardless of how big or small the issues were. They always consulted him for guidance. Ta'Nelle would be returning to the mall on Saturday few days to finish school shopping for the girls.

She would be searching for just the right things for Ja'Nae. She shopped near and far until she found what she considered to be the perfect objects for Ja'Nae's clothes. She wanted to make sure she was not copying anything from a designer. Once she found the items, she planned to work on them after the girls retired for the evening. She needed additional time to finish all the clothes, so she asked Albert to keep the girls busy, she wanted everything finished by the next day. Ta'Nelle was careful to place the items directly where Ja'Nae wanted them.

The next evening while the food was in the oven, Ta'Nelle called Ja'Nae to show her what she had done to her clothes. She placed a large mirror directly in front of Ja'Nae so she could see herself as she tried on her outfits. The more things she tried, the happier she became, in fact, she started singing and laughing. The mood in the Barnesworths' house quickly changed as the girls began to sing along with Ja'Nae. Ta'Nya said, "Thank God, I have my sister back! I have my sister back, thank you, Jesus! Thank you, Jesus!" Albert was so happy to see his girls singing, laughing, and praising God. It truly was a remarkable and miraculous day for the Barnesworth's. Praise the Lord!

Finally, it was the first day of school, and Ja'Nae would make her grand entrance. That morning, Ja'Nae had to try on every outfit, the one she picked the night before just did not seem to fit such a special occasion. Once she made her choice, she started singing her own little song. "It is time to go to school! This is my first day! It is time to go to school. I cannot be late, I am ready to learn from the teacher. It is time to go to sch—ool!" She sang her song over and over until she ate her breakfast. Just when Albert and Ta'Nelle thought they had her figured out she would surprise them yet again. Everything was going great until the next morning, Ja'Nae had to go through the same routine again. She had a style of her very own, Ta'Nelle soon learned that her baby was a fashion ester. She could picture her modeling on the runway. Shortly thereafter, Ja'Nae developed what she called a feel for every day, and that was the end of her impromptu fashion show.

Once in pre-kindergarten, Ja'Nae was prepared for whatever she had to learn. To the teachers' surprise, Ja'Nae was more advanced than she was when she was evaluated a few months earlier. The teacher had a conference with the Barnesworths and the principal to get permission to retest Ja'Nae for the first grade. When the results was returned Ja'Nae was placed in the advanced first-grade class. She was proven to be ready for any task with which she was presented. She was a mover and a shaker that made it her business to get the job done with little or no assistance.

JA'NAE'S VISION
COMES TO PASS

When Ja'Nae was at the tender age of seven, she had developed a deep love for senior citizens. After receiving divine inspiration from the Lord, Ja'Nae formulated a mission statement outlining her goals and ambitions where seniors were concerned. She wanted her plans to be different than anyone she had ever heard of, and be a blessing to everyone involved. If you remember, Ja'Nae was not an ordinary little girl, she had a mind that would shock anyone that knew her. After much consideration, Ja'Nae knew it was time to talk to her parents about the new plan that was remarkably close to her heart. She believed her parents would listen as well as support her once they knew she was following them. She would approach her parents that evening after dinner. As Ja'Nae knocked on the door, Ta'Nelle was sitting on a chair in their bedroom and told her to come in. As they looked at her appearance, they knew she had something of importance on her mind. At that point, they dropped what they were doing. Ja'Nae entered the room and went to her mother's left side as Albert kneeled on the floor to make eye contact with their baby girl.

Ja'Nae said, "I have something that is pressing on my heart, and I can't hold it any longer." They listened as Ja'Nae totally captivated them: they remained completely silent until she was finished talking. At that point, Ja'Nae asked her parents to excuse her for five minutes so she could get something from her room. Albert and Ta'Nelle looked at each other with pure amazement. They could not help but notice how mature she had become, oh such wisdom and compassion that was flowing out of such a small vessel. As Ja'Nae returned to her parents' room, she came equipped with her piggy bank and immediately dumped all her coins on their bed. Then she said, "Mommy and Daddy, I need my vision to happen and because of that, I must be the first person to give. I must show others that I am serious, and I believe in myself even if no one else does. Will you please keep this money for me until I get everything started?"

Albert and Ta'Nelle could not contain themselves any longer. they were filled with joy and peace. After they saw Ja'Nae's faith, they had to help her. Before they knew it, their money was dancing out of their wallets and onto the bed. They were prouder of Ja'Nae that day than ever before and made sure she knew it. There was not a doubt in their minds that they had to offer all the support they could to help push Ja'Nae's vision. She thanked her parents for listening and helping her with her vision. She made sure she told them how much she loves them; they hugged her and said their goodnights. They remembered reading a Sunday school lesson about the importance of having a vision and the difference between a vision and a visionary. They could not contain themselves any longer, they had praise on the inside that they had to get out. They began to praise their Lord for all the things he was doing with their little baby. They were looking forward to seeing Ja'Nae's vision come to pass and how the Lord would use her in the future.

After they composed themselves, they had to make a phone call to their pastor. Apostle Renee Woods would meet with them the next evening while the associate pastor was teaching Bible study to discuss Ja'Nae's vision. After listening to the Barnesworths, Apostle Woods called her secretary, Ms. Butterfield, to inform all the members of the church to be in attendance on Sunday after service for a important business meeting. Apostle Woods could hardly wait to give Ja'Nae the opportunity to present her vision to the congregation. She was optimistic that the vision would help to light a fire under some of the adult members.

On Sunday, after all the visitors had existed out the sanctuary, the meeting was called to order. Apostle Woods said, "I called this meeting because I have been informed about something that I feel is important to this ministry as well as this community. I ask everyone in attendance to pay close attention to what you are about to hear. I want everyone to welcome Alanta Ja'Nae Barnesworth. As you listen to her, remember she is a child, and I ask you to respect her. This child is a true visionary, hear her now!"

Ja' Nae was given the microphone and she started by saying. "Hello, everybody, I want to tell you something. My parents take me and my sisters to the area nursing homes and convalescent centers every Saturday. I loved going there and I want to do something to help make the seniors' lives happier. I want them to know they are loved and appreciated and will not be forgotten. We can learn from their wisdom, knowledge, and life experiences. In addition to learning from them, we can help make the remainder of their days more peaceful and enjoyable. You know we will be a senior, too, one day and we would want someone to do something to help us as well. For that reason, I feel it would be great to start a mission simply to benefit the seniors. The purpose of the mission would be to meet the needs of seniors by ministering to them through gospel music, reading Bible stories, current events, and books that edify the soul, and singing or performing praise dances. However, the praise dancing would only be performed for seniors that are generally able to watch or participate without causing injuries to themselves strictly under the supervision of the nursing home staff. Safety is the number one priority. We would also collect funds to help meet their needs. We cannot give the seniors money, but we can purchase things for them, especially for their birthdays, and holidays such as Mother's Day, Father's Day, Easter, and Christmas.

Ja'Nae continued by saying, "In order for the vision to be successful, I plan to get assistance from other girls my age or a little older. I have four or five female cousins in mind I feel it would be best if the girls will audition to be fair to anyone that wants to participate in this mission. My goal is to get three or four girls to help with this mission. Hopefully, it will keep the girls occupied positively when we are not in school. The mission will be called Girls on a Mission for Seniors (GMS). I have compiled all the information I believe are needed to address any concerns you may have. Once the vision is incorporated, I will advertise on the internet, in the newspapers, and make flyers to post throughout the neighborhood and in the malls. Letters will go to area churches, radio, and television stations, as well as businesses to help with financial support. All money collected will deposited in a bank as soon as we have enough to deposit. I I will need volunteers to assist in getting the girls, to, and from the nursing facilities. To prevent being a burden on anyone, funds will be provided d for all traveling expenses relating to GMS." At that point, Ja'Nae was finished with her presentation. She thanked Apostle Woods and the congregation for giving her the opportunity to share her vision.

Although Apostle Woods heard about Ja'Nae's vision from her parents, she was flabbergasted, after hearing the anointed words flowing out of the mouth of this little babe. Apostle yelled, "Hallelujah! Hallelujah to the most high God! In the Bible, Matthew 21:16 reads, And said unto him, Hearest thou what these say? And Jesus saith unto them, Yea; have ye never read, Out of the mouth of babes and sucklings (infants) thou hast perfected praise?'My God, did anyone hear the wisdom and knowledge flowing out of the mouth of this babe? She humbled herself and waited for confirmation from the Lord for seven nights before she approached her parents. She did not know why she waited, but God was dealing with this child. This babe is not only a dreamer, but she is a visionary! Because of her obedience, God has ordained this ministry. She is in line with the word of God which reads in John 9:4, 'I must work the works of him that sent me, while it is day; the night cometh, when no man can work.' What the Lord wants you to know with this verse of scripture is that when he places a call on our lives while we are young, strong, and able-bodied individuals, we should work it. Do not put it off until we are too old to work, or we may not live to see the vision come into existence. We can miss out on our calling, and our chance to make it into our heavenly home putting things off until tomorrow. No one knows what tomorrow may bring but God! Amen!"

As the Apostle was addressing the congregation, she heard five of the members were murmuring and complaining while jealousy was rising in their hearts. It was revealed to the Apostle what was being said. She said, "Five women in here are questioning this vision. You said, "Why should Ja'Nae oversee the vision? Why should the Barnesworths be involved in everything and collect the money? They will spend it themselves. Why should that child have the final say when making decisions? She is only seven years old, she cannot tell no one what to do! Why can't one of our children be in charge? I am so sick of those girls; in fact, I am tired of the whole Barnesworths family!" "Me too, the Apostle just let them take over the church!" The Apostle said, "Not only did the Lord reveal what was spoken he also showed me who said it. Now I am not going to embarrass you, but I will address your issues!"

Apostle continued by saying, "First of all, this is a child that God has chosen to start this vision, neither for her gain nor glory, but to help others. This child has the gift of helps. Proverbs 29:18 reads, 'Where there is no vision the people perish; but he that keepeth the law, happy is he.' Habakkuk 2:2–3 reads, 'And the Lord answered me, and said, Write the vision, and make it plain upon tables (on tablets), that he may run that readeth it. For the vision is yet for an appointed time, but at the end it shall speak, and not lie: though it tarry, wait for it; because it will surely come, it will not tarry.' She said, "You cannot write a vision if God did not give it to you. If you cannot write it, you cannot run with it. You cannot take something from Ja'Nae that the Lord gave her. God gave her the vision, and it is in her hands she is the only one who can oversee this vision. If Ja'Nae so desires, she can start this vision with or without this ministry, and she can get girls from her family or the school to fulfill it."

"Secondly," Apostle said, "1 Timothy 6:10 reads, "For the love of money is the root of all (kinds of) evil: which while some coveted after, they have erred from the faith (for which some in their greediness have strayed from their faith), and pierced themselves through with many sorrows." The Barnesworths will collect the funds and will be there to support their baby's vision. In fact, they have already contributed to her vision. Now, I want you to know you are not obligated to support this vision, however, I encourage you to do so. Ja'Nae will need financial support, volunteers to transport the girls to rehearsal and to the facilities, and most importantly our prayers. Remember this is a ministry of help Ja'Nae, Psalm 37:1-2 reads, 'Fret not yourself because of evildoers, neither be thou envious against the workers of iniquity (sin). For they shall soon be cut down like the grass, and wither as the green herb.' In other words, baby girl, do not worry about what people say or do. Remember, things may look like defeat, but it is not what it looks like! Ja'Nae, just know that I am so proud of you, and I will do whatever is necessary to push you into the place God wants you to be. Here is a donation from the Woods family."

Despite the negative feedback from five of the parents, most of the congregation agreed to support Alanta's vision. The next Saturday, the girls accompanied by their parents came to the church for the auditions. They received a copy of the rules and regulations for GMS. When Alanta started the auditions, she discovered that the girls had a variety of talents that she believed would be very entertaining to the seniors. She needed assistance from her sister Ta'Nya, and five or six of her older cousins to help choose the girls and place them into the category that would best fit their personalities and talent. Shortly, she had enough girls to get her mission started. The girls would practice twice a week for an hour to get acquainted with each other and master their routines. She also wanted all the girls to be comfortable with their routines and to be committed to her vision.

Everything was going smoothly. Ja'Nae had pictured in her mind what she wanted the girls to wear. Everyone would wear outfits with her signature symbol on the left-hand side of their clothing. Their first outfit would be a red skirt, a white blouse, white tights, and red shoes. She told them she chose red because it represents the blood of Jesus and white because it represents holiness. She wanted everyone to know that the Girls on a Mission for Seniors was inspired, by God and would be used, for his glory. Therefore, everything had to be decent and in order. Their clothes had to fit them loosely, their tights had to be clean without runs or snags. Their shoes could not be scared. She knew the importance of having a good reputation and made sure the girls knew as well. She told them she expected everyone to be on their absolute best behavior including herself.

Girls participating in the mission had to maintain good grades, should be respectable cannot use profanity, or constantly be tardy for rehearsals or events. She refused to accept "it's all about me syndrome" (selfishness), instead, she encouraged the girls to stay focused on Jesus. She wanted the girls to have a profound sense of humor and be able to improvise when performing to keep the attention of the audience. However, the girls had to practice their actions before performing so everyone would know what to expect to maintain a truly spiritual environment. Although it was Ja'Nae's vision, she made sure she kept an open mind. Before long, there were enough girls to have three teams. They practiced for four weeks before performing at the nursing homes. Ja'Nae decided they needed to have a dedicated performance for their parents, the congregation, and their families to make sure they were ready. Instead of having rehearsal the next Saturday, they would perform all their routines. Each routine would last a total of twenty minutes. Once they finished their routines, the audience gave them thunderous applause. At that point, they knew they were ready and scheduled their first appearance as Girls on a Mission for Seniors.

The girls loved GMS and always tried to find ways to improve their routines. They maintained good grades, became more spiritual, and developed high self-esteem. The girls were enjoying themselves, and although they were successful, Ja'Nae knew it was time to go to the media. When the editors and reporters learned that a seven-year-old girl had such an outstanding vision to help improve the lives of seniors, the Barnesworths' phone rang off the hook. Ja'Nae and the girls were asked to do live segments at area churches as well as on TV stations. They wanted to bring awareness to the Girls on a Mission for Seniors (GMS). The stations used their videotapes for future segments on the evening news broadcasts and the audio tapes for radio broadcasts. Ja'Nae also went to the local newspapers and before long, GMS was on the front pages of all the local papers. Her vision was taking off like wildfire. Reporters near and far became a normal fixture at the Barnesworths' home. Ja'Nae and the Girls on a Mission for Seniors' pictures appeared on the front page of various publications throughout the state. Ja'Nae's vision was taking off like wildfire.

Everywhere, Ja'Nae and the girls went, they were treated

like royalty. However, they always reminded the people that it was about the ministry for seniors and nothing else. The funds for the seniors were pouring in from all over the state. Three months after the Girls on a Mission for Seniors was established, the girls were honored as the youngest owners of a senior citizen business by the mayor, the commissioners, the governor, as well as the superintendent of the school in their county. At the tender age of nine, Ja'Nae and the other girls were honored, and she was given a check for five thousand dollars to help fund the organization. Ja'Nae was ecstatic.

The news of GMS traveled quickly throughout the country. Before long, the president of the United States, issue a formal invitation to the young ladies as well as their parents to come to the White House. When Albert received the invitation he believed was a fraud. After three weeks the president had his secretary to call the Barnesworth's home. Ta'Nelle answered the phone and once she acknowledged that she was Ms. Barnesworth, the young lady said, "Please hold the line for the president. At that moment Ta'Nelle motioned for Albert to pick up the other telephone so he could bear witness to the Conversation. Low behold it was truly the president, both Albert and Ta'Nelle recognized his voice. The entire GMS team along with their parents, siblings, and Apostle Deacon Woods were invited to meet the president of the United States, the first lady, and the vice president and first lady at the White House. The president began by welcoming everyone to the White House. He said, "It is a great privilege to meet a group of young ladies with such love and decency for others, especially senior citizens. If only we as adults would think about the needs of others, this world would be a much better place! Ja'Nae, you are a true babe with wisdom and compassion beyond your years. I salute you for a job well done, not only you but all these beautiful young ladies. Because of your faithfulness, I present you Alanta Ja'Nae Barnesworth with a presidential medal of honor for being the youngest African American child visionary to start such a unique organization for the benefit of senior citizens." Everyone applauded.

Next, the president and the first lady presented Ja'Nae and all the members of GMS with a check to help in whatever endeavors they choose, whether it is for college, their own business in the future, or a down payment on a house. They also received plaques in recognition of their outstanding work as faithful members of "Girls on a Mission for Seniors." The vice president and first lady presented the girls with a check of the same amount. Finally, the first Lady said, "Alanta, on behalf of the president and I, we would like to help support your vision with this check for $20,000 for GMS to help finance your vision." Now, you should know the vice president and first lady agreed and gave a sizable check as well.

To show their appreciation Ja'Nae and the girls of GMS performed all their routines for the president, vice president, and all that were in attendance. After their performance, they were all treated to a presidential dinner. The girls as well as their families, the Apostle family, and everyone in attendance were totally flabbergasted. Just when they thought it was time to leave, the girls of GMS were given another check from everyone that attended the dinner. Several of the reporters got permission from their employers to give GMS a donation from their TV stations. GMS was extremely blessed beyond measure, they were given enough money to buy gifts for every patient in all the nursing homes in the entire county They were so proud of all the girls, but especially Alanta Ja'Nae, the true visionary of God!

Regardless of all the accomplishments the girls received and how proud they were of themselves, they remained humble.

When they returned to North Carolina, they received a hero's welcome. Twelve local reporters were waiting to snap pictures and interview the girls, especially Ja'Nae. When she was approached to answer questions, she simply informed the reporters that she had a statement prepared that she was sure would answer all their questions. Alanta Ja'Nae's statement read, "First, I would like to acknowledge the one that gave me this vision. I know some of you may not want to publish what I tell you, but nevertheless, the vision came from my Lord and Savior Jesus Christ by way of a weeklong dream. If it had not been for the Lord, there would not be a ministry for seniors. The Lord made it possible for this vision to come into existence, I simply obeyed the call he placed on my life. I thank God for giving me the girls needed to start Girls on a Mission for Seniors! We want to thank our families, our apostle and Deacon Woods, and special thanks to our parents for allowing us to be a faithful part of this vision. Thank you to everyone that supported and encouraged us. We thank all of you for your help. I know at times, it was not easy. We gratefully appreciate our president, our vice president, and their beautiful wives for their generous donations as well as their gracious hospitality. "To God be the glory and honor. GMS loves you all, especially our precious seniors. God bless you!"

GIRLS ON A MISSION FOR SENIORS UPDATE

All the girls that were a part of GMS went on to become positive and productive young adults. They became business administrators, doctors, nurses, supervisors, entrepreneurs, chemists, educators, and ministers of the gospel of Jesus Christ. However, the parents that opposed the mission were not quite so fortunate. You see, the parents were so busy displaying their rude, disrespectful, nasty, negative attitude toward others that they forgot what they were instructing their children. They were so proud of themselves that they boasted about their actions. They were so busy acting like fools that they were not concerned about the repercussions. Meanwhile, the children sat there with a ringside seat watching their every move. It was funny then everyone had a good laugh, but what about the children?

The Bible clearly states, "Train up a child in the way he (she) should go and when he (she) is old, he (she) will not depart from it. (Prov. 22:6)" The girls started doing exactly what their parents were doing. Remember, it was hysterical until (their children) practiced everything they learned from their parents. One of the sons became a very prosperous drug dealer. So prosperous in fact that Terrance Jr., was arrested, convicted, and sentenced to prison for twenty years. Two of the girls became pregnant at an incredibly young age. By the time they turned sixteen, they were pregnant with their third and fourth child and had no idea who fathered the children. A couple of the other children did whatever came to their minds in the presence of their parents. There wasn't any shame in their game. They walked around the house with barely anything on, even when strangers came to their house, they made no attempts to cover themselves. They dropped out of school in middle school and moved their older significant others in their parents' home whereas neither would work in a pie shop. They warmed the church benches for years, but evidently, no one was listening nor reading the word for themselves. They were so busy bullying others. Proverbs 4:5-7 reads, "Get wisdom, get understanding: forget it not; neither decline (turn away) from the words of my mouth. Forsake her not, and she shall preserve thee: love her, and she shall keep thee. Wisdom is the principal thing; therefore get wisdom: and with all thy getting get understanding." The poor things were so confused they did not have a clue what to do with themselves. They were too bold for any use. They cursed their mother to the point that all she could do was shake from fear. Instead of taking control of the situation while the children were young, the parents let their children take control of them. The fathers were so busy trying to be their children's best friend that he let them run all over him. He could not say or do anything because it was too late. Although his children's partners were celebrating in his house, where he was the provider, he let them live there freely. If he said something to the children, he would have to prepare himself for a beatdown.

Finally, the parents had taken all they could take and called their apostle for assistance. All the apostle could say was, "You trained them! Now you must live with it until you get the courage, (a backbone) and put them out of your house. You cursed everyone that tried to talk to you about your children and refused to hear about anything they were doing that did not sound good to your ears. But you spoke and saw only negative things in others. Galatians 6:7 declares, 'Be not deceived, God is not mocked: for whatsoever a man soweth, that shall he also reap.' You made your bed, now you must lay in it. It's tight but it is right!" The parents did not want to hear the truth however, they knew deep down inside that their apostle was right. They had been a member of the church for fifteen years but, never took the time to experience the true joy of being a child of God. They were in the church (building) as so many are today, but the church (Jesus) was not in their hearts. They were merely bench warmers, but there was hope, they were still living!

The younger siblings watched how their parents were being mistreated and the disastrous lives of their siblings. They decided there had to be more to life than what they had experienced and seen. They made up their minds to be the absolute best person they could be. First, they were going to the church with a new mindset to learn all they could about salvation and how to become the children of God they had witnessed in others. The children not only wanted to see what was so good about the God they heard about, but they also wanted to experience him for themselves. Sadly, the parents now had to learn from their younger children instead of the children learning from their parents. The children that became Christians were remarkably successful and lead a productive, happy life without becoming parents until they were married and ready. They knew someone in the family had to make a change (break the curse) before the entire family was dead or imprisoned for the rest of their lives. Once the parents saw the change in their children, they were ready to follow them. Thank God for his wisdom and understanding, for without him, we would surely live a defeated life, that would cause our soul to burn in the pits of hell forever, and ever!

JA'NAE'S CAREER
TAKES OFF

Once GMS was successful Ja'Nae could move on to other things. She had an interest in learning to sew and once she got the hang of it, she could cut patterns and make whatever she wanted with little or no assistance from the teacher. Ja'Nae quickly fell in love with sewing and was well on her way to becoming an incredibly good tailor. When she entered the sixth grade, she had developed a unique fare for fashion. She tried different scarves, belts, colors, and accessories on various l outfits to make what she believed would be the perfect outfit. Within six months Ja'Nae was designing her own clothing. Everything she pictured in her mind she was able to incorporate. All her friends and family members were shocked when they learned of her newfound talent. The girls of GMS loved Ja'Nae's designs so much that they asked her to make some clothes for them. Naturally, without hesitation, Ja'Nae jumped right on it.

Forget about design school for the moment, Ja'Nae was doing great all by herself. Once she became comfortable with her work Ta'Nya approached her about having a hair/fashion show to feature her designs. Ja'Nae was so excited and agreed to the challenge. The show would be in a three months, which would give Ja'Nae enough time to have her designs completed. She decided on what she believed to be the perfect name for her designs, "Nae Nae's Fashions by Alanta!" A couple of weeks before the show Ja'Nae had completed all her designs. She designed clothing for all occasions from formal wear to casual. She handpicked seven of the girls from GMS, along with a five adults to model her clothing. She was confident that her designs were her best work ever. On the day of the show each model wore a unique style, size, and color that best fit them along with an impressive hairstyle by Ta'Nya. The audience was made aware of the availability of each design, price, size, and color. The show was going just as Ta'Nya and Ja'Nae had envisioned in their minds. The women in attendance were signing up to get the latest hairstyles to wear with the perfect designer outfit. The women were beguiled by all the styles and showed their approval with sighs, and standing ovations. There was one last model that no one had seen. She was waiting patiently in a private room where she watched the entire performance on a monitor. . It was finally time to show off the most anticipated hairstyle and design of the evening. Ta'Nya and Ja'Nae made the best style for the most important woman in their lives, their mother. As Ta'Nelle was led into the room by her daughters, she was covered from head to toe. The audience sat at the edge of their seats as Ta'Nya delicately unveiled her mother's hair. Ta'Nelle's hair had been put up in a bun, with tight spiral curls on the left-hand side of her head. For the final additions, Ta'Nya placed with gold, blue, and white butterflies down the bun.

As the excitement in the room continued to build, Ja'Nae approached her mother and slowly began to untie her cape. Ta'Nelle wore a gold, blue, and white chiffon fitted dress with a while illustrated neckline, sheer long sleeves with a detachable plastic zipper below her knees, with solid gold and blue trim. The dress could be worn, as an evening gown with the right accessories or a prom dress. When shortened to a ¾-inch length, the dress could be worn for dinner parties, for mothers of the bride, or for social events, as well as for Sunday worship services. To top it off, Ta'Nelle wore white pearl earrings, two-inch white pumps, and a matching white purse. In addition to baby blue, the grown could be ordered, in red, mint green, violet, light yellow, or white. The hairstyle as well as the outfit, was designed to knock the audience off their feet and that it did. The hair/fashion show was a tremendous success. Ta'Nya and Ja'Nae scheduled the hair/fashion show around the same time every year for years to come. Each show became more improved than the one before with volunteers of different ages willing to do it all over again. Albert and Ta'Nelle were proud of their daughters. They were very independent young ladies well on their way to happy, productive, and fulfilling lives.

Before long, Ja'Nae was off and running with her new profession. Everything she set her mind to do, she accomplished with little or no thought. While in school, Alanta Ja'Nae completed early college with a bachelor's degree in business administration. Ja'Nae was not satisfied, so she went on to get additional bachelor' degrees in fashion merchandising/marketing. She wanted to learn as much as she possibly could about textiles, science, apparel construction, draping, spec drawing, trend forecasting, fashion illustration, and color theory. Shortly thereafter, Ja'Nae was getting orders from all over the state to design and make clothing. She knew it was finally time to expand her business, so she rented a warehouse, hired twenty staff members, and opened her new fashion house. While the seamstresses were busy working on the orders, Alanta was busy working on new designs. She never complained about her ministry or her business. She knew according to the word of God, "For unto whomever much is given, of him shall be much required: and to whom men have committed much, of him they will ask the more" (Luke 12:48 b). She loved every opportunity presented to her to fulfill the vision God had bestowed upon her.

Ja'Nae's fashions were quickly flying off the store racks. In less than three months, she was on her way to becoming a major designer throughout the fashion world. Although she could afford a home of her own, she decided to live at home with her parents and siblings a little longer. She was traveling from state to state, showing her designs at various fashion shows. She dated occasionally, but her ministry and her fashion house were her number one priority at the present time. She was barely an adult and had many years to date later. Two years later, Ja'Nae was traveling to the east coast, and she met a man that really captured her attention. Although she was not dating, she was not dead either. The two met in a restaurant at one of the local airports. To their surprise, they were both traveling to the state of New Jersey. As fate would have it, they were sitting next to each other on the plane, which gave them the opportunity to chat. The man introduced himself as Matthew Rogers. Ja'Nae decided it would be best to use her first name Alanta Barnesworth so she would not be connected to her fashion house. After chatting for the duration of the flight, Ja'Nae learned that the man lived and worked in the state of North Carolina. He lived about twenty-five miles away from her home, to be exact. He was traveling to New Jersey to visit family members in the union county area. Although he seemed respectable, Ja'Nae was very guarded while talking to the young man as she should have been. She would be in the state for exactly one week to meet with various store executives regarding her designs.

Upon the completion of her business meetings, Alanta returned to the airport to board a plane back to North Carolina. Matthew was also going back to North Carolina but neither knew the exact day nor the time of the other's departure. To their surprise when they boarded the plane, they were on the same flight and sitting directly across from each other. Being cautious, Ja'Nae decided it would be best to exchange email addresses as a point of contact since he wanted to reach her. She was young and inexperienced but nowhere near crazy. Once she returned home, she ran a background check on Matthew. Everything checked out, he was not involved in any criminal activities or bankruptcies. Alanta went back to her fashion house and threw herself into her work.

After two and a halfs, Alanta was finally able to check her emails. Surprisingly to her, Matthew had sent her twelve emails. The last email was dated two days earlier and it really got her attention. Matthew wrote, "Due to the lack of communication, I am informing you that this is my last attempt to contact you!" After reading the email, Ja'Nae responded immediately. She explained to Matthew that due to her busy work schedule, she was unable to check her emails since she returned from New Jersey. They continued to email each other several times a week before going on their first date. Alanta believed Matthew was an upright individual and she did not want to intimate him by telling him she owned her own fashion house. Matthew on the other hand was the lead supervisor at a construction company. He knew from the moment he met Alanta that she was a young lady from the opposite side of the tracks, but he could not help himself. Sparks were flying the first time he saw Alanta and he did not want to waste not one opportunity that was presented to him. He wanted to share so many things with her. However, he did not want to come on too strong and risk losing her before a relationship could develop.

One day while checking her emails, Alanta received a message from Matthew, and she could tell he was extremely excited to see her. After replying to the email, Matthew told her he wanted to take her out to dinner at her earliest convenience. They planned to meet at a restaurant in a couple of days. You see, Ja'Nae's family was very protective of each other, and her cousins knew of her plans and met at the restaurant with their dates. Unknown to Matthew, Ja'Nae's cousins saw her when she pulled up and waited until she had time to be seated, before they entered the restaurant. Shortly thereafter, Ja'Nae's cousins sat at the able across from her on the opposite side of the restaurant. They watched Ja'Nae for any signs of trouble. After dating for four weeks, her cousins believed she was safe; however, they continued to go out with her until she felt comfortable.

Matthew and Alanta were so relaxed with each other that they started sharing their likes and dislikes. A few weeks later, Matthew said, "Alanta, I need to read a scripture in the word of God in the book of Joel 2:28 it reads, "And it shall come to pass afterward, that I will pour out my spirit upon all flesh; and your sons and your daughters shall prophesy, your old men shall dream dreams, your young men shall see visions:" He continued by saying, "As a child, I always loved building things and drawing things, I even drew pictures of my very own dream home. I wanted to one day be an entrepreneur, however, I had no idea that God would bless me so quickly. I remember when we first met, I told you that I was a supervisor at a construction company. Well, my boss informed me that he is retiring and moving his family to Florida. He wants to sell the construction business to me as soon as possible. We had all the paperwork drawn up and signed with our lawyers. In about two weeks, it will be a done deal. I will officially be the owner of my own business!"

Alanta was so happy for Matthew, and she thanked him for thinking enough of her to share such exciting news with her. She said, "Matthew, the Lord has given you favor with your boss.

Matthew 5:16 reads, 'Let your light so shine before men, that they may see your good works, and glorify your Father which is in heaven.' When we first met, I could see the glory of God radiating thru you, and God has put his seal on your dreams and visions. The Lord said that everything you touch shall prosper, and this is your season. According to Ecclesiastes 3:1, "To everything there is a season, and a time to every purpose under the heaven:" The Lord wants you to know out of all the people your boss knew, he offered the business to you. It was not by coincidence, or by chance, it was God's will!"

Matthew began to give God praise for all the things that he had done. He said, "Alanta, I know without a doubt that God is using you to confirm his word. The boss also gave me the first bids on his newly remodeled home. The house has four bedrooms and three full bathrooms, the master bath has double sinks, and there is also a half bathroom. The master bedroom has a large walk-in closet, and there is a huge living room and dining area, and so much more. It sits on a large lot with a three-car garage and too many attractions to name. This truly is my season! Hallelujah! Hallelujah! Thank you, Jesus! Lord, you are so worthy of all the praise!" That night was truly a night of celebration. The Spirit of the Lord filled that establishment. Ja'Nae was so thrilled that she introduced her cousins along with their dates to Matthew. And he invited them to join in their celebration. Before long, it was time to end their date, but not before Matthew prayed for everyone's safe travels back to their homes. The next day, Alanta received another email from Matthew thanking her again for such a formidable evening. He stated he genuinely enjoyed meeting her cousins and would love to go out with her again. He emailed her his cell phone number and asked if she would call him. However, if she did not feel comfortable calling him, she could continue to email him. Naturally, she was looking forward to another date and responded with her cell phone number immediately.

Matthew and Alanta continued to date. After Matthew settled down with the purchase of his new business and acquiring the new home, it was Alanta's time to share. Remember she was a very humble and wise young lady that cared for the happiness and success of others. Although she could have shared her news with Matthew on their date weeks ago, it was not her time. It was truly Matthew's time to shine and that, he did. The couple went to several unusual places on their dates; however, they loved their dinner dates the most. That was their time to really enjoy each other's conversations as they continued to learn from each other. Alanta informed Matthew that when they meet for dinner, she wants to talk to him about something that was important to her. Matthew, like most men, began to wonder what could Alanta want to talk about, was it something good or something bad? As quickly as the thoughts entered his mind, he erased them. He was not going to entertain any negative thoughts because he knew God placed him in the right place at the right time to meet Alanta.

That night, when Matthew laid his eyes on Alanta, he could see the spirit of peace and joy all over her face. He believed with the guidance of the Lord that every date with Alanta would yield more wisdom and clarity into where things were going with the two of them. Although she was a beautiful sight to his eyes, Matthew was more concerned with her spirituality, mannerism, ambitions, and insights. He gave Alanta his undivided attention, he wanted to hear every word that proceeded out of her mouth. Alanta began by saying, "Matthew, I want to be open and honest with you about so many things. First, I know that you are a true man of God and I wanted to get to know you before revealing certain personal things. When we met, you were a nice person however, I was a little skeptical because appearances can be deceiving. As I fore stated, I thank you for sharing your personal accomplishments with me. I am immensely proud of you. Most young men our age want to betaken care of by women. Matthew, you see when you shared your new business adventure with me, I rejoiced with you. I know how excited you were because I experienced that same joy myself a five years ago.

"Matthew, I told you that I worked at a fashion house which is true, but what you do not know is that I am the top designer and the owner of Nae Nae's Fashions by Alanta! Most people in my hometown call me Ja'Nae which is my middle name. I choose to tell people my first name for my safety. When we first met, I was traveling to New Jersey to get my designs in various stores and boutiques. My business is remarkably successful, and I have a staff of fifty including tailors, cutters, and office staff. I am in the process of hiring additional staff as we speak. In addition to my fashion house, I started a ministry as a child that is still in existence today. My ministry is GMS which means Girls on a Mission for Seniors. The Lord has truly blessed me to be able to purchase two brand new vans for GMS transportation to and from the senior citizen's faculties. Although my profession is designing and managing my fashion house, I am always available for my first love, my ministry, GMS."

Matthew said, "Alanta, the book of Matthew 25:21 reads, 'His Lord said unto him, Well done, thy good and faithful servant: thou hast been faithful over a few things, I will make thee ruler over many things: enter thou into the joy of the Lord.' Because you obeyed the Lord when he impressed upon your heart to start GMS, he said he is anointing your hands and mind. He said you have not seen anything yet; you think you can design now but God said you have not even tapped into a third of your anointing. God said go ahead and increase your staff, your fashions will run off the racks. There is an anointing of increase in your ministry, your spiritual walk is going to be dynamite or as people may say off the chain. God is increasing your wisdom and knowledge of his word, and you will preach and teach the word of God. He said the joy of the Lord is your strength, and whatever you desire in this season is yours for the asking. He will not withhold any good thing from you. The Lord is blessing your family beyond measure because your parents trained you and your sisters according to his word. He is increasing their life and their territory."

Matthew continued by saying, "But as it is written, Eye hath not seen, nor ear heard, neither have entered into the heart of man, the things which God hath prepared for them that love him. (1 Cor. 2:9.) 'And the Lord said be careful what you ask for, it shall come to you quickly.' Every design you see in your mind, even in your sleep God is going to bring it into existence. Isaiah 54:17 reads, 'No weapon that is formed against thee shall prosper; and every tongue that shall rise against thee in judgment thou shalt condemn. This is the heritage of the servants of the Lord, and their righteousness is of me, saith the Lord.' God said do not even worry about the naysayers. He has covered you, in fact, if they are not careful every negative thing, they speak over you will fall on their own head. God said according to Isaiah 49:15–16, 'Can a woman forget her sucking child, that she should not have compassion on the son of her womb? yea, they may forget, yet will I not forget thee. Behold I have graven (craved) thee upon the palms of my hands; thy walls are continually before me.' God said step out of your comfort zone." At that moment, Alanta was in tears all she could do is surrender to the Holy Spirit and praise and magnify his holy name. She said, "Thank you, Jesus, for your anointing. Thank you for your confirmation. Thank you, Jesus! Hallelujah to the lamb of God! Hallelujah! I love you, Lord!" Matthew and Alanta weren't ashamed of their Lord and Savior Jesus Christ. When the spirit of the Lord touched them, they let the Lord have his way regardless of where they were. Of course, there were times they could not be as free as they would like, but the Lord was glorified. Matthew and Alanta joined hands in prayer and called it a night.

The next day, Matthew and Alanta decided to invite their parents along with Alanta's cousins to join them at the restaurant on Friday. They wanted their parents to meet the person that has changed their lives and share in what the Lord has been doing over the past few months. Hopefully, they will participate in the festivities. Soon it was time to meet at the restaurant. When they entered the establishment, there were enough people in attendance to fill over half the building. Matthew and Alanta were introduced to each other's parents and siblings. Once they were all seated, the Barnesworths and the Rogers's had ten minutes to get acquainted before ordering dinner. At that time, Matthew and Alanta believed it was a suitable time to inform their family members that the Lord had blessed them with what they considered to be a restaurant ministry. They assured them they would elaborate on it in more detail after dinner.

Matthew and Alanta were truly a welcomed sight to the owner of the establishment, the staff, and the patrons. Whenever they came to the establishment, everyone knew the exact time they would be there. That was the busiest night of the week. They did not have to be concerned about their meals, God had given them favor with the owner, and their food was on the house. Every night after they finished their meal, they always had a word from the Lord for someone. They met every other Friday night at the same place and the same time. On rare occasions, they were late due to their busy work schedules. Regardless of the time when they arrived at the restaurant it was filled. That night immediately after the couple arrived at the restaurant, they were blessed with gifts. Alanta just like her mother was a bucket of water. Before long, the tears were running down her face uncontrollably. The more she wiped her face, the more she cried. She was overwhelmed by the love and affection that the people showed them. Shortly thereafter, Ta'Nelle and Mrs. Lena Rogers were in tears as well; spontaneously, the men reached into their pockets and gave them their handkerchiefs. The three men looked at each other and smiled Albert said, "Oh dear, Lord, we have three of them!"

As they continued to praise their God, Ja'Nae said, "I do not know what the Lord is doing, but every time we come into this place, he meets us here with more and more people. Lord, I do not know what you are trying to tell us, or where you are trying to take us in this season, but Lord, continue to move by your power. Lord, make and mold us into what you will have us to be. Do it Lord Jesus for your glory, and we will praise you forevermore in your name, Lord!" The spirit of the Lord fell, and although it was on Friday night, they had a revival in their favorite restaurant. One thing I know without a doubt, the spirit of the Lord will show up wherever and whenever he is invited. . After the spirit lifted, Matthew asked everyone to stand. He thanked the Lord for his visitation and asked him to give them road mercy as they departed to their separate homes. When Matthew returned to his apartment, he prayed and thanked the Lord again for all he had done and was doing in his life. You see four years before Matthew met Alanta, he made his petition known unto the Lord about his future. He asked the Lord to send him an incredibly special young woman of God to share his life with. For confirmation, he asked the Lord to provide him with his own business and a new home shortly after meeting the woman he was to marry. Everything he prayed for was surely happening.

Although Matthew was a homeowner, he did not live in the home for at least five months. Once Alanta became comfortable with Matthew, he invited her to see his new home. He was very particular about the time they spent inside. Matthew was a true man of God and refused to remain in the home for more than ten minutes. He did not want to do anything to tarnish Alanta's reputation. According to Romans 14:16–17, "Let not then your good be evil spoken of: For the kingdom of God is not meat and drink; but righteousness, and peace, and joy in the Holy Ghost." Matthew wasn't like the average man, he had the spirit of his Lord and Savior Jesus Christ deep down in his heart. He knew how to love, respect, and cherish a woman. Once the tour was completed the couple exited the home and proceeded to lunch.

While Alanta and Matthew were touring his house, their parents were busy getting better acquainted on the telephone. Lena Rogers and Ta'Nelle Barnesworth were busy feasting off the impressive move of God they experienced the night before. Ta'Nelle said, "Lena, who would have thought we would meet the Holy Spirit on the first night we met each other and our children's date? The Lord truly blessed inside a restaurant, no less. Albert and I always wanted to have a son but truly, I believe the Lord will bless us with another new son in a year or less.. And I could not be happier!" Lena said, "Ta'Nelle, I agree. I will have the best daughter-in-law any mother could want for their son. And they do not have a clue that the Lord is anointing them for their new role and their new life together. To God be the glory! Hallelujah!"

The more Matthew and Alanta dated, the more spiritual and anointed they became. They gave the Lord all they had within them. One night after they were finishing their meals, a young man came to the table. The couple could see that the man was excited about something and wanted to share it with them. Matthew told the man to pull up a chair and share with them. He sat down and told them he had a fresh word from the Lord for them and he had to deliver it immediately. He started by telling them how excited he was to be chosen by God to deliver such a wonderful word. He said, "The Lord told me to tell you that he has been preparing you for a life together. And in not so many months, you shall marry, and after your first year of marriage, you will conceive your first child. Matthew, God said that thing you purposed in your heart, he has already done! He is working it out even now. Although you both are happy now, God said you have not seen anything yet. Joy, he is giving you unspeakable joy, receive it now in Jesus's name!" Matthew finally received the confirmation he was waiting for and shortly thereafter, he and Alanta were engaged.

THE BARNESWORTHS
WELCOMED THEIR
THIRD CHILD

Albert and Ta'Nelle were blessed with their third child she was named Jamberlyn Latrice. She was born on September 21 and weighed in at 7 lbs. and 1 oz. Alanta was no longer the baby. She quickly became the middle child, a role she had no desire to fill. However, she adjusted to it very quickly. At first, she was a little jealous, she did not want anyone to take her place with her parents, especially her father. She soon learned that the baby had needs that only her parents could take care of, so she was okay with that. She started helping her parents with Jamberlyn as much as she could. She would get the diaper when she needed changing, tried to assist in her feedings, and tried to sing nursery rhymes. Although Alanta did not display any signs of jealousy, Albert and Ta'Nelle kept a watchful eye on her as much as they could. They knew the best way to prevent jealousy from surfacing its ugly head was to get Alanta involved with the baby as much as possible.

Jamberlyn was growing so fast and becoming more independent every day. Like Alanta, when Jamberlyn started feeding herself, she made a complete mess and was very noisy. As she continued to grow, she wiser than her years. Whenever

Annie Boddie

the girls played too rough around the house, she thought they were fighting and would beg them to stop. Ta'Nya and Alanta included her in their fun and games as much as they could to, assure her that they were playing. As Jamberlyn became a toddler, she was usually the first to rise in the mornings and would make sure everyone knew she was awake. If one of the girls slept in the room with her, she always called their name louder and louder until they acknowledged they heard her. Once she had their attention, she would do whatever is necessary until they were wide awake. You can best believe she was ready, willing, and able to do whatever she had to get all their attention. Talk and talk, she did. Jamberlyn would say whatever came to her mind until she awakened the entire household.

When Jamberlyn was about three years old, her parents gave birth to their final child; another little girl. She was named Anointia Denise. The baby was born exactly on the due date. When the baby entered the house, Jamberlyn hit the ceiling. She changed 100 percent in the wrong direction. She went into full-blown temper tantrum mode. She started throwing things, slamming things on the floor, kicking things, and finally, she fell out on the floor screaming and yelling. She disliked Anointia's name, size, and color, in fact, she did not like her at all. She wanted her parents to take the baby back to the hospital, give her away, throw her away, or do whatever, as long as she got out of her house and out of her life. Ta'Nya tried her best to calm Jamberlyn down and let her know that she would still be their baby. She was not hearing it and she showed a side that her parents did not know she had.

Albert had taken all he could take at that moment. He tried to calm her down by talking to her and telling her that they all loved her, but nothing worked. He called her and asked her to come to him, but she refused to listen, instead of obeying her father, she acted out more. The more Jamberlyn screamed, the more frightened the baby became. Albert got down on his knees and reached out to Jamberlyn and she started fighting him. He said, "All right now, you better stop, I'm not playing with you!" He knew he had to do something immediately to get control of the situation. The Barnesworths was deeply religious, they grew up with the church inside of them and they were determined to raise their children the same way. Albert remembered reading in the Bible in Proverbs 13:24, "He that spareth his rod hateth his son (daughter): but he that loveth him (her) chasteneth him (her) betimes (promptly)." Albert decided to have a temper tantrum of his very own. He spanked her, picked her up off the floor, took her to her room, and put her to bed. Jamberlyn had never gotten a spanking before and she was totally surprised. After five minutes, she quieted down and fell fast asleep.

When Jamberlyn awakened, she got up out of her bed and went to her parents' room. It was as if she had forgotten the spanking, she had received from her dad just a couple hours earlier. She saw her mother feeding Anointia and lost control yet again. She had no idea that Albert was still in the house. She tried to hit the baby and pull the baby out of her mother's arms. Ta'Nelle grabbed Jamberlyn's hand and told her to stop. The poor girl started screaming all over again. She wanted her mother to get rid of the baby right away. She screamed as if someone was killing her. Ta'Nelle had her hands full as she tried to protect the baby from Jamberlyn's rage. She was so out of control that Ta'Nelle had to spank her hands to keep her from hurting the baby. Albert heard Jamberlyn screaming, and he quickly ran into the room to see what was happening. He could not believe Jamberlyn was acting out again. Albert felt it would be best to take Jamberlyn, Ja'Nae, and Ta'Nya out of the house to spend a hour or more time with them. While they were out, he took them to the playground and played with them for hours. He could tell Jamberlyn was not satisfied, she wanted her mother, and there was not anything he could do to change that. On the way home, he stopped at one of the local restaurants and picked up their dinner. Albert and the girls tried their best to pamper Jamberlyn, but nothing worked.

Once they returned to the house, they knew they had to watch Jamberlyn's every move. She was on a mission to get the baby out of the house any way she could and as soon as possible. Family members would often come by the Barnesworths' house to take Jamberlyn during the afternoon and sometimes overnight during the weekends. She gave them a complete fit, she wanted Ta'Nelle every minute of every day. Ta'Nelle spent quality time all her girls until she was exhausted. Albert helped care for Anointia at night so Ta'Nelle could relax and get her needed rest. Jamberlyn was extremely jealous of her sisters however, she quickly learned to leave Ta'Nya and Ja'Nae alone, they proved to be too much for her to manage. She started focusing all her negative energy on her little sister, Anointia, and did not care who knew it. She knew if her parents found her attacking the baby in any way, she would get it good.

One day, while the baby was in her crib fast asleep, Jamberlyn decided it was a suitable time to attack. She slipped into the room, pulled Anointia's hair, and pinched her two times as she asked, "Do it hurt? Huh? Do it hurt?" the baby screamed at the top of her lungs. Jamberlyn ran to her room as fast as her little legs could take her. She functioned as if she was there the entire time. Unfortunately for Jamberlyn, Ta'Nelle was listening on the baby monitor when she entered the room. Ta'Nelle quickly ran into the room, just seconds after Jamberlyn exited the room. Anointia was crying uncontrollably. Ta'Nelle's first order of business was to make sure the baby was all right and then deal with Jamberlyn. While trying to calm the baby, Ta'Nelle noticed that her arm had five or six red marks and scratches on it from Jamberlyn's attack.

After the baby settled down and went back to sleep, Ta'Nelle went to see Jamberlyn with her paddle behind her back. Meanwhile, Jamberlyn was in her room as happy as she could be. She was so proud of herself that she laughed uncontrollably. As she looked around her room, she saw her mother standing at the doorway, and immediately knew she was in trouble. Ta'Nelle came prepared to take care of business and she did. Before she knew what was happening, Jamberlyn's smile quickly turned into tears. Ta'Nelle used Jamberlyn's own words against her she said, "Do it hurt? Huh? Do it hurt?" Jamberlyn was so upset she did not know what to do. As she sat in her room rubbing her bottom, she refused to believe that the baby was hurting as badly as she was. She knew at that moment that she had to find a way to make that baby pay for all the pain she had endured. She did not know how or when she would get Anointia, but one thing she knew with certainty was that she would not rest until that baby paid. The next time, her parents would not catch her.

It was finally time for Albert to return to work. On his way, he dropped Ta'Nya off at school, and Ja'Nae and Jamberlyn off at the daycare. After school, Ta'Nya was taken to the daycare and remained there until Albert got off work. Albert hoped and prayed he would not have any problems with Jamberlyn. He knew the teacher had collaborated with her for almost a month to prepare her for the birth of the new baby. When Albert entered the classroom, the teacher could tell by looking at his face that Jamberlyn was not adjusting very well. The teacher tried repeatedly to help the Barnesworths with Jamberlyn jealously. She had to start from the beginning, everything she taught her before the baby's birth had gone out the window. With love and patience, Jamberlyn seemed to be calming down, but somehow, I doubt it.

One day while everyone was preparing to eat dinner, Jamberlyn produced what she considered to be the perfect sneak attack on Anointia. Once the dinner was on the table, Albert prayed a blessing over the food, and it was on. You see, Jamberlyn knew Anointia would make her normal baby noises while eating. Albert and Ta'Nelle were busily engaged in conversation and before long, Jamberlyn made her move. Anointia was enjoying herself too much for Jamberlyn and within two minutes, Jamberlyn attacked her. Remember she was a little girl on a mission, and she was determined to get all her parents' attention. She reached under the table with her fork and poked Anointia in the leg. Anointia immediately let out a huge scream as she grabbed for her leg.

Ta'Nelle stood up and took Anointia out of the highchair to examine her. As she looked at Anointia's left leg, she saw four puncture wounds on her thigh. She was so surprised to learn that Jamberlyn had poked the baby with her fork. Jamberlyn was fast, but not that fast. Unfortunately for her, Albert saw her as she moved her hand back on the table. She could not win for losing, the poor girl was caught again. Albert said, "Jamberlyn Latrice Barnesworth!" Before he could say anything else she quickly replied, "Daddy I did not do anything! I did not do anything!" He said, "Jamberlyn I saw you. I saw you and I will not allow you to hurt anyone in this house, nor will you lie to me!" She said, "But, but, but, Daddy, I did not do anything! I did not do anything, honest!"

Albert got up from the table and grabbed Jamberlyn by her hand, she grabbed hold of the table leg trying to resist, but she was not strong enough. She kicked and screamed until the two of them were out of the room. Albert grabbed his paddle and quickly introduced it to Jamberlyn's bottom. She thought she had it made in the shade once the paddling was over until it was time to sit on her hurting bottom. At that point, she realized she was reaping the benefits of her actions. Hopefully, she had learned her lesson, but knowing Jamberlyn, you could never tell. She was truly a button pusher that loved to push people to their limit, and Albert was not any exception. Jamberlyn calmed down for a day or two and once again, she was back to her normal mischievous self. One thing was certain, she would not bother Anointia while Albert was at home. One day, all the girls were busy playing peacefully when Jamberlyn decided to strike again. Anointia was busy minding her own business when along came trouble in the form of Jamberlyn. She was out to get revenge for her latest padding, so she grabbed a doll and started hitting Anointia on her back and her shoulders until her sisters entered the room,.

That day, Jamberlyn got more than she bargained for. Anointia let out a horrifying scream immediately. Ta'Nya and Ja'Nae quickly ran to her side. They were determined not to let their baby sister get injuried, Jamberlyn anymore. As they yelled for their mother, they had no other choice but to take matters into their own hands. They reached down and pulled Jamberlyn off Anointia and started hitting her. She was so angry she did not know what to do. When Ta'Nelle entered the room, the girls were engaged in a full-blown fight, she could not believe the way the girls were acting. Anointia was still screaming from the pain she suffered at the hands of Jamberlyn. Ta'Nelle separated the girls and asked, "Why are you girls fighting?" At that moment, Jamberlyn played the innocent role as if she had no idea why she was being attacked by her big sisters. Ta'Nya told her mother what happened to Anointia thanks to Jamberlyn. After checking

Anointia to make sure she had no bruises or scratches, she got her to settle down, Ta'Nelle left the room.

Ta'Nelle was gone for less than five minutes to take several deep breaths. While she was gone, she decided to try another approach to help Jamberlyn to adjust to her baby sister. The Barnesworths tried everything in their power to help Jamberlyn overcome her jealousy. After a two months, they believed Jamberlyn was getting better and was willing to try to be the best sister she could be. She started thinking about all the problems she caused this innocent little child simply because she wanted all the attention. The girls were constantly told to admit to their wrongdoings. Jamberlyn gained what so many people have not gained in their whole lifetime, a conscience.

Jamberlyn knew she had to get things right with her family, especially her baby sister immediately. She swallowed her pride and went to her family. She said, "Ta'Nya and Alanta, I want to tell you that I have been a bad little girl. I have been evil and very fussy to you both, I am so sorry. I know now how it is to be a big sister and I know you both love me. Please do not be mad at me because I did not know that you were trying to help me. I love you with all my heart. I do not want to be mean anymore. I will be a good girl, okay." Jamberlyn's eyes filled with tears. The girls embraced her and showered her with all the love they had. All the girls as well as Ta'Nelle were crying, however, their tears were tears of joy.

Albert and Ta'Nelle took advantage of every teachable moment. Albert said, "We have all done terrible things it is called, sin. But when we know that we are wrong and do not say we are sorry, then God is not pleased with us. That means we have not learned our lesson, and we will do the same things repeatedly. Do you girls remember what we told you about Jesus?" Alanta said, "You said that Jesus loves us and he died for us." Albert said, "Yes, Jesus came here to show us how to love each other and he is happy with you girls right now and so are we. We have everything we need in this family because we have the love of God. Your mother and I are so proud of you, we know that you have listened and you are learning how to be the best little girls you can be. We thank God, he blessed us with such impressive children."

Once Jamberlyn repented to her family she loved people of all races and ages. She became very outspoken, so much so that she never met a stranger or a child she did not like. Because of her personality, she was well-known wherever she went, and she made sure of it. She was not a young girl starving for attention, she was quite the opposite. She was a girl that believed in showing everyone the love and respect she had experienced from her family. . When she started elementary school, she introduced herself to everyone in her class. Once a new student came into the classroom, she made that person feel welcomed immediately. You might say she was a welcoming committee all by herself. She would go to the child and say, "Hi my name is Jamberlyn Barnesworth. What is your name?" She wanted to make sure all the children felt comfortable.

Unfortunately, because of Jamberlyn's unique personality, she experienced jealousy from children in her class (she now knew how Anointia felt). She did not know anything else to do but to be herself by helping others as much as humanly possible. She was a very compassionate little girl that could not or would not tolerate violence from anyone. As she continued to grow older, she frequently intervened when her friends had disagreement. One night before going to sleep, Alanta told her mother she saw Jamberlyn as a well-respected lawyer after graduating from high school. Jamberlyn wanted everyone around her to be at peace with each other. She encouraged her friends to talk about their misunderstandings before letting things escalate and become violent. She informed them that friendships are important to have; however, it is extremely easy to lose a friend for something you could have talked through. She continued by telling them that a faithful friend is a rare commodity that should be valued without causing hurt, harm, or embarrassment. Jamberlyn loved people and believed in resolving things peacefully and she was quickly nicknamed throughout the school "The mediator of peace." She did not know it at the time, but her future as a peacemaker was already taking shape.

Jamberlyn continued to express her love by becoming a youth leader to all the children in their neighborhood, in addition to the children at the church where her family attended. Jamberlyn like her sisters had such a strong passion for people and assisted them in any way she felt would be beneficial. She was intelligent and well-advanced in her classes. She often took time to work with other children in her classroom that were having difficulties. Sometimes, her teacher would ask her to help the other children that mainly were having trouble with math. Regardless of the time, she spent with others she made sure her baby sister was not neglected. The Barnesworth girls would check each other's homework daily.

Jamberlyn was known as a fair and just young lady with an abundance of wisdom and knowledge. She was optimistic of becoming a lawyer after graduating from high school. In her mind, she was well on her way. She was excelling in school quicker than her older sisters and managed to graduate from high school with honors at the tender age of fourteen. She received a full scholarship to one of the best colleges in the country. She knew that to be a lawyer, she had to enroll in undergraduate school, and receive a bachelor's degree to qualify for admission to law school. Although it usually takes a person seven years to finish their studies to become a lawyer, Jamberlyn was looking forward to the challenge. She wanted to make sure she would get all the classes necessary to aid in her career. She started by doing research on the internet. She soon discovered it would be beneficial to take reading, writing, foreign language, history, government, economics, computer science, math, and any classes with public speaking.

Jamberlyn knew her calling in the legal profession would be to defend individuals accused of crimes, so she decided to study criminal justice to get a jump start. After going to undergraduate school, she was looking forward to receiving her bachelor's degree. She was optimistic she would be able to take the Law School Admissions Test (LSAT) in three or four weeks. Everything was working out in her favor; she had her degree. Shortly, she learned that she had passed the admissions test with excellence and would be attending law school in the fall. She was determined to do the best she could to learn as much as possible. The Barnesworths was so proud of their new law student and they knew she would be successful in all her endeavors. When Jamberlyn entered law school, she was barely seventeen and was underestimated and taken as a joke by the other students. They tried everything to intimidate her, but what they did not know was it meant to be a Barnesworth child. All the Barnesworth girls were smart and determined to succeed in everything they set their minds to do. Jamberlyn was more resilient than they could ever imagine, and they would soon see.

Jamberlyn's classmates would say things to discourage her such as: "Little girl, you are in the wrong place, this class is for adults. Why don't you go back to high school where you belong? You can't pass these classes; you don't have the knowledge to be here. You will fail these classes, so you need to go back

home before you make a fool out of yourself! We are not going
to help you when you start failing because you will fail! Go to
secretarial school, just maybe, one of us will feel sorry for you
and hire you after we get our license." Instead of the professors
taking up Jamberlyn, they questioned her ability because of
her age and would join in with the students' harassment. They
would say, "There is no way possible for you to comprehend the
things that we teach here, you are too immature! You are not
smart enough, and I will not waste my time trying to babysit
you!" The entire class laughed and laughed. Jamberlyn was
the laughingstock of most of her classes. They were waiting for
Jamberlyn to bust out in tears, but she was not exactly the crying
type when it came to getting what she wanted. Instead of giving
the class and the professors what they wanted, she let them know
she was stronger than they could have ever imagined. There
was nothing they could do to shake her faith in herself or her
Lord and Savior Jesus Christ. They were fighting a losing battle
but did not have the sense to know it!

Day after day, they continued to harass Jamberlyn in hopes
of making her drop out of school. They watched her facial
expressions every day to see if there were any weaknesses in
her face, but there were not any. So, they decided to try to
stress her out to no avail. Unbeknownst to the class, regardless
of her age, Jamberlyn wanted to be an attorney to help people
of age, race, creed, or color in the criminal justice system. She
did not plan to stand by and let innocent people get punished,
for crimes they did not commit. While her classmates were
so busy trying to find ways to provoke Jamberlyn, she was
busy concentrating on her classes. To everyone's surprise, they
quickly learned that Jamberlyn was not the little weakling they
imagined her to be. She was a strong, intelligent, and focused
young lady that wanted to be one of the best, if not the best

student in the class. And because of her religious upbringing, she knew without a doubt that "she could do all things thru Christ which strengthened her," according to the Word of God in Philippians 4:13. Jamberlyn's parents taught all the girls to be successful, the word failure was not a word used in the Barnesworths' household. While everyone was busy labeling Jamberlyn, she was busy proving herself. Once they realized that she was well deserving of being in the school, they found themselves apologizing to her. Seven of the students humbled themselves and asked the young seventeen-year-old child for her assistance. "Wow! Is not that something!"

There were times when the students had to work as a team, and everyone wanted to work with Jamberlyn. She had been tried, evaluated, and proven to be a true force to be regarded. She was well on her way to becoming a smart and talented lawyer. She became a tutor to those same classmates that believed she was out of her league, too immature to be taken, seriously. In their spare time, the majority of the students formed a debate team. They picked a case that was in their field of study from the newspapers that would shortly be given to the jury. Naturally, they had to study the pros and cons and the remainder of the class would be the jurors. When debating in the classroom, the evidence for both sides had to be so compelling that the mocked jury as well as the instructors had difficulty deciding. If the jury was a hung jury, then the student defense lawyers would get the highest grades. The students were enjoying their classes as well as each other. They became remarkably close friends and before long, it was time to prepare for their upcoming graduation. Jamberlyn and all her classmates blessed the law school with their greatest honor; This entire class graduated as the first class in the school's history of one hundred years on the "A-B" honors roll! Their accomplishments deemed them the most successful law students ever. Jamberlyn was awarded the youngest graduate ever, and she graduated at the top of her class, In addition to their accomplishments they were the first class to be employed on the day of their graduation with prestigious law firms. . Jamberlyn worked with one of the best well-known criminal law firms in the area.

Without a doubt, the Barnesworths was extremely proud of their daughter. She was the first lawyer in the family. Before long, Jamberlyn would be moving into her very own three-bedroom, two-bathroom condominium. It would be a wonderful place to start her life as an independent young woman. Once her clientele started to build up, Jamberlyn planned to venture out and open her own law firm. A year had passed, and everything was going just as she planned. At that point, she knew she needed assistance from her parents, her apostle, and other family members. They started praying for the Lord to order her steps as it is written in Psalm 119:133 which reads, "Order (direct) my steps in thy word: and let not any iniquity have dominion over me." She wanted to make sure her decisions were in line with the plans the Lord had for her life.

Shortly, Jamberlyn, the Barnesworths, their Apostle, and the other family members received the answer they were seeking from the Lord. Jamberlyn was finally ready to establish her own private practice. She rented office space, purchased office furniture, and was ready to open. She named her new practice, "Barnesworths and Associates, Attorneys at Law." She hired two lawyers, three paralegals, two secretaries, and a receptionist. The law firm's clients were satisfied with the representation they received and told all their families and friends. Everything was going just as Jamberlyn wanted. Her business was growing; however, she still had not landed what she considered to be an extremely challenging case for her and her associates.

After about seven months in private practice, Jamberlyn was called to represent one of her friends with a profoundly serious case. It was almost midnight, Jamberlyn was sleeping so peacefully when she received a very disturbing telephone call. To her surprise, the caller was a woman that she had the privilege of going to her wedding five or six years earlier. Beverly was extremely troubled. Jamberlyn assured Beverly that she would oversee the situation. Jamberlyn also told her to tell Brandon to remain silent until she arrived. As she lay there in her bed in shock, she could not help but remember the last time she saw Brandon and Beverly. It was such a joyous occasion. The Fosters were expecting their second child in a few short weeks. Jamberlyn and Brandon attended middle school together and became remarkably close friends from then on. As she continued to lay there, she thought about Brandon and Beverly's wedding. It was a very special day; she could see for herself that the Fosters were madly in love with each other. The Fosters reminded her of her parents. Jamberlyn could only hope and pray that when she marries, she would be blessed to experience that same type of love and devotion. Jamberlyn perceived that her former classmate was a good, decent man, and being violent was not part of his character. Although she did not know the circumstances of his detainment, she was not worried. She considered it to be an honor and a privilege to represent him.

Meanwhile, as Mr. Foster sat at the police department waiting for Jamberlyn, the detectives were on a mission to question him. They so hoped that the man would break down under pressure and confess to the crime. They knew they only had a brief period of time so they brought in their very best detectives. However, Mr. Foster was a well-educated individual that was aware of his rights, his lips were sealed. Once Jamberlyn arrived at the police department, she sprang into action. The detectives informed her that Mr. Brandon Foster had been held under the suspicion of sexual assault and kidnapping. They proceeded to question Mr. Foster for an hour under the watchful eye of Jamberlyn. Finally, she had enough. Jamberlyn informed the detectives to either arrest Mr. Foster or release him immediately. Naturally, the detectives had to comply with her request, and Mr. Foster was released, and returned home to his family. Brandon informed his wife of all that happened at the police station and assured her she had nothing to worry about. Beverly knew it was a case of mistaken identity because she knew her husband was not that type of man.

The next day, Brandon went back to both of his jobs with the joy of the Lord. He was looking forward to his future and the new baby on the way. Brandon informed his supervisors that he wanted a two or three weeks off to help his wife with their new baby in a couple of weeks once the baby arrives. He would let them know the exact date after his wife's next doctor appointment the following week. Both of his employers informed him if she goes into labor, let them know and his leave time would start then, if not before. The next week, Beverly was six centimeters, so Brandon took off work from both jobs for three weeks. He always saved his vacation time for emergencies. The baby was born that afternoon, she was a healthy 8 lbs. and 5 oz. She was named, Briana La'Nae Foster. Bandon and Beverly were blessed to have a little girl to go with their son Brandon Jr. They were so optimistic about their family; they loved each other more than words could say. Brandon was truly a man's man, there was not anything he would not do to help his wife and children. He wanted to spend some quality time getting to know his little girl and help Brandon Jr. get adjusted to his new baby sister Briana.

Before long, it was time for Brandon to return to both of his jobs. Everything was going great you could say, too great. Unknowing to Brandon, the police were watching his every move. One day, they stopped by his home and insisted that he go with them to the police department yet again. Beverly called Jamberlyn immediately and she was told, "Do not worry, I got this!" The detectives believed they had Brandon right where they wanted him. In their eyes, he looked exactly like the man the victim described. One of the detectives said, "I can't tell the difference between those people anyway, they all look alike to me!" Ms. Barnesworth quickly arrived at the police department and was directed to the interrogation room. The detectives were familiar with Barnesworth's law firm. They considered Ms. Barnesworth to be a lightweight attorney that barely passed the bar exam but wanted to be a heavyweight contender. Regardless of how things appeared, Jamberlyn believed she was the best attorney to defend her friend Brandon. The detectives wanted to put Mr. Foster in a lineup with six other men. Ms. Barnesworth nor Mr. Foster had any objections to the request although there was a chance he would be falsely identified. Once the detectives had everyone in place, they called Ms. Barnesworth. She was told to bring (the accused), Mr. Foster, and meet at the police station at 2:00 p.m. the next day. The detectives were sure they had their man. They were so sure in fact, that they used two undercover officers and two men off the streets in the lineup with Brandon. All the men varied in height, weight, and size. They were all African American, light (skin) complexion, muscular men that ranged from 5'7"–6'3" in height. Although Jamberlyn knew there were undercover officers and other personnel along with men off the streets in the lineup, she could care less.

The victim was standing behind a one-way glass petition to see if she could identify anyone in the lineup as her assailant.

The victim stood behind the glass and studied each individual for two or three minutes. It seemed as if she had no idea who to blame for her attack. So instead of saying she did not know or none of the men looked like the man that assaulted her, she produced a plan and set it in action. She finally decided to point to Mr. Brandon Foster. People may say it was unfortunate, but Jamberlyn considered it a challenge that she was determined to win. She could see right thru the victim; she had a deceiving spirit as you will soon see. Mr. Foster was detained, until he met with the magistrate that afternoon. The prosecutor informed the magistrate that the man had been identified out of a lineup by a woman as the man that assaulted and kidnapped her. He wanted Mr. Brandon Foster to remain in custody until the trial. However, Jamberlyn fought for her client. She informed the magistrate that Mr. Foster had never been in any type of trouble in his life and hasn't had so much as a parking ticket. He has been married for seven years with two small children at home, one was born two weeks ago. He works two jobs to provide for his family. He is a well-mannered man that is loved and respected by everyone that knows him. The prosecutor continued to argue for five minutes until the magistrate said, "Save it for the trial! Mr. Foster will be released on bail and remain out on bail until the conclusion of the trial unless he violates his orders. Due to the fact that he doesn't have a prior record, his bond is set at one thousand dollars, and he will pay ten percent which is one hundred dollars and he will report to court two weeks from today at 9:00 a.m. Mr. Foster, if you don't report, a warrant will be issued for your arrest and you will remain in custody until your trial is concluded. Mr. Foster, do you understand?" Mr. Foster said, "Yes, sir!" The magistrate said, "You are free to go after you pay your bond to the clerk."

Ms. Barnesworth and Mr. Foster thanked the magistrate and went on their way.

The prosecutor did not like the ruling, not one bit, but he had to deal with it. He told his associates, "Ms. Barnesworth may have won the first battle, but I will win the war. I am convinced that once the case goes to trial, I will make a complete fool out of Ms. Barnesworth and Mr. Foster. This is an open and shut case as they will soon see. I am a very experienced attorney both in and out of the courtroom and well acquainted with all the judges. To appeal to the female jurors, I have decided to use my top female assistant to question the victim." The prosecutor smelled blood and he wanted to do whatever was necessary to draw the blood from Ms. Barnesworth and Mr. Foster, but would he? Only time would tell! The older folks had a saying, "Don't count your chickens before they are hatched!"

Jamberlyn was not concerned nor was she worried. In fact, she was looking forward to the challenge of representing her dear friend Brandon. She was positive that the case would be the toughest case ever because it would hinge on emotions as well as facts. She understood that the prosecutor would pull out his big guns to make sure he got a conviction. Regardless of what the prosecutor planned, Jamberlyn remembered the oath she pledged and the reason she became an attorney. There wasn't any way possible she would let an innocent man go to prison for a crime he did not commit. Jamberlyn said to Brandon, "The prosecutor wants a fight, and a fight he will get! This fight, I am determined to win. Remember it is not what it looks like! Brandon, I want you to do something that some people would call strange. In fact," she said, "I want you and your family to go on a twenty-one-day fast. I will be fasting with you. We will be fasting for six hours a day. To make sure you know just how important this is, read Mark 9:14–29. It is the story of a man that had a son born with a deaf and dumb spirit, in other words, the young man couldn't hear or talk. Mark 9:17–19 reads, 'And one of the multitude answered and said, Master, I have brought unto thee my son, which hath a dumb spirit; And wheresoever he taketh him, he teareth him: and he foameth, and gnasheth with his teeth, and pineth away: and I spake to thy disciples that they should cast him out; and they could not. He answered him, and saith, O faithless generation, how long shall I be with you? How long shall I suffer you? Bring him unto me.'" The disciples could not help the child, but when the child was taken to Jesus the spirit was cast out of him, and he was delivered immediately. Mark 9:28–29 reads, "And when He (Jesus) was come into the house, his disciples asked him privately, Why could we not cast him out? And he (Jesus) said unto them, This kind can come forth by nothing but prayer and fasting." Jamberlyn informed Brandon that his case was profoundly serious, and he truly needed the Lord's intervention. She did not take anything for granted. Although she believed Brandon was completely innocent, she also knew that innocent people are falsely imprisoned, quite frequently (every day). The fast would start the next day. Brandon was attentive, he listened very carefully to every word Jamberlyn spoke. And he made up his mind that he and his family would obey Jamberlyn to the best of their ability.

Brandon could not get home to his beautiful wife and children fast enough. When Brandon entered the house, he could see that his wife was genuinely concerned about him. He embraced her and held her close and told her how much he loves her. He assured her that everything would be all right. He said, "Baby, we need to talk to our Lord and Savior Jesus Christ. Let us pray. One thing I do know, honey, he (Jesus) will make everything all right!" After the couple prayed, they felt the spirit of peace come

all over them. They knew then that their Lord was giving them
the confirmation they needed to let them know the victory was
already theirs. Although they had the peace that could only come
from their Lord and Savior Jesus Christ, they would continue
to fast and pray as Jamberlyn instructed them. Whenever they
thought about the situation, they praised and worshipped their
Lord with everything in them., There was not any need to worry
about something God had already given victory over. It was time
to continue to walk by faith, praise, and worship the Lord.

The following day, Brandon returned to both of his jobs.
He was an upright individual that genuinely believed in telling
the truth no matter what the consequences. He asked to speak
directly with his superiors as soon as possible. He informed
them of everything that happened to him in the last few weeks.
As the superiors listened, they made up their minds to stand
with him. They volunteered to report to the proceedings and
to speak on his behalf. Being a humble and considerate young
man, he thanked his employers and let them know his lawyer
(Ms. Barnesworth) would contact them soon. Shortly, Brandon
was on his post during the jobs they were paying him to do.

The next day, Brandon's arrest was publicized, it was on the
front page of all the newspapers and on all the local T.V. stations
along with his picture. Every place he went, people that did not
know his character started saying nasty and rude things to him.
When he crossed the street, people tried to run him over or
throw things at him, but Brandon never lost his composure. The
people were convinced he was guilty as charged the moment
they laid their eyes on him. They would yell at him and say, "I
know you did it. I can see it all over your face, it shows even
in your eyes you assaulted and kidnapped that woman! I hope
they lock you up and throw away the key." Or things like, "You
don't deserve to live after what you did!" I am sure you can

testify to the fact that people will believe any negative thing they hear about you, but when it comes to them, they are sweet and innocent. Whatever happened to innocent until proven guilty? That was thrown, out with the bath water! The people spoke such dreadful things that their words and actions cut to Brandon's heart, but he refused to let it get the best of him. He held his head up and continued to go about his business. Regardless of how Brandon felt, he always checked himself before going home. He refused to let his wife see anything negative on his face or hear anything negative in his voice. He could hardly wait until the trial starts so he would be free, and the guilty person would be locked up and punished for such a horrible crime.

The prosecutor was absolutely positive that Mr. Foster was guilty as charged. So positive in fact that he informed the judge that he wanted a speedy trial. He told the judge he wanted Mr. Foster to submit a blood sample to compare the DNA with that found on the victim. Jamberlyn, nor Mr. Foster, had any objections, and the sample of blood was immediately taken after court. The judge scheduled the trial to begin on the earliest date available which would be exactly two weeks from that date. Jamberlyn was busy preparing her case as the prosecutor was walking on pins and needles (anxious). Once the tests returned, the prosecutor was quite disappointed. He believed the best way to proceed with the case was to offer a plea deal to the defendant. Ms. Barnesworth (Jamberlyn) already knew what her client would say before she asked, however, she had to approach him with the offer. The offer was for Mr. Foster to plead guilty to a lesser charge and spend a maximum of three years in prison, and a year of probation. Mr. Foster said exactly what Ms. Barnesworth expected him to say. Brandon said, "Absolutely not! He has lost his mind. One thing I do know it is not what it looks like. I have a God that sits high and looks low. He knows the exact truth, and it will come out in a few weeks, for sure!"

About a week before the trial, the prosecutor called Ms. Barnesworth with what he thought was the perfect deal. He was willing to give Brandon three years in prison and eighteen months of probation only if he agreed to plead guilty before the trial begins. She approached Brandon and his exact words were, "There is no way I'm going to take a plea for something I had absolutely nothing to do with, period!" Jamberlyn said, "The prosecutor is not as bad as he wants us to believe. He has been talking loudly and saying nothing. He has already lost the case, but he wants us to believe he is trying to give you a break. The handwriting is on the wall, his reputation is at stake. He always try to scare the lawyers, and since I am a 'babe lawyer' he wants to take the straightforward way out. And then he would be able to say, I told you that lawyer was not any good! But the devil is a liar! Just hold on, dear friend, we are almost, at the finish line!"

Finally, it was the first day of court, the day to select the jury. It took two days before all the jurors were seated. They managed to select twelve jurors and two alternates. On the third day, the courtroom was filled. Neither the defendant nor the accuser had any objections to allowing reporters in the courtroom. Needless to say, the victim's name had to remain secret, and no cameras were allowed in the courtroom. The prosecutor and Jamberlyn presented their opening statements, and the trial was officially started. The prosecutor called the 911 dispatcher that received the call to testify. He confirmed the date and time of the incident as well as the tone of the victim's tone. When Jamberlyn cross-examined the dispatcher, she wanted to make sure he was certain of the time and date of the attack.

The victim was called, and examined by the assistant

prosecutor. She asked her to describe the incident to the best of her ability. She started by saying, "I was on my way home from the neighborhood store when an African American man approached me. He was driving a red four-door pickup truck. He asked if I needed a ride and I told him thanks, but no thanks. He drove off and turned the corner. I continued to walk down the street. When I turned the corner, the man jumped out of the ally and grabbed me around my waist while placing his hand over my mouth. I struggled as hard as I could to get away from him, but he roughly moved me!" As she sobbed, she continued by saying, "He started dragging me. I fought with everything in me, but I was overpowered by his strength." As the tears rolled down her cheeks, she tried to compose herself. She continued by saying, "Look at me and look at him (as she pointed to the defendant). I could not fight against him. I was totally exhausted. Then at that point, he continued to drag me until he arrived at his truck, where he had the left driver's side door open. He forced me inside and quickly jumped in and drove off." As she sat there fighting back her tears, she resumed by saying, "I tried to get out of the truck on the passenger's side, but the man was holding my arm. He drove for quite some time before turning down a dirt road to a wooded area where he stopped and preceded to tear my clothes off." She let out a huge scream and yelled, "He raped me! He told me if I tried to scream again, he would kill me, and no one would ever find my body. I was so afraid I did not know what the man would do to me. I had no choice but to obey him!"

The assistant prosecutor asked, "Do you remember the time of the assault?" She said, "It was around 7:30 or 8:00 p.m." The AP said, "Can you describe the man? Did the man have any scars or noticeable tattoos on his body?" The victim said, "The man was 5'8 or 5'9 with a light complexion, well-built, about

180–200 pounds with a small goatee and mustache. He was well-groomed with a close haircut. It seems like he had a small tattoo or scare on his right arm." At that time, the assistant prosecutor said she did not have any more questions. Everyone in the courtroom could see the effects the testimony had on the victim. All the women in attendance were in tears, even the men could see the pain the woman had endured. The judge gave her a few minutes to regroup. Jamberlyn believed without a doubt, that the woman was assaulted. Although she could sympathize with the victim, she had a job to do and that was to prove the innocence of her client. At that point, Jamberlyn felt it was best to cross-exam the victim, at a later time if need be. As the case continued, the DNA evidence was presented, however, it could not defiantly prove 100 percent that it matched the accuser. Jamberlyn was very patient with the DA and the witnesses they called. She knew it would soon be her time to present her case. The DA wanted Ms. Barnesworth to believe that he would win the case. Meanwhile, she sat back and watched things begin to unfold. The DA looked at the defendant's table, and in his mind, she had such a defeated look on her face. The more people he called, the more confident he became. He was judging Ms. Barnesworth by the look on her face, he forgot one especially important quote, "Never judge a book by its cover!" He finally rested his case and returned to his seat with a huge smile on his face. But how long would he continue to smile, that is what would tell the story!

THE BARNESWORTH'S
FINAL CHILD

Ta'Nelle was waiting for the arrival of her fourth child, and as usual, Alanta Ja'Nae informed her parents that this would be their final child. The child would also be another little girl. I can only imagine you, the reader saying in your mind, "Why didn't Alanta Ja'Nae let her parents learn what they were having? Well, remember she was a child of God, a visionary, and a dreamer. She was merely telling her parents what she already knew. She was too excited to hold it!" The baby would be born on June 7 and she would weigh 6 lbs. and 4 oz. Once the baby was born, she would be given the name Anointia Denise. Albert and Ta'Nelle could see the similarities with all their children, and they believed Anointia would be like Alanta. If that were the case, only God knows what they would learn from Anointia.

After the baby was t home, she was mild-tempered, but would she continue to be, or would she be smart enough to fool her parents? Only time would tell. One day, while the older girls were at school, and Jamberlyn was at the daycare, Ta'Nelle decided she would get a nap while baby Anointia was sleeping. After awakening from her nap, Ta'Nelle decided to cut the TV on the kid's station while she went about doing her chores. She was careful to place the baby monitor in the room so she could hear the baby when she awakened. The baby was sleeping so long that Ta'Nelle went into the room to check on her. To her surprise, the baby was enjoying the noises from the TV. Ta'Nelle knew it would take time to learn about her baby just as it took time for the other girls. Since the baby was safe and quiet, Ta'Nelle returned to her work. Day after day, Ta'Nelle practiced the same routine with Anointia if it worked, why change it! Ta'Nelle and the girls made sure they watched little Jamberlyn's every move until the baby was old enough to sit up. Jamberlyn was aware of the dos and don'ts where Anointia was concerned.

One day after school, Jamberlyn was the first one in the room with the baby. Since the baby seemed to be asleep, she turned the TV to one of her favorite shows. Immediately after she turned the TV station, the baby let out a horrible scream. Jamberlyn ran as fast as she could to get her mother to see what was wrong with her new baby sister. Jamberlyn said, "Mommy, Mommy, come quick something is wrong with my sister!" Ta'Nelle said, "I hear her, baby, I believe she will be all right, okay? Well, she is not wet, so we do not need a diaper. She is not hungry. What could it be?" As Ta'Nelle looked around there seemed to be nothing to explain what was making the baby scream so violently. As Ta'Nelle stood there trying to please Anointia, Jamberlyn said, "Mommy, I think I know what is wrong. I remember when I came into the room, I thought she was asleep, so I turned the TV station then she started screaming. Did I do something wrong, Mommy? I am so sorry. I do not want my baby sister to cry. Mommy, please make her stop! Make her stop!" She cried. Ta'Nelle replied, "Honey, I know you did not do anything, everything is all right. Now that we have tried everything, let us turn the TV back to where it was, but surely, she has not fallen in love with the TV already!" When Ta'Nelle turned the TV back to the previous station, Anointia stopped screaming. Ta'Nelle could not believe her baby was addicted to the TV in just two days. From that day on, no one wanted to hear that horrible scream coming out of such a small vessel.

She could not wait until Albert came home from work so she could share her new discovery. Shortly thereafter, Albert entered the back door and jumped right into the shower. When he entered the family room, it was just enough time to catch up on the goings-on of the day. Before Ta'Nelle could speak, the girls started speaking all at the same time. Albert was getting bits and pieces and understanding truly little. He said, "Ta'Nelle, what are they so excited about?" As Ta'Nelle explained the situation to Albert, he could not fathom such a thing, he had to see it for himself. At that moment, Albert and Ta'Nelle went into the bedroom where Anointia was and before he could turn the TV, everyone covered their ears except Albert. While turning the TV station, Anointia let out a loud unpleasant scream. Albert could not turn the station back fast enough. Ta'Nelle said, "Albert, brace yourself, we have another peculiar child on our hands. We will be scholars when we learn about these girls, then we will have to start all over again when they start dating. If nothing else, we will have to post a sign stating, 'Watch out, world, here comes the Barnesworths' sisters. Albert said, "Baby, you are right! That's why the Lord did not give us any boys, we have gotten so good with the girls especially since we are not having any more children!"

From that day forward, no one wanted to hear such horrible ear-piercing screams ever again coming out of such a small vessel. Anointia was finally growing up, and the girls could spend quality time with her. Unfortunately for Anointia, majority of the time was educational. By the time she was two years old, she knew enough to start kindergarten. She no longer wanted to be the baby. She wanted to be the little sister, the big sister as well as Jamberlyn's mother. She was born the youngest but loved to switch roles, especially with Jamberlyn. At other times, she wanted to be protective, and a little bossy just like her sisters. You can best describe Anointia as wanting to always want to have her way. Once her siblings started teaching her, she no longer was satisfied watching cartoons. She wanted to learn as much as she could. She quickly absorbed everything the girls were teaching her and was developing a stronger love for education. When she became bored, she would try to play a game until the girls finished their homework.

When visiting family and friends' children came over, Anointia became their teacher. She wanted to make sure they knew everything she learned. Alanta Ja'Nae watched Anointia, and she said, "Mommy, do you remember when you were pregnant with Anointia, and the Lord said she would be the first teacher in the family? Well, I do not know if you have been observing her or not, but the Lord has increased her wisdom and knowledge rapidly. She is becoming so patient and understanding while learning and is willing to teach anyone she encounters. She will be an outstanding educator. I even see her helping the children in her classroom and mentoring older children in things like math and science. I am so proud of her. She gasps things almost instantly. She will excel in her classes faster than any of us did. Education is definitely her calling." Ta'Nelle replied, "Thank you, Jesus! One thing I have learned Ja'Nae is that when God tells you to speak something, you speak it, and it shortly happens. Albert and I are immensely proud of all our girls. You have blessed us in many miraculous ways, we would not trade any of you for nothing. You all have made parenting easy, especially with Anointia. Sometimes, I thought you all were teaching her too fast, but the more you all taught her, the more she wants to learn."

When the Barnesworths children went to their local school, all the teachers were familiar with their family. The children were very well-mannered in most of the time especially the older girls once they learned to resist peer pressure. The Barnesworths would drop in their schools on various occasions to make sure they kept on top of their children's progress. Once they entered the building, the staff welcomed them with open arms. The children that were not so fortunate to have caring parents like the Barnesworths was glad to get a little attention from them also (usually a hug would do the trick.) Whenever the older girls saw a group of children around one of their sisters, they always checked to make sure everything was okay. They would look at their sister's face, and if she did not look like her normal self, they would ask, "What is wrong? Why are you all surrounding her? And what are you trying to do to her?" You can best believe they better answer quickly and say the right thing. They were very protective of each other, sometimes too protective, that is what true sisters do!

When Anointia began kindergarten, her sisters had taught her as much as her little brain could absorb. They were very patient and enjoyed every minute with her. At the tender age of five, she developed a love for teaching. She informed her parents that she wanted to be an elementary school teacher as well as a Sunday school teacher at their local church when she grows up. Anointia made up her mind that she would follow in her sister's footsteps. She would do her absolute best to become a straight "A" student to continue to help others. She wanted desperately to understand and pass her classes with ease. She became the teacher's helper. In her spare time, she landed her first job tutoring the other students in her class as well as children in the neighborhood. She was helping the other children to reach their goals. After entering high school, one of her grades dropped for a semester to "B." She was so disappointed in herself that she became depressed. She was a person that needed to work out her own problems, so she worked as hard as she could and the next semester her grades were back on track. Albert and Ta'Nelle were immensely proud of Anointia and the way she had grown up in such a short period of time.

   The older Anointia became, the stronger her love for teaching increased. She mastered her classes like a sponge absorbing water. She knew without a doubt that she would tutor children of various ages. As her love for teaching grew, she also wanted to teach the young adult Sunday school class at their local church in the not-so-distant future. Anointia developed into a mature and lovely young lady and started to tutor high school students as well as senior citizens. She went on to graduate high school/early college with a full scholarship. She continued her education in childhood development and received her master's degree in education. She had completed everything she needed to become an elementary school teacher. She applied to eight local school districts, but she was optimistic of teaching at the elementary or middle school she attended as a child. Before long, Anointia received the news that she had been waiting for. When the school opened for the new year, she proudly walked into her very own classroom. Although she could instruct elementary students up to the sixth grade, she was overjoyed to be able to start with the second and third graders. She wanted to make sure her students had a solid foundation so they would have all the principles needed to excel. She would practice the same format that she was taught as a child by encouraging the students to be the absolute best they could be by working hard. After Anointia started teaching, her dreams of becoming a Sunday school teacher became a reality. Due to the enormous growth at her church, she was given the opportunity to teach the young adult class. Every opportunity was given to Anointia to be a tremendous success. She loved her life and continued to be effective in the minds of every child that the Lord has entrusted her with.

There were times that were more challenging than others when she wanted to give up. However, she was reminded that no one gave up on her and she was not a quitter, but a winner. Anointia knew that if she gave up on the children that were considered the difficult or problem children, they would give up on themselves. And because of low self-esteem, they would drop out of school and become lost to the streets by committing crimes, going into the prison system, becoming gang members, and killing others or being murdered themselves. She knew that was not what God had called her to do. She welcomed a challenge and she was determined to meet every challenge head-on. She thought about how her sisters loved her enough to commit themselves to teaching her doing their spare time. And because of her upbringing, she refused to let any child assigned to her give up on themselves and later in life become a high school drop-out, a criminal, or a drug dealer/addict standing on the street corners with extremely low self-esteem, locked up behind the prison walls, or laying in the morgue. Anointia genuinely believes if we are never challenged we will never reach our full potential. Anointia was a noticeably young inexperienced teacher with a heart of pure gold. However, because of all her accompaniment, the board of education recognized her as the county's most influential teacher of the year for eight years.

The Barnesworths was so pleased with all their girls, they were all mature independent young ladies living incredibly happy and fulfilling lives. One summer, Anointia and nine of her co-workers' friends went on vacation in the mountains. While there, they had the opportunity to attend educational classes to learn the best way to deal with students with behavior problems. Anointia and her co-workers were determined to do everything they possibly could to help all children. There were educators from the east coast as well as the southern areas of the state including professors and parents dealing with abused and neglected children. Anointia and her group decided to sit with someone they did not know to make the classes more enjoyable.

While attending the classes, Anointia met a man name Steven Thornburger. He was a prominent professor at one of the local colleges for the past few years. The two started talking and soon learned that they had four things in common. First, and most importantly, they were both Christians and because of their religion, they believed in obeying God to the fullest. Secondly, they were educators that loved children of all ages. And thirdly, they both graduated from high school as well as college years earlier than they expected. After the classes were over, Steven decided he wanted to get to know Anointia better. The two of them started dating. And although their feelings were starting to grow stronger for each other, they wanted to take their relationship slowly. After three months, they were totally in love with each other and unknowingly, they started praying the same prayer. Things were going exceptionally well and the two were optimistic that one day they would become spouses, but only if it was approved by God.

Steven and Anointia had been dating for almost two years. They were so in love with each other and was optimistic that their relationship would soon move to the next level, however, the choice was out of her hands. On their first anniversary, Steven decided to take Anointia out to celebrate at one of their favorite restaurants out of town. He had everything planned a month in advance to make sure he reserved the best section in the establishment. When they were escorted to their table,

Matthew had a dozen yellow long-stem roses waiting in the seat next to where he would be sitting. The table was lit up with seven tall candles. Anointia was told to order whatever she wanted, but the dessert was already ordered. Once the meal was finished, the waiter brought their desserts which were Anointia's favorite devil food chocolate cake with a scoop of vanilla ice cream with whip cream and a cherry on top. Steven ordered a banana split fully loaded. While Anointia was eating her cake, Steven was busy examining his final surprise. He knew exactly how he wanted things to preceded, he had rehearsed it in his mind repeatedly.

As Anointia was eating her cake and ice cream, Steven placed a dozen of yellow long-stem roses on the table directly in front of her with the ribbon facing her. Unaware to Anointia, there were two violinists playing soft music from the moment they were sitting. Anointia was so busy admiring Suddenly, she started admiring the roses, she thanked Steven and told him how beautiful they were. As she picked the roses up to smell them, something caught her eye. She said, "What is this wrapped up around this ribbon? Steven, there is something sharp, ouch, in this ribbon!" Steven stood up and made his way next to Anointia and said, "Can you see it? Give it to me so I can see what it is. It's probably a thorn!" Anointia said. "Oh my god! Oh my god! Steven, is this what I think it is?" Steven replied, "What do you think it is?" At that moment, Steven kneeled down and said, "Anointia, honey, I know that today we are celebrating our first dating anniversary. But I know what I want, you have been my sunshine in my darkest days. When I am alone, you are constantly on my mind. When I am watching the games, I see you on the court or on the field. While at work I have called out your name. Honey, will you bless me and give me the honor of being my wife?" She grabbed

Steven by his neck and hugged him so long and so hard that the poor man could not breathe. As he tried to grab her arms she began yelling to the top of her lungs. She yelled, "Yes! Yes! Yes! Yes! Dear god, yes!" Poor Steven was trying to enjoy the moment, but how could he? His neck was still under in distress! Steven knew without a doubt that Anointia loved him with all her heart, but at that time, although he appreciated her, he just wanted her to give him a break and remove her arms quickly! Finally, the violinists hit an ear-piercing key, and immediately Steven was a free man. Steven had everything planned just the way he wanted but he forgot to get a video of his proposal. Thankfully, there were nine of the patrons at the restaurant had it all captured on their phones.

Unknowing to Anointia, the Barnesworths and the Thornburgers was at the restaurant in the formal dining area waiting to help Anointia and Steven celebrate their engagement. One thing is for sure, all the Barnesworth women had enough strength to choke an ox. When the women became excited about anything the men would try to run for cover. Majority of the time, their running was in vain. When the Barnesworths and the Thornburgers heard Anointia's yell, the servers opened the sliding doors to the formal dining room. Steven said, "Mr. and Mrs. Barnesworth, I absolutely love this woman right here, but if she is this strong when she is happy, Lord, help me when she gets upset. One thing is for sure, I am going to try my absolute best to keep her happy every minute of every hour of the day! Anointia, along with all the women, in the establishment were in tears thankfully to God those tears were joyful tears. Only God knows what would happen to men in a room filled with angry women. One thing is for sure, the word in Proverbs 25:24 states, "It is better to dwell in the corner of the housetop, than with a brawling woman in a wide house." In other words, it is better to be single than to be married to an angry woman. If you marry out of lust, you will be miserable for ninety nine percent of every day, month, or year. Have you ever heard the saying, "Happy wife, happy life?"

The Barnesworths and the Thornburger's believed their children had the person God ordained for them. Whenever they spoke of each other or saw each other, their faces lit up like a one-hundred-watt light bulb. They were married the next year with an outside backyard wedding with an indoor reception. They would be moving into a condominium after returning from their honeymoon until they decide where they wanted to live permanently. Steven and Anointia were awfully close to their families and decided to build their new home within a few minutes from them. They married the following year, three days before their second dating anniversary. They had an outdoor beach wedding with a large reception. Anointia was the third Barnesworths daughter to marry. In their second year of marriage, they decided it was time to start making plans to enlarge their family. They did not know just how many children they wanted, but one thing is for sure, they wanted their final child to be a little girl. However, as faith would have it, they would have five children and they were named, Steven Jr., Armando, Stephan, and their twin girls, Angel and Angela.

WHEN THE UNDERDOG BECOMES A CHAMPION

As you may remember, the time has passed since Mr. Foster was arrested, for kidnapping and assaulting a young woman. I decided to take a station break to introduce Barnesworths' final child. All the Barnesworth's daughters were in their early twenties when Jamberlyn was hired to represent Mr. Foster. The prosecutor has presented his case, now it is Jamberlyn's time to present hers. For her first witness, she called the defendant, Mr. Brandon Foster. She started questioning him extensively, everything that she believed the prosecutor would ask she asked. Once she finished the prosecutor, Mr. Silverman had his chance to cross-examine Mr. Foster. He was so pleased to get the opportunity to examine Mr. Foster, he was acting like a child at Christmas. Mr. Silverman believed he had the experience and the expertise to break Mr. Foster down and make him confess to the assault. He tried as hard as he could to make the man change his story, but Mr. Foster stood his ground, he refused to confess. Mr. Silverman was so upset and frustrated with the man's testimony that it became apparent to everyone in the courtroom. He yelled and yelled at Mr. Foster, but nothing worked. The more he yelled, the calmer Mr. Foster became. Mr. Silverman continued to yell and said, "Mr. Foster, were you this patient when you assaulted Ms. Doe? Did you assault her for the fun of it or to prove your strength? Couldn't you find a woman on the street corner to entertain you?"

Jamberlyn had more than enough she stood up and said, "Objection, your honor, Mr. Silverman is badgering the defendant!" Mr. Silverman was boiling hot; he was hotter than a forty-five! The judge said, "Sustain! Sustain! Mr. Silverman, if you continue, I will hold you in contempt and you will be thorn in jail for two weeks!" Mr. Silverman knew the judge meant just what he said, and he apologized to the court, Ms. Barnesworth as well as Mr. Foster. At that time, he reframed from questioning the defendant. Jamberlyn was a very smart young woman, and the opposing counselor would soon realize it. When calling her witnesses, she made sure none of them were in the courtroom until it was time for them to testify. Once they finished their testimonies, they remained in the courtroom unless they had to return to their jobs. She called ten friends of Mr. Foster, his pastor, ministers, and members of his church for character witnesses. There were so many witnesses that wanted to testify on behalf of the defendant that Jamberlyn could only mention their names. Mr. Silverman refused to believe anyone had that ten or more friends and loved ones willing to speak on their behalf. During his questioning, Mr. Silverman tried to get seven of the character witnesses to admit they were promised some type of incentive to lie for Mr. Foster, needless to say, all his efforts failed.

Next, Jamberlyn called Mr. Foster's, co-workers so she could verify his whereabouts on the night in question. Once again, Mr. Silverman tried his best to discredit the witnesses, but he was fighting a losing battle. He believed he had the right person on trial but at that time, he was having a challenging time trying to prove it. Jamberlyn on the other hand was determined to keep her composure by being cool, calm, and collected. She called the employees, the supervisors, the payroll clerks as well as the plant managers. After those witnesses, Jamberlyn entered into evidence fifteen sworn statements from other co-workers. She gave copies to the judge as well as Mr. Silverman. Finally, she rested her case. And due to the late hour, the judge adjourned for the day and the case would resume at 9:00 a.m. on the following morning, beginning with closing arguments

Jamberlyn was given the opportunity to give her closing arguments and she started by saying. "Ladies and gentlemen of the jury, I honestly believe Ms. Doe was kidnapped, raped, and dumped in the woods, however, my client, Mr. Brandon Foster, is not the guilty person. Mr. Foster is a man who loves people, and as you have heard from twenty witnesses, it is impossible for him to be in two places at the same time. You have heard Mr. Silverman ask every question that he could, and he still got the same answers. I deliberately had the witnesses questioned, and they remained in this courtroom or returned to their jobs, so no one knew what I was going to ask, nor their answers." At that time, Mr. Silverman said, "Your Honor, Your Honor, can we approach the bench?" The judge said, "Mr. Silverman, it is highly unlikely to interrupt a lawyer while she is giving her closing arguments." Mr. Silverman said, "Your Honor, this is very important, there is new evidence that was just brought to my attention, which will change everything!" The judge asked Ms. Barnesworth if she had any objections to Mr. Silverman's request. She replied, "No, Your Honor!" As the lawyers approached the bench, Mr. Silverman informed the judge that another woman had been kidnapped, raped, and assaulted in the same manner as Ms. Jane Doe several hours ago. "The man fits the same description and there is no way possible that Mr. Foster committed it. He is still wearing a monitor, and according to all the proven witnesses that have testified, he is not capable of doing such a thing. I honestly believe it is impossible for Mr. Brandon Foster to be guilty of the crime that he has been charged. Currently, I want to drop all charges against Mr. Foster and address this court, with your permission, of course, Your Honor!"

The judge said, "Due to the circumstances and the time, I will address the court immediately. Ladies and gentlemen of the jury, due to the information that was brought to my attention a few minutes ago, I want to thank you for your service, you're free to go!" After the jurors exited the courtroom, the judge said, "Deputy Thompson, will you please remove the monitor off of Mr. Foster's ankle? Mr. Foster, please stand. First, I want to inform you that you are a good man. Unfortunately, you were accused of a crime you did not commit. I have presided over hundreds of cases, and I have not found anyone with the love and compassion you displayed in this courtroom. Unfortunately, you were inconvenienced, for a crime you truly did not commit. I was given some terrible news that, yet another woman has been assaulted and raped by a man with the same description as the one that assaulted Ms. Doe. I came into this courtroom with a clear mind so I could get all the facts and would be able to judge you according to the testimonies. Although your case was dismissed, I already knew by the evidence that you were innocent. I cannot erase what you have been thru, but I can bid you God's speed. Wherever you go in your life. you can be a witness that God still delivers! God loves you, young man, and so do I!" The judge and Mr. Foster shook hands, and Brandon prayed for him and bid God's blessings over the judge and his family!

Mr. Silverman apologized to Mr. Foster for all the pain and suffering they caused him and his family. Mr. Silverman and his staff also apologized to the Fosters for all they endured from the investigators and the assistants. The judge and the prosecutor agreed to allow a statement to be released to the reporters in order to clear Mr. Foster's name. Mr. Silverman also wanted to congratulate Ms. Barnesworth for a job well done. As he shook her hand he said, "Ms. Barnesworth, you are indeed a force to be reckoned with You will no longer be considered a lightweight attorney but you are one of the absolute best. Anyone that goes up against you will have a hug fight on their hands. Although the case was not finished, I want you to know you were winning, and there was not anything I could have done to reverse it."

Once Mr. and Mrs. Foster and Jamberlyn Barnesworth and her staff along with their extended families left the courtroom, they were surrounded by reporters from states as far away as Texas to Connecticut Mr. Foster's story was going to be put on the front page of all the newspapers. There were TV cameras and camcorders airing the story immediately. The reporters said, "Mr. Foster, how do you feel about the victim? Can you forgive her for being arrested and jailed for a crime you did not commit? Did you ever think you would be convicted for rape and kidnapping? What are your plans now that you are a free man? And what do you think about your lawyer, Ms. Jamberlyn Barnesworth?" As the Fosters stood there embracing each other with tears in their eyes, Mr. Foster said. "First, I want to thank my Lord and Savior Jesus Christ. I give him all honor and praise for delivering me. He said in his word, 'If ye have faith as a grain of mustard seed, ye shall say unto the mountain, Remove hence to yonder place; and it shall remove; and nothing shall be impossible unto you (Matt. 17:20).' I want you to know we believe God and he did just what he said he would do. 'God is not a man, that he should lie; neither the son of man, that he should repent: hath he said, and shall he not do it? or hath he spoken, and shall he not make it good? (Num. 23:19)' Thank you, Jesus! Thank you, Jesus! Thank you, Lord, for delivering me! Hallelujah! I was facing a huge mountain-prison time, we could not work this out on our own, but God heard our cry and saw our faith. He moved our mountain! There is nothing too hard for our God, nothing! I thank him, he gave us our life back. We thank him for giving us this wonderful lawyer, and dear friend, Ms. Jamberlyn Barnesworth. She instructed us on what to do. Whenever things were getting worse, she always encouraged us by telling us to hold on and watch God turn things around. And she constantly reminded us that, 'Things are not always the way they appear!' She was right, now look at God! He did it! He did it! He broke every chain that had us bound. My God is not dead He is still alive! Thank you, Jesus, for delivering us! I recommend anyone that is looking for a defense attorney to call Barnesworth & Associates Law Firm, you will not be disappointed!"

Mr. Foster continued by saying, "As for the victim, we have no hatred toward her. She has suffered at the hands of someone that calls himself a man. A real man does not hurt a woman. He has hurt her dearly and to the point that she will have a tough time trusting a real man again. Do I forgive her? There is nothing to forgive, she just wants justice for all the pain and suffering she has endured. The male species that did that to her, although he has been arrested, we pray that he will be punished to the full extent of the law. She has nothing to apologize for. My family will do everything in our power to help her as our Lord and Savior Jesus Christ leads us. We also want to say to her, young lady, you have not done anything wrong, a wrong has been done to you. Hold your head up, God has your back! God loves you and so does the Fosters! Go in peace and keep God in your heart. My family and I are praying for you. In fact, I want to pray for you now, God wants you to have his peace!"

When he finished praying for her, she received Jesus as her personal Lord and Savior. Before leaving, he closed with this final statement, "Now I am looking forward to going home and enjoying every passing moment of quality time with my wife and children. I want to thank my Lord and Savior Jesus Christ for delivering me from a jail sentence. And I thank God for my pastor, ministers, church family, my friends, co-workers, plant managers, supervisors, Barnesworth Law Firm, my neighbors, and everyone who prayed and stood by me and my family in this trying time. Thank you! Thank you and God bless you all! Jane Doe had an opportunity to approach the Fosters. She said, "Mr. and Mrs. Foster, I want to apologize to you and your family for all the turmoil I caused. I truly did not know who to pick from the lineup but I choose you. I know it sounds crazy, but I thought they would find the right person before going to trial. I have never been assaulted, and I hope it never happens to anyone ever again. You see when I saw you, I saw a smartly dressed, well-groomed man. There was something about you that caught my eye and I never felt that way before. All I knew is I wanted to see you as much as possible. I felt something drawing me to you in hopes of developing a friendship/relationship with you. However, the more I saw you, the more I was drawn to you as a father figure or a big brother. You see, my father abandoned my mother leaving her to take care of six children, I am the oldest. I am eighteen, my birthday was the same day as the assault. My mother does not know what happened to me. I did not tell her because I did not want her to worry about me or cause her any more pain. As I stand here, I ask you both to please forgive me, I am so sorry! I know I cannot erase the pain and suffering I caused you and your family. I am so, so, sorry! One thing I know for sure there was something missing in my life. I did not know then, but I know it now, it was Jesus! Thank you both for leading me in the right direction!"

Brandon Foster said, "Young lady, my wife and I are here for you, and anything we can do to help you to better your life we will. All we want is that the man that attacked you and the other women to get what he deserves." Beverly agreed with her husband, and she said, "Honey, you have been through a terrible ordeal, and we are not going to make you suffer any more than you have already. We will mentor you, whenever you need to talk to someone, we are here, and we will adopt you as our little sister." All Ms. Doe could do was cry. She never met anyone that showed her the love and the understanding the Fosters were showing her.

After Ms. Doe received the Lord Jesus Christ as her personal savior, she had a new lease on life. When she went back to court for the second trial, she was determined that she would go in armed and dangerous with the word of the Lord (the Bible). So, she joined a Holy Ghost-filled ministry and totally became a faithful woman of God. Although she was a babe in Christ, she knew she needed prayers from the Fosters, the Barnesworths, and countless others to join with her faith to aid in the man's conviction. She prayed three or more times a day and she was ready for the entire ordeal to come to a conclusion in her favor as soon as possible. The man was convicted and sentenced to life in prison without the possibility of parole due to being a repeat offender. After the trial was over and done with, whenever Ms. Doe (Rebecca Ann Hawthorne) traveled with her church, she always testified about her completion. Rebecca went from church to church and place to place telling everyone she encountered about the ordeal, and her victorious outcome thanks to her Lord and Savior Jesus Christ. After Brandon Foster's case was all over, the news Jamberlyn was well respected in the courtroom. From that day on, Jamberlyn Barnesworth was no longer classified as a weakling, but she was "The Underdog That Became Champion!"

JAMBERLYN FALLS IN LOVE

Things profoundly changed for the better for Jamberlyn. After the trial, she was one of the youngest and most outstanding lawyers in the area. Jamberlyn's law practice grew rapidly. Two years after opening her own business, Jamberlyn had more clients than she and her associates could manage. Once again, it was time to seek the Lord for guidance for a new location. She believed at that point it would be best to build rather than rent another building. Although Jamberlyn was a grown woman, she did not feel at ease making such a major decision without getting the aid of her parents. Albert and Ta'Nelle's opinion were extremely important to her. She wanted their wisdom and expertise before going forth with her vision. After they received the approval from the Lord, she contacted a realtor.

Jamberlyn and her parents came to a unanimous decision, she continued with her plans. Once she obtained the land and the building was finished and ready to move in within six months. After the building was started Jamberlyn placed a sign on the property advertising the opening of the new law firm. She also placed a help wanted notice for attorneys. Jamberlyn started taking applications immediately. When she received an estimated date of completion, she started interviewing all the applicants and hired the ones she believed would work best in her firm. Due to the attorney/paralegal relationship, Jamberlyn asked the attorneys to hire their own paralegals. She hired the secretaries and the receptionist. Things were moving along very smoothly, and before long, they were occupying their new offices. Jamberlyn was so pleased, everything was coming together just as she pictured. The new law firm was built in the main section of town, which truly worked in their favor.

Jamberlyn and her associates often went to business luncheons with lawyers as well as doctors. Those luncheons were very productive for everyone involved. At the beginning of the business luncheons, everyone were asked to stand and introduce themselves. When Jamberlyn stood up, she could tell that she captured the eye of a particular young man. Ten minutes later, the man was given the opportunity to introduce himself, he said, "I am Dr. Peter Tomberseed from TOMBERSEED'S OB/GYN." The luncheons were once every two months at various restaurants.

After a two months, Jamberlyn was running errands when she bumped into the man again. As their eyes met, he said, "Are you the lawyer that was at the luncheon two months ago? Your name is Mrs. Barnesworth if, I am not mistaken!" She replied, "Ms. Barnesworth, and you are?" He said, "Hi I am Peter, Peter Tomberseed, I have a private practice about five miles from here. It's nice seeing you again. I was wondering if you would go out with me sometimes if you aren't in a relationship. We could meet for lunch or dinner whatever is best for you!" She replied, "I would love to!" They made a tentative date for Friday night. Peter would call her on Thursday to make sure they were still on for the next day.

Jamberlyn remembered very clearly when she introduced herself at one of the luncheons and how Peter watched her almost the entire time. She believed there was a little spark, but she had no intentions of acting on it. She genuinely believed that the man chases the woman, and not vice versa. She was confident that whatever God's plans were for her life, it would happen. Jamberlyn was not concerned about where Peter would take her to the establishment or not because the Barnesworth's family were frequent patrons at all of the businesses. Remember, Jamberlyn was an exceptional lawyer that made it her business to stay on top of her game. Although Peter seemed to be a nice person, she wanted to make sure he was on the level. She ran a background check to make sure he did not have any skeletons in his closet including marriage, divorce, abuse, alcohol/drugs addiction, or a nasty custody battle. Once the report was returned, she was quite pleased with the results. Peter was single, not divorced, has no children, or any outstanding warrants, not even a parking ticket. That Thursday, Peter called just as promised. He wanted to make sure, Jamberlyn felt comfortable, so he suggested they meet at the restaurant.

The next day, Peter made sure he arrived at the restaurant at 6:40 p.m. He went inside and gave instructions to the waiter. At 6:45 p.m., he returned to the front entrance to wait for Jamberlyn to arrive. To his surprise, she had arrived and was making her way to the entrance of the establishment. Peter quickly ran to the door and opened it just in time. He greeted Jamberlyn with a deep baritone voice and a warm smile. Then he gently placed her left arm in his right arm, and the two were escorted to their table. Once at the table, Peter made sure Jamberlyn was sitting comfortably before he went to his seat. He presented her with a bouquet of long stem red roses. She was overly impressed. She said to herself, "Wow, a girl could really get used to this!"

Peter and Jamberlyn dated for eight or nine months and they were truly getting to know each other. She soon learned Peter was a respectable God-fearing man. Wherever they went, Peter made sure, Jamberlyn had his undivided attention, nothing or no one else mattered to him while they were together. He could see that she was an incredibly special young woman the first time he laid his eyes on her. He found himself developing feelings for her. The more time he spent with her, the stronger his feeling became. Before long, he was falling head over heels in love with her and believed she was falling in love with him as well. He was quite certain that she would become Mrs. Jamberlyn Barnesworth-Tomberseed in the not-so-distant future.

Although Jamberlyn had her own home, she made plans with her parents earlier in the week to spend the night at their home in her old room, across the hall from her baby sister Anointia. While Jamberlyn was out enjoying herself on her date, Ta'Nelle and Albert could not help but discuss how joyful Jamberlyn seemed the last few months. They had no thoughts of prying into their daughters' personal life. They believed she would talk to them when she was ready. As they sat in their living room watching TV, Jamberlyn arrived from her date. She was in a world of her very own, you could say she was on cloud nine. She was extremely happy. In fact, her parents had never seen her that overjoyed after a date ever. She was bubbling with joy and was ready to talk and talk she did.

Jamberlyn began by saying, "Mom and Dad, I have been dating a man named Peter Tom-ber-seed whoa! He is an OB/GYN, and he has his own practice. He is three years older than I am." The Barnesworths listened to their daughter speak of the man, they could tell she was quite smitten with him. The more she talked, the more excited she became. She said, "We have been dating for a year. Oh, Dad, when we go out, he treats me like royalty. He opens the door for me, escorts me to the table, pulls the chair out for me at the table and remains standing until he is sure I am sitting comfortably. Oh, and Daddy, oh, oh, after our date, he walks me to my car, opens and closes my door, and follows me home. He opens my car door, goes with me to my front door where he unlocks my door and goes with me inside. After entering my home, he checks every room including the garage. When he finishes, we say our goodnights. He stands outside the door until he makes sure I am locked in. Oh, what a man, what a man! And Mom, he sends me flowers, cards, notes, candy, and fruit baskets at the office at least once or twice a week. All my co-workers are so envious of me. They ask me if he has any brothers, cousins, or even an adult nephew would be great! I just laugh and tell them I do not know, one thing is for sure, they will not get my man, Peter! When we go out, he brings me a long stem rose. I declare, Daddy, Peter Tomber-seed has totally spoiled me, and I love it! I love it! Do not be alarmed, I have not compromised! Oh, and the girls want to meet Peter, I boldly told them they will not meet my Peter until the wedding if it is the Lord's will that we marry. They can dream and fantasize about him all they want but he is mine, all mines! I totally trust Peter, but I know what women will do if given a chance. And it just is not going to happen!"

"Oh, Mom, he reminds me of you and Dad. I cannot wait for the both of you to meet him. We are thinking about doing something on Wednesday night, and I was wondering if the two of you could meet me at my house for dinner at 7:00 p.m.? I just want you to meet him so badly I just know you will love him!" The Barnesworths noticed how Jamberlyn's eyes lit up every time she mentioned Peter's name. They believed if a man could make such an impression on her, he had to be a special man, and they would be honored to meet him. Shortly, Jamberlyn was ready to retire for the evening. She told her parents she was going to take a shower and go to bed.

She said, "By the way, I can't wait to talk to Peter tomorrow. I am so excited, and I believe he will be as well. I am so glad you will be coming over so you can finally meet him. He is such a good man and he is so sweet, just wait until you meet him. Just think I have my own doctor as a boyfriend. I must find myself something to wear, may I go shopping. I need something nice, but not too nice. I hope Peter likes what I wear, I should get Ta'Nya to do my hair. I do not want to scare the poor man to death, what if my hair gets out of -lace? Should I invite Ta'Nya and Alanta, or should I wait? Oh, I think I will wait, I do not want to overwhelm Peter, but then again, I do not w, I just do not know! What do you think, Mom?"

Before Ta'Nelle could say a word, Jamberlyn had left the room. All Ta'Nelle could do was laugh. She said, "Albert, I certainly, hope she can make it to Wednesday. She has a one-track mind, Peter, Peter, Peter, Peter, and Peter. She is going to dream about him all night. Jamberlyn may not know it yet, but she has fallen in love with Peter. She will have a great sleep tonight because she will see Peter in her dreams, I hope he does not hurt her." Albert said, "Honey, how do you know that Jamberlyn is in love with Peter?" She answered, "Have you forgotten how we acted toward each other when we first met? We tried to fool ourselves but deep down inside we knew we were hooked, still are!" Albert said, "Yes, baby, you are so right! I love my Ta'Nelle and there is not a thing you can do to change it!" Albert did not think twice about the dinner on Wednesday, to him, it was a normal dinner, no big deal. However, Ta'Nelle knew it was especially important to Jamberlyn. It was Jamberlyn's way of getting Peter to realize that she was not only great in the courtroom, but in the kitchen too. In other words, she was determined to score big, she wanted to totally sweep Peter off his feet. Without saying a word, she was auditioning for the part of a lifetime, the role of Mrs. Peter Tomberseed.

The next day, when Jamberlyn talked to Peter, she was more
excited than ever. Peter accepted the invitation to meet the
Barnesworths on Wednesday night. Things were going exactly
as Jamberlyn pictured in her mind. She decided to go out of her
way to make what she believed would be the perfect meal. As
much as Jamberlyn enjoyed being with Peter, she was determined
to make sure her clients were taken care of. She rearranged four
of her appointments from Wednesday to Thursday so she could
go home early. Everything was falling into place. She cooked
baked chicken, a small roast with onions, chunks of potatoes
with carrots and gravy, mashed potatoes, string beans, and
sweet tea. For dessert, she prepared homemade peach cobbler
and a scoop of vanilla ice cream was given to whoever wanted
it. My, my, it seemed that Wednesday came very quickly. Albert
and Ta'Nelle arrived at Jamberlyn's house at 5:30 p.m. Ta'Nelle
made herself available to help Jamberlyn prepare dinner if
needed. Once she saw that Jamberlyn had everything under
control, she set the table while Albert relaxed in the living
room. Before long, Peter was the topic of conversation. Ta'Nelle
knew that it was important to let Jamberlyn talk so she grabbed
a chair at the table smiled and listened to her every word. At
6:40 p.m., everything was completely done. The meal was just
the way Jamberlyn wanted it. So, she turned the oven down
to warm so when Peter arrived, everything would be exactly
right. Jamberlyn and her mother entered the living room to sit
down with her father, and suddenly, the doorbell rang. To their
surprise, it was Peter aka "Mr. Punctual" as Jamberlyn called
him. She could not wait to get to the door however, she did
not want Peter, or her parents to know that she really wanted
to run and greet him. She tried to play the part of the slow
patient type. She was nervous, but excited at the same time.
As Ta'Nelle watched her go toward the door, she could see her

knees knocking. The poor girl was so nervous, Ta'Nelle did not want to make matters worse, so she laughed under her breath. She knew how Jamberlyn felt because she experienced the same thing when she met Albert's parents for the first time.

As Jamberlyn walked toward the door, she started praying softly to herself, "Lord, give me the strength to make it through this night." She convinced herself that once she saw Peter's face, she would be nice and calm. Ta'Nelle leaned over and whispered to Albert, "The way that girl is going to the door, it is as if she is walking down the aisle at the church. Well, I guess you could say she is getting her practice in now." Albert laughed and said, "Girl, you are still crazy as you were when I met you." Ta'Nelle replied, You liked what you saw after all, you married me! There has never been one complaint from you and there is no sense you are acting up now! Amen, somebody!" Jamberlyn finally made it to the door, and she let out a deep breath. She looked in the mirror to make sure she looked her absolute best. Then she turned to her parents, and they assured her with two thumbs up that she was beautiful. She opened the door for the man of her dreams. Peter wore a nice black leisure suit and black shoes and he had a fresh haircut. Jamberlyn was dressed comfortably in a red A-line short sleeve dress with a black belt and red and black one-inch stilettos. Ta'Nya styled her hair with a simple but beautiful updo that was guaranteed to impress. As their eyes met, they both let out a huge smile. Jamberlyn was at ease, her nervousness disappeared immediately. She looked up toward the ceiling and said silently, "Thank you, Jesus." Peter could not help but notice how gorgeous she looked.

Peter and Jamberlyn stood in the doorway admiring one another, they truly forgot about the Barnesworths. Albert cleared his throat while Ta'Nelle started coughing, but they could not manage to pull Peter and Jamberlyn's eyes away from each other. Albert decided to go to the door and try to break the trance that captivated the couple. He said, "Hello, I am Albert, and this is my wife Ta'Nelle. We are the parents of this beautiful young lady that you came here to meet. I am aware of the fact the two of you are into each other, but can you please come in and close the door? And besides, we are ready to eat, do you mind? Or should we start eating without the two of you?" At that point, everyone started laughing. Poor Peter could not comprehend how he would get himself out of the dilemma he had fallen into. The Barnesworths immediately acknowledged the fact that Peter was totally smitten with their daughter. After composing himself, Peter apologized for their temporary lack of knowledge where they were concerned. There was not any straightforward way to recover so Peter felt it would benefit him if he simply told the truth. He said, "Okay, you caught us!"

After Peter and Jamberlyn's dramatic stare down at the door, everyone was completely relaxed, and that was a good thing. Peter presented Jamberlyn and Ta'Nelle with a bouquet of long stem red and white roses. He gave Albert a bottle of cologne and a bottle of sparkling white apple cider. Peter could see where Jamberlyn had gotten her good looks and great personality. Peter and the Barnesworths was so comfortable with each other, it was as if they knew each other all their lives. As Albert and Peter were getting acquainted with each other, Jamberlyn and Ta'Nelle excused themselves to go into the kitchen to put the finishing touches on their dinner. The food was placed in the dining room at approximately 7:00 p.m., the women went to get their men. After a thankful prayer led by Peter, dinner was served He believed Jamberlyn was a good cook, but he could not imagine the depths of her talents in the kitchen. As Peter started eating, Jamberlyn paid close attention to him, she knew he was enjoying the meal by the expressions displayed on his face. Before long, he set his approval on the meal by moaning and groaning. Unknown to Peter, everyone heard every sound he made. Finally, Albert said, "Peter, son, are you all right?" He replied, "Yes, sir, this food is so delicious. Jamberlyn, you are an excellent cook." When the main course was finished, Jamberlyn served peach cobbler and vanilla ice cream. Peter was full after he ate the cobbler, he said, "Jamberlyn, the entire meal was fabulous. Thank you so much for inviting me!"

The dinner was an absolute success. Jamberlyn had accomplished her goal Peter was completely satisfied. She made sure she prepared Peter a plate for him to take home for later or lunch the next day. You may have heard the saying, "The way to a man's heart is thru his stomach." That night, it proved to be true, especially where Peter was concerned. While Ta'Nelle and Jamberlyn were in the kitchen cleaning up, Peter and Albert were in the living room getting better acquainted. Albert wanted to know exactly how Peter felt about his daughter and what was his intentions. Peter expressed his undying love for Jamberlyn and told Mr. Barnesworth that he was optimistic of marrying her if it was okay with him and Mrs. Barnesworth. He continued by telling Mr. Barnesworth that he had not mentioned anything to Jamberlyn about his plans, he wanted to meet them and get their approval first. He also wants to take Jamberlyn to meet his family and explore the possibility of becoming a part of each other's family before moving forward.

The following week, Peter had a dinner party at his house for Jamberlyn and his parents. When she arrived, Peter came to the door adorning a full-length apron. She believed Peter put on the apron as a practical joke to help her feel comfortable around his parents. Although she was comfortable, that was far from the truth. He introduced her to his parents, Robert and Jessica Tomberseed, and the rest was history. Jamberlyn assumed

Peter's mother had prepared the meal, but she soon learned that Peter could burn in the kitchen. In fact, Peter enjoyed cooking since he was a teenager and often prepared food for the family. He prepared steaks, with baked potatoes, tossed salad, and succotash. For dessert, he made a homemade two-layer red velvet cake. Jamberlyn said, "Oh my goodness, a doctor and a master chef, impressive!" Peter gave her a humongous smile and said, "Thank you, my dear!"

After dinner, Jamberlyn assisted Peter's mother (Jessica) in the kitchen. While getting acquainted, they learned that they liked cooking, running, family gatherings and most importantly, they both loved the Lord with all their heart. Mrs. Tomberseed could see that Jamberlyn was madly in love with her son and believed he felt the same about her. She especially loved the fact that Jamberlyn was well-mannered, well-educated, and a pillar in the community. After the dishes were placed in the dishwasher, everyone returned to the living room. Mrs. Tomberseed could not help but engage in a conversation about the life of her son, after all, no one knew Peter as well as she did. Jamberlyn was extremely interested to hear about the Tomberseeds' version of Peter's dream of becoming a doctor. Jessica said, "Peter was a very enthusiastic young man that had a love for medicine. At the tender age of three, Peter announced to Robert and me that he wanted to be a doctor when he grows up. Of course, we just thought it was a passing phase and we would just play along with him. One day, he decided to bandage our dog with an old rag he found in the trash. He tied the rags around the dog's neck and around his leg. The poor dog yelled until we rescued him. The dog became afraid of Peter and managed to stay out of his reach for quite days

Robert picked up the story and said, "Whenever Jessica and I sat down in the recliner to get a quick nap, Peter would spring into action. He would place his little hand on our foreheads and say, 'How do you feel? Do you have a headache? Does your tummy hurt? Oh, you have a fever. You need to drink something, and you will feel much, much better. I will be right back!' When he returned, he had all his medical equipment. He brought a large rag, a cup of orange juice, and a cup of water. Of course, two-thirds of the water would be spilled all over the floor. He would say, 'Hold your head back please!' All we could do is obey the doctor and try not to laugh. Without a doubt, when he finished you sported a large rag around your forehead and given a cold drink of your choice. He would say in his little boy voice, 'Now I am going to pray for you so close your eyes. I know you will feel better. Jesus, my mommy, and daddy are sick. I did everything I know to do, now it is time for you to do your part. Lord, I want you to touch them from the top of their big heads to their long, long feet. It may take a little more time for my daddy 'cause his feet are so much bigger than my mommy's. Lord, I sure hope you hear me because I need me a snack and something to drink now. Thank you, Jesus, and amen!'

"Immediately after the prayer, Peter would ask, "Do you feel better?' We would say yes! He would say, 'See, I told you God answers prayers. Now it is time for your nap, you look tired. I will be back to check on you in a minute, all right?' We said, 'Yes, Dr. Peter, we feel good now! Thank you so much.' He said, 'Okay, its nap time, no more talking, night, night!' We replied, 'Okay, night, night, Dr. Peter!"

All Jamberlyn could do was laugh until she became tickled. Peter said, "All right, that's enough, she will never let me forget this, Mom and Dad." But naturally, Jamberlyn wanted to hear more so Jessica and Robert started to tell her more. Jessica continued by saying, "We always had an adventure when we took Peter to the doctor. The doctor visits turned out to be a learning experience for the doctor as well as Peter." Jamberlyn said, "What did Peter do? Please tell me what he did?" Mrs. Tomberseed said, "Before the doctor could examine, Peter, he had to be examined. Peter would take the doctor's vital signs by looking into the doctor's mouth. He pulled up the doctor's pant legs to check his knees, he investigated his ears, and stared into his eyes. Then he would question the doctor and finally, after gathering all the information, he gave his diagnosis. Usually, he would say, 'Well, Doc, ah, I have some shocking news for you. You better sit down.' The doctor would say in a trembling voice, 'What is it? What is wrong?' Peter would scratch his little head and say, 'I do not know how to tell you this, but . . . hum mm, hum mmm. Your knees look funny, you have too many knots to count. Your eyes are big and red, they look like red tomatoes. And you have bugs in your teeth!'" Jamberlyn laughed and said, "Bugs in his teeth? What in the world?" Jessica said, "The doctor had fillings in his teeth. Peter had never seen fillings before and he went on to say, 'But I think you will be fine. You need to get the bugs out of your teeth, do not worry I am going to pray for you. Close your eyes, Lord, please touch this doctor, he is sick. Touch his big red eyes, his funny-looking knees, and please, please get the bugs out of his teeth. Please touch him so he can feel so much better Jesus, okay? Amen.' The doctor said, 'Thank you, Peter, and thank you, Jesus!'" Jessica said, "We would all break out laughing. The doctor was getting a kick out of Peter and God knows we were!"

Mr. Tomberseed said, "The older Peter became, the more determined he was to practice medicine. We had no clue that he would one day be an OB/GYN with his own private medical practice. After Peter graduated from high school, he had a scholarship to go to one of the best colleges where he studied pre-med. While in college, he studied as hard as he could but he also practiced everything he learned with whomever that would allow him to. He went on to one of the best medical schools in the country, where he became the doctor, he is today. He is the only doctor in our family, and we are so proud of him." Jamberlyn giggled and giggled as she listened to Peter's fascinating childhood. She said, "Mrs. Tomberseed, that reminds me of the stories my parents told Peter about my childhood." Mrs. Tomberseed said, "I would love to hear about your childhood, I'm sure you kept your parents on their toes." Jamberlyn said, "Oh yes, I did. No one can tell those stories like my parents."

At that point, it was time to bid good night. Jamberlyn, the Tomberseeds, and Peter all left the house at the same time. Peter followed Jamberlyn to her house and escorted her inside. After he saw that everything was safe, they bid each other good night. The next day, Peter went to his parents' home to get their thoughts on Jamberlyn. The Tomberseeds knew Peter and Jamberlyn loved each other very deeply. While eating their supper, Robert and Jessica began to talk to Peter about Jamberlyn. He was told that Jamberlyn was a very well-mannered, intelligent, respectable, charming, beautiful young woman that loved him and the Lord Jesus with all her heart. Jessica was wondering what Peter's Thoughts were concerning Jamberlyn, and before she could say a word, Robert said, "Son what are you feeling right now about this young lady, Jamberlyn? How serious are you about her and how long have you been dating her exclusively?" Peter said, "Mom and Dad, we have been dating for a year, and she is the only one I want. I have never dated anyone like her. When I first laid my eyes on her, I knew she was unique, a woman that respected herself and was very independent. In other words, she is a very diligent worker, she is a criminal defense lawyer. She has her own home, and she owns the law firm Barnesworths and

Associates Law Firm. She really makes me happy, and I cannot see myself without her in my life. I want to make her my wife until death do us part."

After Peter and Jamberlyn were introduced to each other's family, they became more inseparable than ever. To the delight of their parents, Peter and Jamberlyn became engaged a two weeks later. Jamberlyn and Peter set their wedding date for July 3, at 4:00 p.m. exactly six months from that day. They would invite two hundred and fifty guests. Once the list was completed, Jamberlyn had her staff prepare and mail the invitations with the RSVPs (respond if you please) within the next two weeks. They wanted the RSVPs returned no later than May 31. The couple decided to keep both of their homes to use for rental property. They wanted to start their new life together in their very own brand-new home that would be purchased by the two of them. They would move into their home after returning from their honeymoon. They contacted realtors about their plans for a new home as well as their individual homes to be leased out no later than June 1. They would live with their parents until after they returned from their honeymoon. Peter and Jamberlyn were so excited about their upcoming nurtures. Nothing would please them more than becoming Dr. and Mrs. Peter Tomberseed. Jamberlyn on the other hand was busy practicing what name would best suit her. She did not know whether she wanted to be called, Mrs. Tomberseed or Mrs. Barnesworth-Tomberseed. All that really mattered to her was being married to the man of her dreams.

July 3 was just a week away. Jamberlyn was so excited. She began to check her list of things to have finished before the wedding. She said, "Let's see now, luggage packed for the honeymoon, both homes have been leased, our new home finished, and we have the keys, furniture delivered and in place, food in the cabinets, refrigerator stuffed, blinds closed, doors locked, and the alarms are set, and my beautiful wedding dress has been completed and hanging in Alanta's fashion house! All I must do is tie up loose (designate eight cases)ends at the office, and make sure all my clients are very well taken care of until I return from my honeymoon as Mrs. Peter Tomberseed!"

Finally, it was the day of the wedding, the most important day of Jamberlyn and Peter's life together. They were so excited it was as if time had flown by. The wedding would be large with all their families, close friends, and co-workers in attendance. The RSVPs was returned almost immediately, there would be five hundred guests witnessing their marriage. Peter and Jamberlyn were so excited about their upcoming nurtures. Nothing would please them more than becoming Dr. and Mrs. Peter Tomberseed. Finally, it was time to march down the aisle. There were seven photographers and five videographers taking pictures and taking videos to make sure they caught every moment of the wedding. Truly, Peter and Jamberlyn had the wedding of their dreams and during the reception, they excused themselves to change out of their wedding attire. Once they returned, the bouquet and the garter belt were tossed out to the guests. Thankfully, all the women remained in the standing position. The couple was finally ready to bid their guest's farewell. They would walk a small distance where they would board Peter's friend's (Harry and Susan Broomdale) private jet and go off to their romantic honeymoon destination. Harry and Susan Broomdale would return in a week and take the Tomberseeds to their second destination. Harry and Susan were going on their second honeymoon on the island of Maui, Hawaii, so they dropped the Tomberseeds off on the island of Honolulu, Hawaii, where they would honeymoon for one week. Jamberlyn had no idea where they were going until that very moment, but it really did not matter as long as she was with her Peter. Peter wanted Jamberlyn to know that he was going to start their new life off on the right foot by pampering her from the very being of their marriage. There wasn't anything he would not do for his new wife. They were a very loving and devoted couple. After a two and a half years of marriage, they were honored to become the proud parents of four adorable children: Peter Jr., Jazmine, Ja'Nice, and Robert Albert (named after his grandfather's Robert and Albert)., Jamberlyn adjusted her work schedule to accommodate her children whenever necessary. There wasn't anything more important than her family. The couple married the mate that the Lord had ordained for them, and they lived happily ever after until death did, they part.

ALANTA JA'NAE
GETS MARRIED

Although it appears that Alanta Ja'Nae was the third Barnesworth daughter to marry, that was not the case. In fact, she was the first to marry, however, I choose to place her at this point to continue the story, "Out of the Mouth of Babes Revived a Family's Ultimate Challenge." Alanta is the visionary that started Girls on a Mission for Seniors, which is an organization that tries to meet the needs of senior citizens as well as entertain them. Whatever she dreams for days, happens just like she dreamed it, and whatever she put her mind to do, she succeeded in it. She never met a stranger, and she was the school's very own welcoming committee. She was often misunderstood by adults as well as children, and sometimes, they became jealous of her. She was a child that wore her heart on her sleeves even in adulthood. She would much rather hurt herself than hurt others. At the senior citizen's homes center, if she saw a resident that looked sad, she would check to see what was wrong before leaving. While in school, she learned to sew by pattern. Shortly thereafter, she developed a love for sewing, and everything she pictured in her mind, she was able to make without a pattern. Alanta Ja'Nae's ministry was Girl's on a Mission for Seniors, however, her occupation was Nae Nae's Fashions by Alanta which she owned and made successfully.

Now that you have catch up on Alanta Ja'Nae, we can get back to her upcoming wedding. Traditionally, the bride's parents pay for the wedding, however, this is not a traditional wedding nor traditional families. You see, according to Matthew's parents, they were so incredibly pleased to get Alanta as their daughter-in-love that they chipped in to help pay for the wedding. They loved Alanta from the first time they met her. Matthew and Alanta would be having an outdoor wedding, but the reception would be inside to another location. The Barnesworths knew Alanta had a unique style and that made things easier. All they needed were her colors and the number of guests expected. While Alanta was busy picking her colors and designing what she considered to be the most stunning gowns, Matthew was busy picking the honeymoon location. Naturally, Matthew had to enlist help from Ja'Nae's family to assure he did not take her to any place she had already visited. He wanted their honeymoon to be a new and adventurous journey, one that she would never forget. Once he decided, he did not reveal the location to anyone, regardless of how hard they tried to pull it out of him. Before long, everything was completed, and they would be married in a few short weeks. Matthew made sure he signed all the necessary paperwork needed for his company and gave the supervisor the instructions to fulfill their obligations while he was away. The couple would be gone for two weeks. Ja'Nae made sure she had all her designs ready for the tailor and that the orders would ship out on time as promised.

At last, it was Matthew and Alanta's wedding day. There were almost a thousand people in attendance. Alanta dressed her mother in a gold A-line free-flowing floor-length dress with a short white shawl and a gold and white necklace with matching earrings and a bracelet with white pumps and a gold and white purse. Matthew's mother wore a cream floor-length dress with gold and white overlay and a short white coat. She wore a gold bracelet with the necklace and earrings to match, in addition to gold pumps with an identical gold purse. As you can tell, everyone was stunning! Alanta dressed her seven bridesmaids in gold gowns and black belts with a large bow in the back. They were three-inch black pumps and carried gold, black, and six creamed-colored rose bouquets with gold and white ribbons. The maid of honor wore a cream gown with a large gold-and-black belt with a four-inch Black angel wing directly on her left shoulder and black six-inch pumps. She carried a cream, gold, black, and white rose-colored bouquet with white ribbons. The seven groomsmen wore a black tuxedo with a gold bow tie, gold boutonniere, white shirts, black socks, and black patent leather shoes. Matthew, his best man, and the ring bearer wore black penguin tuxedos with a gold cummerbund, gold bow ties, a white shirt, black patent leather shoes, and a gold boutonniere.

Alanta dressed her three flower girls in gold and white knee-length dresses with silk bottoms covered with small gold, black and white roses, and half-inch black pumps. Their baskets were filled with fresh gold, black, cream, and white rose petals. Alanta wore what she considered to be her personal masterpiece that she would never duplicate. She wore a beautiful white gown with a three feet detachable train detailed with a large white embroidered angel's wing with gold and white one-and-a-half-inch pumps. For her headdress, she wore a silver tuck comb covered with silk and trimmed with white lace. She was absolutely stunning. As she walked down the aisle, all she could hear was woos and wows from the women in attendance.

The wedding was over in less than an hour and before long, they were enjoying their reception. Matthew and Alanta had four large tables filled from the floor to as far as they could safely stack with wedding gifts, and there were even more gifts coming. They opened a thirdf the gifts, but due to the abundance of gifts, they had to postpone opening the others until they returned from their honeymoon. It was time to throw the bouquet, and all the single ladies quickly took their places. Oh, did I tell you that the bride carried three bouquets and wore three garter belts? Instead of one lady going home with the bouquet, there were three. There were at least seventy single ladies at the wedding. Ja'Nae said, "Wow, this should be very interesting!" Ja'Nae threw the first bouquet, and the ladies were pleasant. So, she waited until the first lady that caught the bouquet returned to her seat before throwing the next one. When Alanta threw the second bouquet the ladies were fur furious. The ladies remaining would have one final time to catch the final bouquet. Well, Ja'Nae gave the ladies two minutes to h activate a plan and to catch their breath. Then she counted to three, threw the bouquet, and ran for safety. The single ladies were giving it all they had, no one wanted to surrender. It was down to three ladies, they were on the floor, rolling, pushing, and pulling until the plastic bouquet holder was broken into pieces. Naturally, there were one third of the ladies going home upset and disappointed, well there is always another wedding .ng it all in, they were to diviner to even think about acting like the ladies! Are you sure about that? Let us just wait and see! Matthew had the floor and everyone's attention. He said, "All my single men, please come stand in front of me. The young man that catches the garter will put it on the young lady's leg just above her knee. And the ladies would come in the order in which they caught the bouquet. The lady that has the largest piece of the plastic bouquet holder will be the lady whom one of the men will put the garter just above her knee. Now guys, do you all understand the instructions?" They yelled yes! Matthew said, "Now ladies, you know exactly why I had to ask that question, right?" They replied, "Yes, we know, Matthew!"

Matthew turned around and threw the first garter. Once the man caught the garter, he went in the opposite direction and attempted to place the garter on a young lady that was sitting with her legs crossed. As he leaned over to touch the woman's leg, she said, "Excuse me, young man, you are supposed to be (as she raised her arm and pointed) all the way over there to your left!" He said, "My bad, I am so sorry, sweetheart!" Everyone in attendance busted out laughing. He leaned over toward her and gave her his business card, and said, "Call me!"

Matthew said, "Now ladies, this young single man has been mesmerized by all you beautiful single women in here. Now, brothers, I know it is almost impossible to listen to dear old me, but Alanta and I have a plane to catch tonight! I will tell you what we will do after we finish our business, listen very, very carefully. If this establishment manager approves, I will pay for an extra hour for the reception hall so you singles can mingle. However, there will be no alcoholic beverages served, and if anyone starts to get unruly, or irritate everyone, will have to leave this establishment immediately! I have already sent a message to one of the servicers, and when I get an answer, you will be informed asap." On the count of three, the second garter belt was thrown. At last, the final bouquet was thrown, and I am pleased to say all the young single men were obedient. Matthew said, "May I have your attention please. The establishment has approved my request for one additional hour. Remember how you manage yourselves will help Alanta and me or hurt us. If you want to marry in the not-so-distant future, you must practice what you preach. Just as I said, you have an extra hour, and you will be told by the staff when your time expires. I would appreciate it if some of you men would be so kind as to help load our gifts into the truck while we excuse ourselves to change out of our wedding attire into our traveling clothes."

While Matthew and Alanta went to change clothes, the best man and the maid of honor accompanied them. . Once Matthew finished changing, his best man took the tuxedo so it would be returned to the rental shop on Monday. Alanta's wedding attire would be put in the cleaners on Monday by the maid of honor. to be cleaned and preserved. Matthew and Alanta returned to the reception hall to tie up any loose ends before they leave for the airport. They made sure their marriage license was signed and witnessed so the Apostle could take it to the clerk's office on Monday. After everyone had returned to the reception hall, the Rogerses stood and addressed their guests. Matthew thanked everyone for attending their wedding and their hospitality, their gifts, and all the love they showered on them. They had already given instructions to their family members and given a set of keys to their new home to their parents. At that time, everyone was asked to hold hands as the Rogers's prayed over all their guests. They bid their farewell and turned to the door when their guests grabbed them both and carried them to the limousine, singing, and rejoicing. (Thank God, Alanta was dressed in pants.) They wanted to send the Rogers's off with the joy of the Lord! And yes, everyone departed the reception hall happier than they had been in quite some time.

Shortly thereafter, the couple was checking in at the airport in preparation to start their honeymoon as Mr. and Mrs. Matthew and Alanta Rogers. They were looking forward to seeing what the Lord had in store for them soon. After everyone boarded the plane, they were off on their first trip together to a place they had never been before. Matthew planned an impressive trip to Madrid, Spain. The day after their arrival, the couple took time to rest and enjoy each other's company. The following day, they were up and ready to tour the city and the surrounding areas. They wanted to experience all that Madrid had to offer. They went to the botanical gardens, museums, the Royal Palace of Madrid, and the Golden Triangle of Art. They rode on a hot air balloon just to name a few things. They especially loved their evening strolls as they stopped to watch the stars and take in the scenery. Naturally, being a Barnesworth woman, Alanta had to shop until they dropped. They took lots of pictures and videos to share with their families, friends, and their future children. Although it seemed like it was yesterday, it was time to return home. The honeymoon may have been over in Spain, but they vowed to be on a honeymoon for the rest of their lives.

As Matthew and Alanta pulled up to their new home, they were pleased to see their family members waiting to help unload the truck that was filled with their wedding gifts. Alanta had only been in the home one time, but she was excited to get settled and put some of her designing skills to work. After parking the car, Matthew helped Alanta out of the car, he gently picked her up and carried her over to the threshold of their home. Unbeknownst to Alanta when they went into the home, Matthew had the home completely remodeled. He informed Alanta that everything in the home was specially designed with her in mind. He wanted to make sure she knew how much he loved and respected her. There was nothing too good for his new bride. Alanta was totally flabbergasted seeing all that her husband had done to welcome her into their new home. She was moving into her own personal mansion. Once again, Ja'Nae, Ta'Nelle, Lena, and all the women in the home were in tears, but thank God, those were happy tears. Shortly thereafter, the entire family broke out into praise.

After everyone regrouped, the men began to bring in all the wedding gifts. Matthew and Ja'Nae had initialed China, stemware, cups, towels, bath cloths, bedding, personalized bathrobes, two microwave ovens, two toaster ovens, diverse types of grills, three irons and ironing boards, pressure cookers, slow cookers, air fryers, gift cards from major outlet centers, and three coffee machines in addition to many items too many to name. They were abundantly blessed beyond measure; however, Alanta made a list of things needed/wanted so there would not be any duplicates. They were very thankful their families spent several afternoons helping them place the items in what they considered to be the correct place. She mailed special thank you cards every day for three weeks to let her guests know just how very much they appreciated their gifts and their presence at their wedding.

MATTHEW AND ALANTA EXPECT THEIR FIRST CHILD

Ja'Nae's House of Fashion and Matthew's construction company continued to prosper. Regardless of their businesses, they always made sure they closed at 5:00 p.m., and were closed on the weekends. They continued to meet their friends and family at their favorite restaurant to fulfill all their obligations both spiritually and personally. After being married for about a year, Ja'Nae became pregnant with their first child. They were overjoyed and they decided to wait unto the baby was born to find out what they were having. The couple jogged or walked several times a week. The doctor believed it would be okay for Alanta to continue if she weren't having any discomfort. She had a nice little baby bump and was almost five months. Due to her small frame, you would not know she was expecting unless she told you.

One afternoon, Ja'Nae called Matthew to let him know she was going jogging and would call him when she returned. She was going to try to clear her head. Although she was feeling great, she was having a little trouble concentrating on the direction of a new design. She informed Matthew that she would have her phone, a couple of dollars, and her identification on her. Ja'Nae had been running for about twenty minutes when she finally got the answer she was looking for. She stopped at the local store and purchased a drink and a snack before returning to work. She was so happy. While eating her snack, she took a few minutes to draw some designs on a paper towel and took pictures of the drawings with her cell phone before leaving the store. She could hardly wait to get back to her desk to put her final touches on the drawings.

Although Ja'Nae was anxious to return to work she made sure she paid very close attention to her surroundings. She was determined not to take any unnecessary chances that may cause harm to herself, but most importantly to her unborn child. Ja'Nae was a few blocks from her fashion house when she observed a car headed toward her going at high speed. Drivers were blowing their horns and the pedestrians were yelling trying to get the driver's attention. There were a couple of drivers that tried to sacrifice their vehicles in hopes of preventing the young lady from getting injured or even getting killed. Ja'Nae was so terrified, there was no place for her to go. Within seconds, the driver hit her, and she was knocked unconscious. Someone called 911 and informed the dispatcher that a young woman was hit by a car and is lying on the side of the road unresponsive. And they need help immediately. The person on the phone asked if anyone knew her and no one had a clue who she was. The lady also told the dispatcher that the man that hit her was pinned in his vehicle and they would need help for him as well.

There Ja'Nae lay at the side of the road with no movement. Instantly, she started bleeding from her mouth and nose. Ja'Nae's face was turning black and blue, her left leg was turned sideways, and her body was turned in an awkward position. Thankfully, the police and the ambulance/rescue squad were on their way, but it seemed that time stood still. Several people ran to the lady's side, and one of the women started screaming at the top of her lungs as the tears rolled down her face. She knew not to touch her or try to move her, at that point, she wanted to see if the woman could hear her. There was no response, so the woman started praying to her Lord Jesus Christ. Others quickly joined in and was praying with all their hearts. A young man took his suit jacket off and covered Ja'Nae to make sure she was warm and no debris would get in her wounds. At that point, several individuals kneeled down in front of the victim and prayed as hard as they could for the Lord to save her life, and that he would give her a new testimony. The women knew time was of the essence and although help had not arrived, they knew someone that could help her immediately. The women started calling out to the Lord. They knew if the Lord could not help them, no one could. As the tears continued to roll down the women's faces, they cried out:

"Lord Jesus, we come to you as humble as we know how. Lord, before we ask you for anything, we just want to say thank you. Thank you for being so good to us. Thank you for being our healer and deliver and so much more! We know that you said in your word according to James 5:14–16, 'Is any sick among you? let him/her call for the elders of the church; and let them pray over him/her, anointing him/her with oil in the name of the Lord: And the prayer of faith shall save the sick, and the Lord shall raise him/her up; and if he/she has committed sins, they shall be forgiven him/her. Confess your faults one to another, and pray one to another, that ye may be healed. The effectual fervent prayer of a righteous man/woman availeth much. Help, Lord! Lord, we need you right now! Lord, two of your children are hurting. We do not know them, but we know you do. We ask you to touch them in the name of Jesus. Lord, give them another chance, heal their bodies, their hearts, and their minds. Please,

Lord, help them if it is your will, and do not let them die. God, you are a healer and a deliver. You are the doctor that never lost a case, send help now in Jesus's name. Lord don't let them suffer, and please Jesus stop the bleeding. Lord, I know you can because you said in your word according to Isaiah 53:5, 'But he was wounded for our transgressions, he was bruised for our iniquities: the chastisement of our peace was upon him; and with his stripes we are healed.' We aren't praying for ourselves but we are coming on behalf of two of your wounded, unconscious children. You said in your word that we are to pray and seek your face and we humbly yield to your commands. Lord God, we know that you are not a man that you should lie nor the son of man that you should repent: 'Hath he said, and shall he not do it? or hath he spoken, and shall not he make it good? (Num. 23:19) So therefore Lord God we stand on your word, knowing that you have the final say where these victims are concerned. You also said according to your word that 'Many are the afflictions of the righteous: but the Lord delivereth him out of them all (Ps. 34:19).' Lord God, these two are suffering right now due to this accident. Father God, I do not know if these individuals have accepted you as their Lord and Savior or not, but I ask you as I stand on your word to deliver them for your glory. (Oh Lord, where is that ambulance or rescue squad? Why is it taking so long?) I know without a doubt that you are a God of miracles because you performed miracles in your word whereas, the blind man washealed (Matt. 11:5), and you unstopped the deaf ears and surely, surely Lord, you can deliver these injured victims. You raised Lazarus from the dead four days after his death for the glory of God (John 11: 38–44), all you did was call his name and Lazarus had to answer. My Lord God as we continue to pray, I am reminded of your word in John 11:41–42: 'Father, I thank thee that thou hast heard me.

And I knew that thou hearest me always: but because of the people which stand by I said it, that they may believe that thou hast sent me.' Now Lord as your wailing women (Jer. 9:17–20), we are praying and seeking your face for these wounded victims. We ask that you let their spirits connect with our spirits as we step out on faith and touch and agree with your word that you will speak thru them for your glory that others may hear and believe in you. It is written in Matthew 18:19: 'Again I say unto you, That if two of you agree on earth as touching anything that they shall ask, it shall be done for them of my Father which is in heaven. For where two or three are gathered together in my name, there I am in the midst of them.' Lord Jesus, there are several people here praying and lifting up your children in your name, and I know that you will answer our prayers. We have no one to turn to but you, Lord Jesus! We are humbling ourselves to you on behalf of one of your sons and one of your daughters. Lord, everything I do and everywhere I go, I go under your direction and something I do will help lead others to you. Even now as I come to you on behalf of your children, I ask you to heal, deliver, and make them whole for your glory. Lord as we the wailing women continue to pray, we ask that as our spirits connect, that you will speak through them for your glory so that others may hear and believe in you. As we praise and call out to you, have your way, Lord.

Before long, the women were praying and speaking in unknown tongues as recorded in Acts 2:1–4. "And when the day of Pentecost was fully come, they were all with one accord in one place. And suddenly there came a sound from heaven as of a rushing mighty wind, and it filled all the house where they were sitting. And there appeared unto them cloven tongues like as of fire, and it sat upon them. And they were all filled with the Holy Ghost, and began to speak with other tongues, as the Spirit gave them utterance."

As the women began to listen for the Spirit to speak, the ambulances finally arrived. The troopers were quickly taking control of the situation. One of the officers directed the traffic while the others were accessing the scene. Since the women were praying for the victims, the officers allowed them to stay where they were. Once the EMT's emergency medical technicians unloaded the stretchers, the unconscious woman began to speak out of her spirit as the Lord spoke thru her in unknown tongues! The man started groaning and moaning in a peculiar tone. Everyone that was at the scene began to praise and worship God. The Lord Jesus Christ along with the Holy Spirit showed up and showed out for the glory of God. Although the victims were still unconscious, according to the man, they were very much alive in the name of Jesus! Ja'Nae was the first victim to get taken to the hospital. The EMTs was incredibly careful lifting Ja'Nae off the ground and putting her in the vehicle. They tried to question her, but she was busy speaking in unknown tongues, and they did not have a clue what she was saying.

Once the young lady was off to the hospital, the EMTs was waiting for the firefighters to finish using the jaws of life to pry open the man's car door. The wailing women continued to pray for the man's life. Although they did not know his condition, they knew he still needed the Lord's intervention. The crowd that was standing around was listening and witnessing things they have never seen before. The women prayed until everyone in the area had gotten clarity about the power of their Lord Jesus Christ. Once others understood the importance of having the power of the Lord, they did not know how to get it, but they wanted it. They cried out saying, "Lord, I do not know any other way to talk to you, but I need your help right now. I see what the women are doing, and I have learned enough from what I have seen to ask you to help. Lord help me to speak in that unknown language, so I can pray the way these wailing women are doing!" And one of the praying women turned to the group and started praying, "Lord, you said in your word according to Matthew 7:7–8, 'Ask, and it shall be given you; seek, and ye shall find; knock, and it shall be opened unto you: For every one that asketh receiveth; and he that seeketh findeth; and to him that knocketh it shall be opened.' Now, Lord, these people want to be filled with your precious Holy Spirit with the evidence of speaking in unknown tongues Lord God we believe by faith that they shall be filled according to their faith and your word in Psalms 84:11, 'No good thing will he withhold from them that walk uprightly.'" And the Lord did exactly what he said, and there were seven souls saved at the scene of the accident. Wow, look at God! The people came as bystanders, and they left filled with the Holy Spirit with the evidence of speaking in (unknown) tongues as the Spirit gave them utterance. What a mighty God we serve! Hallelujah!

Once the fire department finished opening the man's car door, the EMT reached the car with a stretcher. They noticed the man was stooped over the steering wheel, suffering from a head injury, semiconscious, and he was humming. The police officers noticed several open containers on the floorboard and an open container in the cupholder. The man smelled strongly of alcohol. He was carefully lifted out of the car onto a board and onto the stretcher before transporting him to the hospital. When he was examined, his blood was drawn as well as his urine. The test was returned, and he assessed positive for driving under the influence of alcohol and prescription drugs. He also had a deep cut on his forehead, his right foot was fractured and heavily bruised. He was admitted to the hospital, and a police officer was stationed at the door of his hospital room. After a thorough examination, the doctor found the man had internal bleeding in his abdomen. Naturally, the man had to undergo exploratory surgery to find where the blood was coming from. The surgeon stated that the bleeding was caused by the deployment of the airbag. He also had to have surgery to repair his foot and toes and he would have physical therapy to help him walk correctly.

Meanwhile, as the doctors were busy at the hospital, the police and state troopers were still on the scene of the accident talking to the witnesses and recovering any evidence they could find. Shortly after a few minutes, the officers heard a phone ringing, and it was found in the ditch above where the young lady was found. To their surprise, the phone belonged to (Ja'Nae) the victim. As the officer answered the phone, a man said, "Hello, who am I talking to?" The officer responded, "This is Officer Frederick Cornbread from the North Carolina State Highway Patrol. Who am I speaking with?" The man said, "I am Matthew Rogers, I was calling to check on my wife. Where is she? Is she all right?" The officer said, "Sir, the young lady was hit by a car about ten minutes ago, and she was rushed to the Collardfield Medical Center on 1325 Walkaround Blvd. Sir, I know you have lots of questions, but if you will get in contact with your family members, I will meet you all there in a few minutes. Sir, please hurry!" Matthew said, "Officer Frederick Cornbread, please let them know my wife is pregnant!" Officer Cornbread replied, "Yes, sir, I will tell them right now!"

As the secretary heard the conversation, she jumped on the phone immediately. Matthew had all the emergency phone numbers on speed dial and within minutes, the Barnesworths and Rogerses were on their way to the Collardfield Medical Center. As Matthew hung up the phone, all he could do was call on the name of the Lord and plead for his wife and unborn child's life. Matthew's supervisor was also in the office, and he quickly drove Matthew to the Collardfield Medical Center and remained by his side until Alanta was out of surgery. The supervisor had complete confidence in his staff and knew if any problems aroused, they were quite capable of handling them. Matthew was beside himself; he could not get to his wife's bedside fast enough. Once he arrived at the medical center, he went directly to the receptionist to gather any information he could get about his wife. The receptionist buzzed the men inside to a waiting area where someone from the medical staff would meet with him as soon as possible. Matthew did not know whether to sit, stand, or pace back and forth, but one thing was certain, it was praying time. He fell on his knees and began to cry out to his Lord and Savior. He knew the way to get God's attention was to pray his word back to him. Matthew could care less about the people that were in the waiting room, or what they heard him say! All that mattered to him at that moment was to reach his heavenly Father and welcome him into that Collardfield Medical Center.

Matthew said, "My Father God, which is in heaven and on earth, I humble myself before you with outstretched hands. First, I want to thank you for another opportunity to call on your holy and righteous name. Lord, I thank you for being my God, my healer, and my deliverer. Right now, I need you to intervene on my behalf. Lord, you said in your word according to 1 Peter 5:7 that I can cast my cares upon you, for you careth for me. In other words, I can give you all my worries, my distractions, my burdens, and my anxieties. I need you to stop by this medical center right now in the precious name of Jesus. Touch, Lord, every family member in the waiting room in the name of Jesus. You said in Matthew 18:18, 'Whatsoever ye shall bind on earth shall be bound in heaven: and whatsoever ye loose on earth shall be loosed in heaven.' Now Father, in the name of Jesus," Matthew Rogers continued, "I ask you to touch my wife and baby and every patient in this medical center that is fighting for their life from the crown of their head to the soles of their feet. Lord, guide the doctor's hand in the operating rooms. I know that you are a God that is too wise to make a mistake, and if it is your will, please turn every situation around for your glory and your honor. We will be so careful to give you all the praise. I love you Lord with all that is within me, you are the first in my life and I trust you. I believe every word that you have spoken thru your word. Everything I have asked of you has happened. You said when a man finds a wife, he finds a good thing and obtaineth favor of the Lord (Prov. 18:22). Now, Lord, I just do not believe you gave me my wife to take her away after a short period of time. I know you are the one and only God that has never lost a case. You are a doctor above all doctors. You created us and you can put things in place that are out of place. You can mend nerves, organs, bones, and tissues, you can turn any situation, regardless of what the doctors say or do you have the final say. I humbly ask you to restore our loved ones and bring them back to their families in the mighty name of Jesus I pray. Hallelujah! Hallelujah! Thank you, God! Thank you! Thank you! Amen!"

Matthew cried and prayed until he completely lost his voice. Everyone in the waiting area was in tears as they tried to control their emotions and console him at the same time. As the family members arrived, they could see that Matthew was in great distress. They surrounded him and began to pray for his strength as well as deliverance for Alanta Ja'Nae and their baby. Shortly thereafter, Matthew said, "Lord, I know according to the world, men are not supposed to cry but Lord we hurt too. I am not ashamed to cry because of the love I have in my heart for my wife as well as others. Although my heartaches, I know I am not alone. Lord, you said in 1 John 5:4, 'God is with you, wherever you may go no matter what life brings.' Psalms 139:14, "Be strong. Be brave, Be fearless. You are never alone." Lord, I thank you for restoring my strength. Thank you, thank you, Jesus!"

It seemed as if time had stood still. Finally, after nearly four heart wrenching hours, the receptionist buzzed Matthew's monitoring machine. He went to the desk and was told the doctors would meet with the family in a private waiting area within the next five minutes for updates on Alanta's condition. Shortly thereafter, Matthew, Alanta's parents, her sisters, Matthew's parents, and their pastors went into the waiting area to wait for the doctors. The doctors were very professional and polite as they addressed the families. The surgeon introduced himself and told them he had to return to surgery in a few minutes. Dr. Saul Stubaker said, "During the accident, Mrs. Rogers was knocked on conscience and she twisted her left knee which caused her to sustain a torn ligament in that knee. I had to perform surgery to remove the loose fragments and stabilize her bone. Due to her physical condition before the accident, I expect her to fully recover from the surgery in eight to ten weeks. However, she will suffer severe pain at times and will need to take pain medication for a few weeks or more. I have given her an injection of cortisone after I finished the surgery which should control the pain hopefully for at least a week or more. She will be given a walker in a few days, and the physical therapist will come in and work with her. In the beginning, she will sit up on the side of the bed several times a day until she can sit without assistance. Then she will move on to standing. She will have difficulty trying to stand, and that's okay, but as time passes, she will be able to stand. When the therapist thinks she is ready to try to walk, they will assist her. Once she starts walking, she may walk with a limb which may, or may not be permanent. It is extremely important that she has someone with her at all times and that she obeys the instructions of the therapist to prevent injury to herself or others. Does anyone have any more questions or concerns?" No one had any questions, so Dr. Saul Stubaker said, "Now, I know you need time to process everything so if you need me to explain anything later, just inform the nurse and I will gladly come and address them. I will excuse myself and let the other doctors talk to you."

Dr. George Pinsnicker greeted the family and stated he would be totally honest with them. "When Mrs. Rogers arrived at the hospital, she was unconscious due to the trauma from the impact of the accident. In addition to the injuries she sustained that caused her surgery, she was severely bruised in her abdomen. Sad to say, we were unable to save her unborn child. After a thorough and complete examination, we discovered that she has an abnormal uterus which has a center wall dividing it into two cavities (called a septate uterus). Unfortunately, she will not be able to conceive again. I know this is a term that physicians don't normally use, but it was nothing short of a miracle that she was able to get pregnant at all. She is in recovery, and you will be notified when she will be taken to a room where she will be monitored for any signs of infection or other complications. In a couple of hours, you will have the chance to see her for a short period of time, however, she will be heavily sedated. She probably won't respond to you and if she awakens, she may be talking out of her head. Tomorrow, she won't remember anything that happened not even the accident. The most important thing is that she gets as much rest as possible."

As Matthew listened to the doctor, he took several deep

breaths as he tried to fight back his tears. Matthew as well as their families were totally devastated by the horrific news they were told. Everyone's emotions were all over the place but without a doubt, they were all distraught, angry, and frustrated. In a calm voice, Matthew asked, "When she awakens and asks questions about the baby, what should we tell her?" Dr. Pinsnicker replied, "Try to keep her calm and tell her as little as possible until you feel she is strong enough to handle it. Please have the nurse in the room with you when you decide to tell her so she can sedate her if need be. Two of you can spend the night with her if you desire, she will need you to help get her through this. However, if you feel that you can't handle being here with her, please leave. You all know who she leans on the most when she gets hurt or upset, I suggest you are the one that she will need here other than her husband."

The driver of the car was so intoxicated that he didn't know what happened, nor where he was for two days. On the third day, he was awakened by the warmth from the sunlight shining on his face. He opened his eyes and tried to reach his aching head when he noticed he was handcuffed to the bed. The poor man thought he was having a bad dream. As he blinked his eyes several times, he looked around the room and realized what he thought was a dream was truly the beginning of his worst nightmare. He screamed to the top of his lungs, "Lord, somebody, please help me! Help me! Help me, please!" Suddenly, the nurse and the police officer entered the room to see what seemed to be troubling the man. The nurse asked, "What's wrong? Are you in pain? What do you need?" The man answered, "What happened to me? Why am I here? Why am I handcuffed?" The officer informed the man that he was involved in an accident and would be charged upon his release from the hospital. The man stated he knew nothing about an accident, and the officer had confused him with someone else. Once the officer enlightened the man on all that had taken place two days before, he became inconsolable. The man burst out screaming and yelling uncontrollably. He said, "Oh my god! Oh my god! What have I done? What have I done? Lord, you should have taken me instead of that innocent little baby! Lord, I destroyed a family, and a new life. Lord, have mercy on that family, have mercy, Lord!" When the doctor made his rounds that morning, the man was released from the hospital into police custody at 10:30 a.m. He was immediately escorted directly to the county jail. That afternoon, he went before the magistrate where he was formally charged with (DWI) driving under the influence, inflicting serious injury, speeding, and death of an unborn child. He wanted to hire his own attorney and was ordered to remain in custody until his first court appearance in a few days. Although he was visibly and extremely upset, the magistrate refused to give him a bond for fear that the man would try to commit suicide. As the officers returned the man to his cell, the entire staff was informed that the man was to be placed on suicide watch 24/7.

Meanwhile, as the man was being processed, Alanta was coming out of the heavy sedation. As she started moaning and groaning, the first thing she did was reach for her abdomen. However, she was in such severe pain that all she could do was cry. When she noticed Matthew and her mother were by her side, she cried for her mother. Although she was a grown woman at that time, she wanted the love and affection that she experienced from her mother. Matthew couldn't bear to see the pain on his wife's face, so he exited the room and went to get the nurse. When the nurse entered the room, Ja'Nae was in her mother's arms. Although she was still in pain, just knowing her mother was there made the situation much more bearable. Once the pain medication was put in the IV, Ja'Nae started to feel a little better, and shortly, she was fast asleep. On the third day after the accident, Ja'Nae with the assistance of the nurse was able to sit up on the side of the bed for five minutes. While trying to sit up, she felt her abdomen and realized that her stomach was no longer hard and there weren't any signs of a heartbeat. Matthew and Ta'Nelle looked at each other, they knew the time was at hand to prepare themselves for the questions and more importantly for the dreaded answers. Thankfully, the nurse was standing next to Ja'Nae. Remember, Ja'Nae was a very smart and observant young lady. As she looked around the room although Matthew and Ta'Nelle were smiling, she could sense that there was something they were keeping from her. Sadly, Ja'Nae believed she had delivered the baby early and wanted to know if the baby was a boy or a girl. Before they could answer her, she asked, "Where is my baby? How much did the baby weigh? When was the baby born? Who does the baby look like? Does the baby have any health issues due to being premature? What happened to me? Why am I in so much pain? What happened to my leg? Why haven't I seen my baby?"

Quickly Ta'Nelle said, "Baby, you are asking too many questions at one time, and we will answer every question, but first we have to tell you what happened." Matthew told Ja'Nae everything that happened before the accident, and she remembered it all. As he continued to take her through the accident scene, Ja'Nae began to tear up and before long, she was totally dismayed. She became so agitated that the nurse had to call for assistance to help restrain her so she could be sedated. Ja'Nae's blood pressure was off the chain, extremely high, she was hyperventilating and in a full-blown panic attack. Albert was coming down the hall when he heard his baby in distress, he ran as fast as he could to get to her room. Outside of Jesus, Albert was the only one that could console Ja'Nae. He entered the room just in the nick of time. He said in a strong soothing voice, "Alanta Ja'Nae, baby, it's going to be all right. Baby, please calm down, they are trying to help you, listen to me. Remember God said in his word according to Psalm 34:19 'Many are the afflictions of the righteous: but the Lord delivereth him out of them all.' Baby, according to the word of God, you are one of the righteous. Remember Ja'Nae it's not what it looks like nor as bad as it seems. Honey, God has the final say. Don't get discouraged, God is working in your favor. He has not forgotten you. He has craved you in the palm of His hands according to Isaiah 49:16. You know God has a plan and a time set for our lives, and thou you are burdened and grieving now, don't let your emotions blindside you, baby. Whose report are you going to believe? The doctor said you shouldn't have gotten pregnant the first time, but God! Baby, I believe the report of the Lord!"

Albert grabbed Ja'Nae's hand and said, "Honey, listen to daddy. Do you remember reading in the word of God about a man called Legion? Legion was a man that lived in the tombs and no man could bind. Every time they chained and shackled him, he would break the chains and pull the shackles apart. Everyone was afraid of him. He was treated like a wild animal, a lunatic which means he was mentally unstable. Neither the doctors nor anyone could heal or calm him. One day, he came into the presence of Jesus, and he started worshipping him. He cried out loudly and said, 'What do you want with me Jesus, thou Son of the most high God? Don't torment me!' He was afraid of Jesus because he knew that Jesus was the true and living God, and he knew what was about to happen. Jesus looked at the man and saw the lunatic spirit in him, and command the spirit to come out of him. Do you remember what Jesus did?"

Ja'Nae said, "The spirits in the man asked Jesus to send them into the swine (pigs), and Jesus did. There were two thousand spirits in that man and when they entered the swine they ran off the cliff into the sea and was drowned (Mark 5:1–20)." Albert said, "Sweetie, if God delivered that man from all those spirits, don't you know he will deliver you! This is just a light affliction baby. God's got this!"

Ja'Nae said, "Daddy, I am so glad God blessed me to have such amazing parents as you and Mommy, and my awesome, loving husband. As I sat here listening to your every word, God began to quicken my spirit. It's not important what the doctor said because his knowledge is limited. The doctor studied medicine, but God created man in his own image, and he knows what is best for us. God has a plan that no man can cancel, his plans override any diagnosis. I was raised on the Word of God and I have faith in him because in him, I have my being. The doctor may have operated on my body but without God's intervention, I would have died in the operating room, or while I was lying on the ground. Doctors practice medicine yet God is the chief physician, he never loses a case. I trust the God that lives on the inside of me, and although I lost it for a few minutes emotionally, I believe everything will be all right. I know Matthew and I will grieve over the loss of our precious baby, but we believe in the report of the Lord Jesus Christ. Hallelujah! Hallelujah, thank you, Jesus!"

Ja'Nae continued by saying, "Nurse Rosalyn, I want to apologize to you, my family, and the entire staff for the way I acted. I am grieving the loss of our baby, but we will get through this. God said this is not the end, I will go thou some extreme pain both physically and emotionally, but I am in recovery now. I don't need to be medicated because God, my husband, and our family is all the medicine we need. I know the doctors and the medicine has their place, but right now, I need the meds that only Jesus can supply. I would like very much if you would join me and my family as I lead in a word of prayer. She started by saying, "To my holy and all-wise God, I want to thank you, for another day's journey. Lord, I want to you for touching my family in this most difficult time. Thank you for the EMTs, the police officers, as well as the North Carolina State Highway Patrols, the doctors, and all the hospital staff that aided me after the accident. Thank you, Lord, for blessing me with such awesome families and a loving husband. Thank you for every prayer that was prayed on behalf of Matthew and I, our baby, and also the driver of the car. Thank you, Lord, for taking our baby into your loving arms and giving him or her rest. Lord, I ask you to forgive me for all my sins, all the unpleasantness I bestowed on others. Lord, as we continue to recover from this horrible situation, I ask you to mend our broken hearts and heal from the crown of our heads to the soles of our feet. Continue to lead, guide, and direct the doctors and the entire staff to be a blessing to each patient and the families that enter this establishment. Lord, touch them in a way that only you can, meet their needs spiritually, physically, emotionally, as well as financially. Ease the troubled minds, send peace and healing now to the driver of the car that hit me, and have mercy on him and his family. If there is anything or anyone that I failed to pray for, please charge it to my mind and not my heart, send peace now Lord in Jesus Christ name. Amen!"

Nurse Rosalyn said, "Thank you, Mrs. Rogers, for that powerful prayer. You are such a strong woman of God and a great and powerful inspiration to me. I thank God I got to meet you and your family but I wish it was a happier occasion. Nevertheless, I will never forget you and your family. I am looking forward to seeing you all in the future with your babies.

By the way, I love your designs and I will defiantly let everyone I know to make sure they buy your clothes. I feel as if I have known you for years. If you need anything, just ring. Now try to get some rest because your physical therapist will be in to see you this afternoon." Ja'Nae replied, "To God be the glory! I am only a vessel that is being used by God. Without the spirit of God inside of me, I would be nothing. Thank you so much, Nurse Rosalyn, I am so much better now, I am going to sleep." Once Ja'Nae became comfortable, she slept for hours.

Albert could focus his attention on his wife. Ta'Nelle was totally unnerved after witnessing the pain and discomfort her child was experiencing. She tried to keep her emotions intact, but once Ja'Nae was sound asleep, she cried uncontrollably until she ran out of tears. She said, "Albert I know we all have to go through trials and tribulations, but I wish I could have boar this for Ja'Nae and Matthew, I hate to see my children suffer. I thank God you came in when you did, Matthew and I tried everything to calm her down. Matthew, Albert, and I have learned a lot of lessons from our daughters, now this was a new one for me. You are a part of the family so let me tell you, brace yourself, there is never a dull moment with the Barnesworth girls (women). If you want to change, you have to go with the flow. I birthed those girls and I am still amazed at the things I am learning from them. Alanta truly is a daddy's girl if Albert can calm her down, you and I can forget it!"

Matthew said, "Mom and Dad, I am so sorry I should have been there with Alanta, I could have protected her from the impact. I would have much rather taken the hit than let her get hurt. You entrusted your beautiful daughter to me, and I have failed you all. I can't undo what has happened, but I will take better care of her from now on." Albert said, "First of all, we all feel the same way about this situation, unfortunately, we can't be with her all the time. We have joy knowing that we serve a God that sits high and looks low. A God that has blessed us with Ja'Nae, he is a healer and a deliverer. Did you see how God comforted our baby and caused her to regain her faith? She is going to be all right as a matter of fact, she is on the road to recovery as we speak. Let us thank God for what he has done and is doing on her behalf. Amen!"

Finally, Ja'Nae was well enough to be released from the hospital. A nurse's assistant along with the physical therapists was hired to aid in Ja'Nae's recovery until she was well enough to walk without assistance. While Ja'Nae and Matthew were still grieving over the loss of their first child, they managed to comfort each other as they continued to rely on their faith in their Lord and Savior Jesus Christ. The time they spent together proved to be quite valuable, their love and devotion to one another became stronger than they ever thought possible. The Lord continued to bless the Rogerses. While at home recuperating, Ja'Nae scheduled meetings with her staff to show them her new designs and make sure everything was going smoothly at her fashion house. Matthew stayed close to Alanta by designating his out-of-town jobs to his foreman until she was comfortable returning to work. He was determined to make sure she was safe before they both returned to work full-time.

At long last, Ja'Nae was released to return to work full-time in a few days. Matthew would return to his full schedule the same day as Ja'Nae. Things were slowly returning to normal, everything Ja'Nae visualized in her mind, she was able to incorporate, and the designs became top sellers. Regardless of the demands at work, Ja'Nae and Matthew continued to clock out at 5:00 p.m. and neither worked on Saturdays unless they were on location out of state. Their companies were prospering tremendously, so much in fact that they had to hire additional workers to keep up with the demands. Girls on a mission for Seniors was expanding as well throughout the United States. The ministry was changing the lives of the elderly as well as the girls. While the girls were ministering to the seniors, the seniors repaid them by telling them stories from their childhood as well as stories told to them by their parents from the early 1900s until the present time. The Rogerss continued to frequent their favorite restaurant and ministered to the patrons as the Lord directed.

Everything was going just the way Matthew and Ja'Nae wanted. They were happier than they ever imagined and they would soon be celebrating yet another anniversary. While making plans to surprise Matthew, Alanta received the phone call she had been dredging for over a year, a call from the district attorney's office. She was informed that her case would be tried in two weeks. After hanging up the phone, Alanta called Matthew and the rest of the family to schedule a meeting for the following evening.

The next evening, Ja'Nae and Albert told their families what the Lord wanted them to do in regard to the accident. While the Rogeres were recuperating from the accident and the loss of their first child, the driver of the car remained incarcerated. The man, Josiah Sanders, was given a one-hundred-thousand-dollar bail, however, he chose not to post bail. Naturally, due to the dilemma, the man found himself in he became deeply depressed, yet remorseful. As the man paced back and forward in his small jail cell, he remembered all the times his parents talked to him about drinking. He thought he had everything under control, but he soon learned he couldn't control the alcohol, especially after taking meds from his doctor. He truly underestimated the power of the drugs and alcohol combination and he almost killed himself, the Rogerses' unborn child, and Alanta. He was so very wrong!

Mr. Sanders had many thoughts inside, and before long, he started talking to himself. "If only I would have listened, the young lady would not have gotten hit or lost her baby. How in the world can I make this up to that family for all the pain and heartache I caused? What if she can't get over the loss and never be able to have another baby? Oh my god! Oh my god! What have I done? Lord, I should have died in that car! Why? Why? Why?" He screamed and cried. "Why did this have to happen? Why didn't I learn from others? Wow, why am I so hardheaded? Why am I so stupid? Why am I so selfish? I should have known better, I'm not a kid anymore. I am a grown man! I can't believe I let something so small and worthless get the best of me! What was I thinking? Clearly, I wasn't thinking!" The man cried and trembled as he continually wiped his nose. He cried himself to sleep. When he awakened, he could hardly see out of his red swollen eyes. Within minutes, he was crying, screaming, and trembling all over again. It was a new day, a new hour, but the same old heartache. Day in and day out, the man went through the same routine. It seemed as if time had stood still, he was in the same small cell for almost a year, yet to him, it seemed like eternity.

The closer it came to the court date, the more distressed and disillusioned the man became. When Mr. Josiah Saunders was arrested, he weighed two hundred and forty-five pounds, muscular build, and could be considered a heavyweight contender. As the time was drawing nigh (closer), the more depressed and restless the man became. Mr. Sanders's nerves were torn all to pieces. He couldn't control his bowels, he couldn't sit or stand without his knees knocking, and he couldn't eat without throwing up. The man was messed from the floor up. Forget about sleeping, the more he tried to sleep, the bigger his eyes became. The man was seen by the prison nurse and given some medications to calm his nerves and to help control his bowels. The weight he carried into the jail had now dribbled down to one hundred fifteen pounds, the muscular build was now skin and bones (no wonder he didn't have any strength).

Finally, it was time to get prepared to face the judge and the young lady that he hit along with her family members. Mr. Sanders was visibly disheartened, upset, and physically exhausted to the point that he had to be pushed into the courtroom in a wheelchair. Once he entered the courtroom, he kept his head down so he wouldn't see the anguish and disgust on the Rogerses' faces over such a senseless and preventable act. The man wanted the situation resolved as soon as possible without causing any further pain or sorrow to the families. He was, without a doubt, the guilty person and was ready to take whatever punishment the judge deemed appropriate.

Once the court proceedings started, the man completely lost control, especially after learning there were other cases before his. What he hoped would be a quick turnaround proved to be very time-consuming. Mr. Sanders wasn't concerned about himself, but certainly, he dredged the agony he believed the Rogerses were experiencing because of his ignorance. Unfortunately, due to his emotional state, the man had to be taken out of the courtroom several times to be cleaned up. The last time Mr. Sanders was taken out of the courtroom, the judge informed the deputy to let him remain in the holding cell until his case was called. The court cases were longer than the judge expected, so Mr. Sanders was informed his case would hopefully be heard the next day. Once again, Mr. Sanders had to try and prepare himself for another sleepless, torturous night. It was as if that night was the first night he spent in jail. He tossed and turned, cried, yelled, and threw up to the point that everything came out of him at the same time. He was totally miserable. I am sure you too can attest to the fact that when you are tired, frustrated, worried, afraid, and in physical pain, you can't sleep. Some say to count sheep, but when you start counting the sheep, they seem to be missing in action. The closer it gets to the time to get up, the sleeper you become. "Amen somebody!" Before long, it was the break of dawn, time to prepare for whatever the day would bring.

Once again, Mr. Sanders was pushed into the courtroom and he desperately wanted everything to come to an end that day, but would it? The sheriff's deputy pushed the defendant, Mr. Sanders, to the defendant's table. The court was called to order by the judge and the judge asked Mr. Sanders if he could stand. He said, "I will try my best, Your Honor." As he attempted to stand, the judge could see that the man was dangerously weak, so weak in fact that one of the deputies and his lawyer grabbed him to prevent him from falling. The judge said, "Let him remain seated. Mr. Sanders, would you like to postpone these proceedings until a later date?" Mr. Sanders replied, "No, sir, this family has suffered enough. I want to plead guilty to all charges?" The judge said, "Mr. Jamal Redgrave, have you advised your client of the consequences that go with a guilty plea?" Mr. Redgrave replied, "Yes, your honor, he has been well informed and he chose to enter a guilty plea." "Very well!" the judge replied. He turned to the prosecutor and said, "Mr. Wallace (Thomas, III) are you ready to call your first witness?" "Yes, Your Honor, I would like to call Mrs. Susanna Gumshield."

Before the woman could be sworn in, Mr. Redgrave stood up and said, "Your Honor, if there are no objections, my client would like to make a statement to the court and also to the family." Mr. Wallace said, "Your Honor, can we approach the bench?" "Yes," the judge replied. Mr. Wallace said, "Your Honor, this family has been through enough, and I don't want this man to willfully hurt them by his ploy to get less time." Mr. Redgrave said, "Your Honor, I assure you this young man has nothing up his sleeve. He is an emotional wreck over his bad choices. He is willing to do whatever sentence you impose. He has no desire to say or do anything to cause this family any more unnecessary pain, nor cause the taxpayers any more money. He wants this case over as soon as possible." The judge said, "I will allow it, but if I hear just one word that I feel is inappropriate I will stop it immediately. Have I made myself clear?" Mr. Redgrave said, "Perfectly, Your Honor!"

The judge looked up and said, "Mrs. Gumshield, you may return to your seat, but we reserve the right to call you at a later time if need be." She said, thank you as she returned to her seat in obedience. The judge then looked at the defendant and said, "Deputy Wrinwater, please push the defendant to the front of the witness box. Thank you. Mr. Josiah Sanders, you have the floor, but I don't want you to ramble on for fifteen or twenty minutes because I will stop you immediately." "Yes, sir!" Mr. Sanders said. He started by saying:

"Your Honor, I made the biggest mistake of my life the day I decided to drink and drive after taking prescribed medications." He cried. "I'd much rather hurt myself than hurt this young lady and take her baby's life." As the tears rolled down his face, he said, "I have no excuses and I will not try to offer any. My parents always told me to stop drinking before I hurt myself or someone else. Mom and Dad, I am so, very sorry, I should have listened." With a weak voice, he finished, "But at the time, I was so busy trying to prove that I was a grown man. You always told me, 'If you make your bed hard then you have to lay in it!'

I did exactly what they told me not to do!" He sobbed and said, "Momma, don't you worry about me while I am incarcerated, you and Dad did the best you could to raise me into a young man. I did this to myself! I have to pay for my own mistakes. It's not your fault, you hear me? I did this! I did this to myself! Momma, don't shed not one tear for me. I will be all right! I am the guilty one, I did this!

"Your honor, I was stubborn and very hardheaded. Once I became eighteen, I started 'smelling myself' as the old saying goes. And because of my age, I believed I could do whatever I wanted to without answering anyone. I was going in the wrong direction. I am not trying to have a pity party. I don't want anyone to feel sorry for me because I wasn't pitiful when I got behind the wheel of the car after drinking and taking medications, and I am not pitiful now! (He wiped his eyes and blew his nose) Mr. and Mrs. Rogers, I want to offer my sincere apology for all the agony (sniff, sniff, sniff) and sorrow I have caused you. If I could turn back the hands of time, I would, unfortunately, that is impossible. One thing I have promised to myself, I will promise to you and to this court, I will not drive under the influence ever again. As matter of fact, I will not drink again, life is too precious, and once it is taken, it can't be restored."

As he continued to speak, tears were flowing down his face as his voice became weaker and weaker. He said, "I know, (as he pointed to his chest) I know that the judge has the authority to sentence me to serve time for as long as he sees fit according to the law. However, I can't let another second go by (he cried out) without asking you all to forgive me (sobbingly) for this agonizing situation. I am truly sorry. Please, please, please, forgive me, and maybe, (he paused) just maybe one day, I will be able to forgive myself. Thank you! Thank you!"

The judge asked Mr. Wallace if he had any questions for the

defendant. As Mr. Wallace approached Mr. Sanders, he said, "Mr. Sanders, that all sounds extremely magnificent, and I have to give you a hand clap (he claps) for such an outstanding performance. Do you genuinely expect this court to believe that you are sorry for the accident and the death of the Rogerses' unborn child?" Mr. Sanders replied, "Sir, I can't control what you may or may not believe. I can only tell you the truth, I am truly sorry if I could have hit a tree, a parked vehicle, or an unoccupied storage barn I would have, even if it cost me my life! I can't give a life, and I had no right to take a life, but unfortunately, I did. Mrs. Rogers was on the side of the road (the bike lane) running, minding her own business when I, with my intoxicated self, hit her with my vehicle. I am in no way proud of my actions, but I am the guilty one!" Mr. Wallace did all he could to make Mr. Sanders crack in order to prove it was all an act. He refused to believe the defendant was remorseful, but all his efforts failed, the man was unshakeable. Mr. Sanders tearfully yelled, "It was my fault! I did it and I should be punished! What else can I say or do? It was my fault, all my fault! I am not running from this, but I am facing my punishment head-on! I take full responsibility for the accident. Your Honor, do what you want to do with me, do what you feel is best, it's in your hands! It's in your hands!" He continued to yell and sob uncontrollably. The judge sent for the inmate's nurse so he could come and sedate the poor man so he would calm down. Mr. Sanders could be heard yelling and screaming in the other courtrooms. People were curious to find out who was crying so terribly sad and why. As they opened the door to the courtroom and started looking around, they could hear and see the women crying, and yelling at the top of their lungs. Once they saw the shape of the man, it broke them down emotionally.

Normally in the courtroom, the district attorney (DA)

has the opportunity to present his case first, however, there wasn't anything normal about this case. Due to the fact that the defendant, Mr. Sanders, wanted to end the case before it started, the judge without any objections from the DA listened to what he wanted to say. Mr. Wallace didn't object because he wanted the opportunity to let the man cook himself, so could rake him over the coals and the judge give him the maximum sentence. Mr. Wallace had a reputation for being ruthless, insulting, nasty, and he rarely lost a case, but at that moment, he was feeling a little bruised. As he started presenting his case, he called Mrs. Susanna Gumfield as his first witness to help lay the foundation. Mr. Wallace asked Mrs. Gumfield to start by telling what she saw on the day in question. She said, "I saw the victim, Mrs. Rogers jogging down the street. As she approached the corner, she jogged in place while waiting for the light to change. She was very mindful of her surroundings and watched every vehicle in the vicinity as well as the traffic lights. Mr. Sanders was coming down the road and (sniff, sniff) he umm, (as the tears rolled down her face) he, missed the curve in the road and was weaving back and forward headed directly toward Mrs. Rogers. Oh my god, the other drivers started blowing their horns, but Mr. Sanders wasn't paying attention or didn't hear them. Whatever the case may be, he continued driving directly toward Mrs. Rogers. Lord, Lord please help her! (Sadly, she yelled) Stop! Stop! What's wrong with you? Don't you see that young lady? At that point, Mrs. Rogers tried her best to get out of the path of the car, but there was no place for her to go. Shortly thereafter, Mrs. Rogers was hit, knocked unconscious bleeding from her mouth and nose. As I looked at Mr. Sanders, it appears he was knocked unconscious as well behind the wheel of the vehicle. I screamed for help and started praying for Mrs. Rogers as I remained by her side until help

arrived." Mr. Wallace didn't want to pressure Mrs. Gumfield
because he didn't want to replay the entire gruesome accident
in the presents of the Roger family.

Next, Mr. Wallace called the doctors in hope of scoring
points with the judge. If you remember, I already informed you
the readers about the injuries Ja'Nae sustained. Finally, Mr.
Wallace called Mrs. Alanta Ja'Nae Rogers. She stated, "Your
Honor, I was jogging and was on my way back to my place of
employment when I approached the stop light. I was jogging in
place waiting for the traffic light to change. As I was looking
in front of me, I saw a vehicle coming in my direction, the
driver was weaving from side to side. I was so afraid, I didn't
know what to do, I tried my very best to get out of the path of
the vehicle but I was unable to (with tears in her eyes she wept
and continued). The next thing I knew I was waking up in the
hospital room with my family surrounding me. I could see on
their faces that they were very worried (she wiped her eyes). As
I tried to sit up, I was so weak that I fell back on my pillow and
was fast asleep. I don't know how long I was asleep but the next
thing I remember was the excruciating throbbing pain running
throughout my body. Although I was hurting, nothing (she
paused), nothing could compare with the pain and discomfort I
experienced after I was informed that my precious, oh my god,
my precious little baby was dead. And the doctor said I will
never be able to carry another child. But I am so glad my God
has the final say!"

"Oh my god!" She cried out in a long devasting tone. "Oh
my god! I was hurt, I was unreasonable and unbearable to
be around. I was extremely upset with myself as well as Mr.
Sanders. My flesh wanted to die! And just let me be real about
Mr. Sanders. I wanted to hurt him badly. As a matter of fact,
I wanted him to suffer until the last breath left of his body. I

couldn't bear looking at my husband because for a minute I believed I failed him by putting myself and our baby in danger. You see, I lost it for a while, yes I let my flesh take control until my Heavenly Father Jesus Christ sent my earthly father, Albert Barnesworth, with a fresh word, the exact word I needed to calm me down. After bringing my flesh under the submission of my Heavenly Father, I was able to hear what the Holy Spirit was saying. Your Honor, Matthew and I have had time to grieve the loss of our child (she paused as the tears ran down her face) and we will always have pain in our hearts because of the loss. However, we have prayed, cried, and thought long and hard about the situation we have been living in for almost a year. After much prayer, fasting, and soul searching, Matthew and I are totally satisfied with the answer we received. We realize you have the final say in this matter and we aren't in any way trying to overstep our boundaries. Your Honor," she continued, "we have no anger, resentment, or ill feelings toward Mr. Sanders. Yes, he was wrong for taking medication, drinking, and driving, but who are we to judge him? Who are we to be hardheaded, hateful, and unloving? Matthew and I have caused others pain by being disobedient to our parents and saying things about others with no regard for their feelings. We weren't concerned about the pain we caused or the trouble we brought on others. We aren't exempted, we are human beings and our Lord and Savior forgave us and still forgives us of all our indiscretions. As we sat in this courtroom listening to Mr. Sanders and seeing the stat he is in, we felt his pain and we know he suffered and is still suffering the same Matthew and me as we experienced the loss of our first child. Our God tells us in his word according to Romans 3:23, 'For we all have sinned and come (fallen) short of the glory of God;' Do I drink and drive? No, but nevertheless, I have sinned! I have read in the book of John in chapter 8 about a woman that was caught in the very act of adultery. She was brought before Jesus, and the men wanted her to be stoned to death. Keep in mind that the woman wasn't committing adultery alone, but the men wanted to make point out her sin. As Jesus listened to the men, he stooped down and wrote on the ground. The men were getting impatient and they wanted Jesus to do something immediately. Jesus stood up and said, "He that is without sin among you, let him first cast a stone at her." Jesus stooped back to the ground and when he stood up, there was no one there but the woman. He asked her, 'Where are you accused?' The men were convicted of their own sins so they left. Jesus told the woman to go and sin no more. All the woman had to do was repent for her sin, be godly sorry and never do it again, she did exactly what she was told."

"This may seem strange to some of you that don't have a personal relationship with the Lord." She continued, "But Matthew and I saw Mr. Sander suffering in his jail cell, and we heard his cries. No, we haven't physically visited him, we have never seen him before these court proceedings. God was dealing with Matthew and me on this man's behalf. We haven't taken anything that happened to us lightly, but our God has told us to forgive this man, God has work for him to do, if we refuse to obey God, then we will continue to suffer. We serve a true and living God. A God that loves us in spite of our imperfections, our faults, and our sins."

After several deep breaths, she continued, "Your Honor, we Rogers and the Barnesworth families ask that you please have mercy on Mr. Sanders when you sentence him. We believe this man has suffered enough, and he has learned from his mistakes. Furthermore, we believe it wouldn't serve any purpose for Mr. Sanders to sit in prison for months or years. He can be rehabilitated and become a witness to teenagers at the schools, universities, and outreach facilities about his experience. As I forestated, we have totally forgiven you, Mr. Sanders. If my Lord and Savior Jesus Christ forgave the men that crucified him, surely, we can forgive you, Mr. Sanders."

Alanta turned to the defendant and proceeded to talk directly to him. "Mr. Sanders, you don't have to cry anymore, you can rest and hold your head up! The Lord gave and the Lord hath taken away; blessed be the name of the Lord (Job 1:21). Sometimes, God allows things to happen to get us to the place where he wants us to be. Matthew and I don't know what would have happened with our baby, but God does and he never makes a mistake. We love you, Mr. Sanders. Do you hear me? Don't let your past circumstances dictate your future. We love you and the word of God states, 'For if ye (you) forgive men their trespasses (to commit an offense or sin; err), your heavenly Father will also forgive you: But if you forgive not men their trespasses, neither will your Father forgive your trespasses. (Matthew 6:14-15)" Alanta said, "Mr. Sanders, look behind you!"

Mr. Sanders was a little hesitant at first, but when he turned around, all the Rogerses and the Barnesworths stood up one by one and smiled at him. A few minutes earlier, Mr. Sanders was depressed, hopeless, heartbroken, and in torment, but God was working in his favor. Suddenly, everyone in the courtroom was in tears. Mr. Sanders was weeping from the shock as well as being overjoyed from the circumstances that had just happened in the courtroom. He thought he was in the middle of a dream but rest assured if he was dreaming, he didn't want to be awakened. The judge said, "Out of the mouth of babes and sucklings thou hast perfected praise! Truly, I have never witnessed such love and compassion from a victim to a defendant in my entire life either as a lawyer or a judge. This is unprecedented, I am totally in awe. I don't know what to say or what to do at this moment.

However, I don't want to react to emotions, so I will take a five or ten-minute recess to give everyone an opportunity to calm down and recover from this amazing testimony. Everyone, please remain in the courtroom. I will give my decision when the court reconvenes."

Due to the pleasant and peaceful atmosphere in the courtroom, the deputy sheriff's allowed the families to approach Mr. Sanders. As the families surrounded Josiah Sanders, it was as if they were having a family reunion with a family member they hadn't seen in many years due to military deployment. It was truly an amazing experience that no one in the courtroom would ever forget. The Sander family never felt so much love in their entire life, they knew it had to be the love of God. Alanta asked the families to join hands as her father, Albert led them in a powerful word of prayer for Josiah's quick release. That day, the three families created a bond that they would cherish for generations. While the court was in recess, the spirit of the Lord was having his way moving from person to person.

The judge has the authority to call for a recess whenever he deemed it necessary. However, the recess was different than any normal recess. The judge couldn't get out of the courtroom fast enough. He reached his chambers just in the nick of time. You see, the judge felt the Holy Ghost praise coming on. As he closed the door to his chambers it was on, the spirit of the Lord was all over him. Forget about pondering over a decision for the moment, he had praise on the inside that he had to get out. As the officer stood at the entrance of the courtroom, he could hear the judge yelling and dancing at the same time. Without a doubt, the judge was giving God all the praises that were built up during the proceedings. The judge began speaking in unknown tongues as it is written in the book of Acts chapter 2. Everyone that knew the word of God, and heard the judge would truly believe that the day of Pentecost had fully come in the judge's chamber. Truly, the judge was in his chambers cutting the rug as the older people would say. For those that haven't heard that before, it simply means that the Spirit of the Lord was having his way with the judge. He was dancing, jumping, and talking to his God regardless of who heard him. He truly was not ashamed of the gospel of Jesus Christ! When the Spirit of the Holy Spirit lifted off of the judge, he was soaking wet. Thankfully, he had a full bathroom in his chambers and a change of clothes. What was meant to be a five or ten-minute recess soon became thirty minutes, just enough time for the judge to shower, change, and pray before returning to the courtroom.

Finally, the judge re-entered the courtroom. He had such a glow on his face. "And as he prayed the fashion of his countenance (appearance of his face) was altered (Luke 9:29)." Once the Rogerses and the Barnesworths saw the judge, they knew he had a spiritual encounter with the Lord, and they were confident that everything was going to be all right. After the court was called to order, the judge said, "I have listened to all the incredible testimonies and I am ready to rule in this matter. This has been at the least the most surprising, stimulating, and unusual set of circumstances in any case that I have ever presided over. First of all, I would like to say to the Rogerses and the Barnesworths families that I am extremely sorry for your loss."

The judge turned to the defendant's table and said, "Mr. Jamal Redgrave, due to the defendant's fragile condition, he can remain seated as I read my decision." Mr. Redgrave said, "Thank you, Your Honor!" The judge said, "Mr. Josiah Sanders, I want you to know that drinking and driving along with medication is never a good combination. Due to your actions, Mrs. Rogers was not only hit and injured, but she lost her unborn child. All three of these things come with a punishment. When you came before the magistrate about a year ago, you were given bail. Your parents were ready and willing to bail you out, but you chose to remain incarcerated for almost a year. In my opinion, Mr. Sanders, you manned up and refused to take the situation lightly. As I watched and listened to you today, Mr. Sanders, I could hear the remorse in your voice and see it in your eyes, it also showed in your body language. You were very emotional, and I believe you meant every word you have spoken in this courtroom today. Furthermore, I am confident that you have learned your lesson about drinking, driving, and medicating. I have reviewed your records from the time you were arrested until today. Most of the time, you had to be watched to make sure you didn't attempt to hurt yourself. Although you are still very weak from lack of eating and not sleeping, I am so happy you have managed to pull yourself out of the rut you were in. Thankfully, you realized your death would only cause more pain for your family as well as the Rogerses. You have suffered tremendously with the accident and all the things that transpired as a result of it. While being held in the jail, you were assaulted and abused by the inmates and you refused to retaliate."

The judge cleared his throat and continued addressing Mr. Sanders. He said, "Mr. Sanders, I see this is your first offense and prayerfully, this will be your last. Therefore, I will credit you with the time served, and you will need to perform forty hours of community service. In case you don't know, you are a blessed young man. I have never seen a victim as forgiving, loving, compassionate, and understanding as the Rogerses, and that is partly why I am being so lenient on you. Please consider yourself warned if you are caught driving under the influence of alcohol and medication within the next five years, you will

be incarcerated. Make no mistake, you will do hard time at
one of North Carolina's facilities if the judge sees fit according
to the law. Have I made myself clear?" Mr. Sanders said, "Yes,
sir! Your Honor, can I please say something?" "Yes, you may,"
replied the judge.

Mr. Sanders said, "Thank you, Your Honor. I have been
given an awesome opportunity to get my life together and
I promise myself, you, my parents, the Rogerses and the
Barnesworths that I will do my very best to make a difference
in the lives of young people. I have learned a lot during this past
year some things I hope to forget and others that I will always
remember. Your Honor, when I was younger, I often heard
people talk about a man named Jesus, unfortunately, I didn't
believe them. I thought Jesus was a fairy tale that people made
up to have something to hold over their children's heads as a
scare tactic and to it was complete foolishness. Boy, was I wrong!
You see, I wanted to keep up with my so-called friends and I
believed I had everything I needed and wanted, there wasn't
any place in my life for a man named Jesus. However, he cried,
after everything that has happened in my life during these court
proceedings, I know Jesus is alive and well. He has truly moved
in here today! I have been to church in my younger years, but
at the time, I couldn't care less what was going on. Today, you
all opened my eyes, and (sniff, sniff) I am not the same man that
entered this courtroom several hours ago! I was totally weak,
weighted down, and had no hope for the future. I thought I was
worthless, and I had nothing or no one to live for so I thought,
but thanks be to God, I now have a purpose in my life. Now I
truly understand why people say everything in your life happens
for a reason. I was in the right place at the right time for my
miracle! Thank you all, thank you, thank you!"

The judge said, "Does anyone else have anything to say

before we adjourn?" Alanta stood up and said, "Your Honor, I just received a text from my doctor that Matthew and I are pleased to announce that we are expecting a baby in seven months. The doctor said we should not have conceived our first child and never be able to conceive again but God! Matthew 19:26 reads, 'With men this is impossible; but with God all things are possible.' Who wouldn't serve a God like this? Mr. Sanders, we would be honored if you would be our child's godfather!" Matthew and Alanta asked him together. Mr. Sanders said as he was crying, "Thank you so very much, I am completely overjoyed. I consider it an awesome privilege to share in your family's joy!"

The judge said, "Truly, I am at a loss for words with all the generosity that has been displayed throughout this trial. This case should have been recorded and used as an educational tool for our teenagers. I have witnessed things that I could have never imagined, things that weren't taught in law school. I am ecstatic for being during such awesome families. To the Rogerses and the Barnesworths, it has been my pleasure having you in my courtroom. You have been a great inspiration not only to me but to everyone in this court. I have never seen so many people shedding tears in the courtroom that started off sad and ended up being tears of joy, I bid you all God's speed! Mr. Sanders, I expect great things from you. You are free to go as soon as the appropriate papers are signed. This court is adjourned!"

I Know a Change Is
Going to Come

After being released, Mr. Sanders went home with his parents. That was the best day of his young adult life, and he was determined to make a difference in everyone's life that he came in contact with. That night, he made a list of the things he wanted to accomplish in his life within the next three years. At the top of his list was to surrender his life to the Lord. Secondly, he wanted his community service to be used by spending time talking to teenagers and young adults about the consequences of drinking, driving, and using drugs. Josiah was optimistic of becoming a positive role model to help others to accomplish their goals in life by learning from his mistakes. Thirdly, he wanted to enroll in college to master in computer engineering. To start his plans, Josiah called Matthew Roger and asked if he could meet with them the next day at their earliest convenience. They were going to meet at the Rogerses' home at 9:00 a.m.

The next day, Josiah was so excited that he remembered the last thing Matthew told him the day before. Matthew said, "If you ever need anything, feel free to call us, and we will help you in any way we possibly can!" Once Josiah got to the Rogers' home, he was welcomed with open arms. Matthew said, "We are friends and as such, we will call each other by our first names, after all, that's what friends do!" Josiah said,

"I do not want to waste your time beating around the bush so I will get to the point. I did not come here for a handout, but I came for a hand. You see, what I want is more valuable than anything I have ever wanted. While in the courtroom, I witnessed several miracles performed and I was utterly amazed. I don't understand the power of God, but I want to be able to experience God for myself. So, I came here to ask you to help me surrender my life to your God and lead me thru the process. Can you tell me what I must do or say? All I know is I am at a loss, and I need direction. The strangest thing happened to me yesterday, something that I cannot quite explain, but honestly (as he scratched his head), it's like peace and hunger came all over me. This hunger is not like a hunger for food, but I know something is missing. It is like a huge piece of the puzzle that I can't quite put together by myself. Can you help me?"

At that moment, Matthew and Alanta had to take a praise break. That was the best news they had heard in an exceptionally long time; they were overflowing with pure jubilation. They could scarcely believe what they were hearing. Without any hesitation, they began to talk to Josiah. Matthew said, "First, let us pray for God to direct us to explain to you what salvation truly is and how to achieve it." After the prayer, they were led to these scriptures: Jeremiah 18:1–6, NKJV, "The word of the Lord came to Jeremiah from the Lord, saying, "Arise and go down to the potter's house, and there I will cause you to hear My words." Then I went down to the potter's house, and there he was, making something at the wheel (potter's wheel). And the vessel that he made of clay was marred (ruined) in the hand of the potter; so he made it again into another vessel, as it seemed good to the potter to make. Then the word of the Lord came to me saying: "O house of Israel, can I not do with you as this potter?" says the Lord. "Look as the clay is in the potters' hand, so are you in My hand, O house of Israel!" Romans 9:20–to21, "But indeed, O man, who are you to reply against God? Will the thing formed say to him who formed it, "Why have you made me like this?" Does not the potter have power over the clay, from the same lump to make one vessel for honor and another for dishonor?"

Matthew said, "Josiah, the Lord uses his word as a parable which means a simple story that was designed to help us understand his word easier. What this story means is that we were created by God for God! And although we sin or turn away from what God has purposed us to do, he gives us an opportunity to get it right by the way of repentance. As the potter was making something (an image) out of the clay, the clay was not coming together as he wanted it to, so the potter destroyed it and started over. God created man out of the dust in his own image, and although he is our creator, he can mold us and make us into what he desires. However, our God is a perfect gentleman. He gives us a chance to live our lives the way we desire. Joshua 24:15, KJV, reads, 'And if it seems evil unto you to serve the Lord, choose you this day whom ye will serve; whether the gods which your fathers served that were on the side of the flood, or the god of the Amorites, in whose land ye dwell: but as for me and my house, we will serve the Lord.' We all came from dust, and we shall all return to dust, but while we are here on earth, we have a purpose, and it is totally up to us to fulfill that purpose. God's plan is for us to live a holy committed life for him. He died on the cross so that we may have the right to the tree of life which is a right to salvation. He wants us to choose him. Because you are here seeking our Lord and Savior Jesus Christ the Son of the true and living God, you are in the right place at the right time. God is calling you to come into the fold so that you will have a seat in heaven. Just like the potter and the clay that God is drawing you into your purpose. The reason you are here is to receive him, you want your soul delivered, am I right, Josiah?"

Josiah replied, "I want the God I witnessed in the courtroom! I want the god that has given my peace! I want the God that has given me favor with you and your families! I want the same God that has touched me with the finger of love! I want the God that had mercy on me! I understand everything you have explained to me; now how do I get to the next level with this God? I do not know what to do next, but I know I am ready to experience everything God has to offer. I am tired of drinking and driving. I am tired of hanging in the clubs! I am tired of chasing women for sport! And I am ready to settle down to make something of myself, something I can be proud of. I am tired of causing my parents grief! I am tired of making my mother cry because of my immaturity! Please," he cried, "please tell me how I can get from point A to point B! I do not know the way, but I believe you and Alanta can lead me to the way of righteousness. Can you or will you help me?" he cried.

Matthew put his hand on Josiah's shoulder and said, "Man, you are on your way. God is drawing you and you are ready, willing, and able." "Honey, will you get the scriptures? Baby, read the scriptures please!" Alanta began to read Romans 10:9–to10 aloud. "That if you confess with your mouth the Lord Jesus and believe in your heart that God has raised Him from the dead, you will be saved. For with the heart one believes unto righteousness, and with the mouth confession is made to salvation." Matthew said, "Josiah, all we want you to do is believe what you say, and God will do the rest. Will you stand and repeat after me? Lord Jesus, Lord Jesus, please forgive me of all my sins, please forgive me of all my sins, and come into my heart. And come into my heart. Lord, I believe you died on the cross. Lord, I believe you died on the cross, for the remission of my sins. For the remission of my sins. And on the third day you rose, and on the third day you rose, that I may have a right to the tree of life. That I may have a right to the tree of life." Matthew and Alanta knew that Josiah was real for God. As he finished repeating the prayer, he started praising God, he started jumping up and down and yelled, "Thank you, Jesus! Thank you, Jesus, for saving me! Lord, I am not worthy of the nails that were nailed in your hands and feet nor for the thrones that were placed on your head! Hallelujah! Hallelujah! Thank you, Jesus! Thank you, Jesus! Thank you, Lord, I am saved! Matthew, I am saved! Alanta, I am saved! I am saved! Thank you, Jesus, for putting this family in my life! Hallelujah! I am saved! Thank you! I feel the weight dropping off me! Thank you, God! Lord, I don't know what you are doing to me, but keep on, Lord! Keep on, Lord, thank you!"

After Josiah finished praising God, Alanta read, Matthew 5:6–8, "Blessed are they which do hunger and thirst after righteousness: for they shall be filled. Blessed are the merciful: for they shall obtain mercy. Blessed are the pure in heart: for they shall see God." The Rogerses were praising God and rejoicing with Josiah. After Josiah calmed down, the Rogers hugged him and congratulated him. Matthew said, "Josiah, welcome to the fold, you are not only our friend, but you are our brother is in Christ for Luke 15:10 reads, "Likewise, I say unto you, there is joy in the presence of the angels of God over one sinner that repenteth." Hallelujah! Hallelujah! Hallelujah! Josiah said, "Matthew, when you and Alanta were talking to me in the courtroom, I did not quite understand why you both would forgive me, I was so afraid to face you in the courtroom. I heard some of the inmates in the jail talking about me and they said if they were you, Matthew they would get a gun and kill me for hitting your wife and causing the death of your baby. I understand now, it was the God in you!" Matthew said, "Josiah, our God tells us to love one another. People talk about taking someone's life because they are the children of the devil. The Bible tells us to do unto others as you will have them do unto you. Jesus is love, and he loved us enough that he died on the cross so that we may have a right to the tree of life. Romans 12:17–19 states, 'Recompense to no man evil for evil. Provide things honest in the sight of all men. If it be possible, as much as lieth in you, live peaceably with all men. Dearly beloved, avenge not yourselves, but rather give place unto wrath: for it is written, Vengeance is mine; I will repay, saith the Lord.'"

After Josiah became a Christian, he landed a part-time job, enrolled in a university to complete his degree in computer engineering, and did his community service. He was baptized in the water and continued to grow in his faith. He sort the Lord so he would be filled with the Holy (Ghost) Spirit with the evidence of speaking in an unknown tongue as recorded in the book of Acts 2:2–4. Within a few weeks, Josiah was equipped with the power he needed to endure whatever life threw his way. He was ready to do whatever the Lord had planned for him. At that moment, Josiah knew that God had His hands on him and yelled, "Lord, whatever you are doing, please don't do it without me!" He was on fire for his Lord and Savior Jesus Christ!

Meanwhile, as Josiah was growing in the Lord, Matthew and Alanta were preparing for their new baby. You may remember that the doctor told the Rogerses they would not be able to conceive another child. As a matter of fact, according to the doctor, she should not have conceived the first time, but God! This reminds me of Elizabeth, John the Baptist's mother. Luke 1:36–37 "And, behold, thy cousin Elisabeth, she hath also conceived a son in her old age: and this is the sixth month with her, who was called barren. For with God nothing shall be impossible." Matthew and Alanta's baby was due any day, they were so excited. The baby was born on the third day of the seventh month at 3:36 a.m. He weighed 6 lbs. 7 oz. He was named Matthew Devon Rogers, Jr. After three years, Matthew and Alanta were blessed with their second son, and he was named Maurice Javon Rogers, and their third child was named Alana Yvonne Rogers.

Although Josiah was a babe in Christ, he was willing to learn and was determined to be the best man of God he could be. His whole life changed after he met the Rogerses and Barnesworths families. He soaked up every word of God that the pastor preached about. His dreams and desires were happening quicker than he ever imagined. Every opportunity he was given to witness to others, he made sure he told his testimony. People were amazed at how dedicated he was to his Lord and Savior Jesus Christ. As his former friends tried to pull him out of the church and back into his old way of living, he did not have any problems standing his ground.

He never forgot his old ways and his jailhouse experience, and how God had changed his life. His parents and family members were so enormously proud of his accomplishments. He was no longer the man that was too grown for any use. It took his trials and tribulations to get him to the place where he is and he never turned back. Yes, he looked back only to remind himself where the Lord had brought him from. That is how he saw himself, and he could truly confess to everyone that he came in connection with that, "I know that my change has come!"

THE FINAL WORDS
FROM THE AUTHOR

Now that you have read "Out of The Mouth of Babes Revived A Family's Ultimate Challenge," what are your thoughts? Could you forgive Josiah Sanders if you were the Rogers? If you were arrested for a crime that you did not commit, would you forgive the accuser, or would you want the person to suffer too? What has happened in your life that were so challenging that you haven't forgiven yourself or others? How long will we let our past circumstances/mistakes dictate our future? We only have one life to live, will we waste it on hate, jealousy, envy or will we forgive and forget? The choice is yours, I choose to forgive.

As sure as we are born, we will all go through challenges. Those challenges are made to make us stronger and wiser. Therefore, if we are never challenged, we would not be able to walk, talk, feed ourselves, or become independent. Whatever we partake in makes us who we are today. If we do not teach our children the value of a dollar, they will always be poverty stricken. We have the authority to instruct our children the difference from right from wrong and when they are disobedient then there are consequences that must be applied. In Proverbs 13:24, "He that spared his rod hateth his son/daughter: but he that loveth him (punishes) chasteneth him betimes." Proverbs

19:18, "Chasten (discipline or correct by punishment) thy son/daughter while there is hope and let not thy soul spare for his crying." No discipline, no foundation, and without a foundation, your child will do whatever comes to their mind. If there is no discipline at home, then the teachers will not be able to teach them, and they become unteachable. And yes, their mind will be destroyed/wasted on things that profit them nothing. Can you live with that? The Barnesworths children were not perfect, no one here on this earth is perfect, but the Lord Jesus Christ! He is perfect, He is the true and living God! No one can compare to Jesus, but we have a road map to follow if we want to raise obedient, loving successful children. We must follow the instructions God left us in His Holy word, the Bible. Amen, Somebody!"

I pray that something you have read in this book "Out of the Mouth of Babes: A Families' Ultimate Challenge" will help you realize where you are in God! And if you do not have a personal relationship with him, get it right while you still have the blood running warm in your veins! Do not wait till you are old because God is calling the roll every minute of every hour of the day. And just in case you think you have it made in the shade because you are a member of the church, think again. God wants true worshippers, think about that while you are rejoicing over other's challenges. And some are wondering why they are not happy! Your happiness does not come from your beauty, or lack thereof, nor your friends, or your possessions, but true happiness can only come from receiving Jesus Christ as your Lord and personal Savior to live the life God has ordained for you! Only what you do for Christ will last!

ABOUT THE AUTHOR

Annie C. Boddie was born in Tarboro, North Carolina. She attended Edgecombe County Public School until she completed the third grade. She was relocated to Elizabeth, New Jersey, where she attended the Union County Public School and graduated from Battin High School in Elizabeth, New Jersey. She attended Union County Technical Institute before returning to North Carolina in 1981, where she resides. She is a wife, mother, grandmother, and great-grandmother. Annie is considered a character by everyone that truly knows her. She firmly believes in saying something or doing something to lift people's spirits. She is very outspoken and truly believes in always telling the truth. She is a visionary as well as a writer. She is dedicated to her Lord and Savior Jesus Christ, her husband James of thirty-seven plus years, her children, grandsons, and a great-grandson, as well as her family and friends. She never meets a stranger; for her, treating people as strangers is a total waste of valuable time that can never be regained. To all who will buy this book, she prays that something you read will help you overcome your many trials and tribulations! Thank you so much! Remember, we all are facing tests, be angry, and sin not! Let us strive to treat others the way we want to be treated. Love covers a multitude of sins. We all want to be loved, happy, and successful if your plan is not working it is time to change what we are doing. Hate brings more hate

CITED SOURCES

The American Heritage Dictionary of the English Language
All scriptures were taken from the "Spirit Filled Life Bible," King James
Version, and The New Open Bible, New King James Version," published
by Thomas Nelson Publishers.